PRAISE FOR ANGIE F

5 Stars! "This second MASH book is even better than the first!"

5 Stars! "It has all the right touches—love, laughter, suspense, action and surprise twists!"

5 Stars! "Finished this in one night!"

5 Stars! "The cast of characters is amazing, the world Petra lives in is fascinating. You cannot read this book fast enough to learn what happens next."

5 Stars! "Love Love Love! What else can I say?"

ALSO BY ANGIE FOX

THE MONSTER MASH TRILOGY

The Monster Mash

The Transylvania Twist

Werewolves of London

THE SOUTHERN GHOST HUNTER SERIES

Southern Spirits

The Skeleton in the Closet

The Haunted Heist

Deader Homes & Gardens

Sweet Tea and Spirits

Murder on the Sugarland Express

Pecan Pies and Dead Guys

The Mint Julep Murders

The Ghost of Christmas Past

Southern Bred and Dead

The Haunted Homecoming

THE ACCIDENTAL DEMON SLAYER SERIES

The Accidental Demon Slayer

The Dangerous Book for Demon Slayers

A Tale of Two Demon Slayers

The Last of the Demon Slayers

My Big Fat Demon Slayer Wedding

Beverly Hills Demon Slayer

Night of the Living Demon Slayer

What To Expect When Your Demon Slayer is Expecting

SHORT STORY COLLECTIONS:

A Little Night Magic: A collection of Southern Ghost Hunter and Accidental Demon Slayer short stories

THE TRANSYLVANIA TWIST

ANGIE FOX

THE TRANSYLVANIA TWIST

ISBN: 978-1-939661-76-0

Warning: This book contains a Star Wars-obsessed werewolf, an adorable hellhound, demigods in peril, action, romance, and friends who put each other first—in a MASH camp where everybody knows your business.

CHAPTER ONE

MEDUSA, serpent goddess, executioner of men, scourge of Kisthene's plain, stabbed a clawed finger in my direction. "Tell me the truth, human," she hissed. "No more lies."

I straightened my spine and fought the urge to rub my temples in a most unprofessional way.

Why did the gods have to be so dramatic?

Medusa coiled on the examination table in front of me, wearing a light blue open-backed gown. She stared at me, her eyes glowing red as her clawed hands shredded the white sanitary paper.

"I am outcast," she said in a gravelly voice. Her rattlesnake's tail swished, nearly taking out my freestanding EKG unit. "I am the damned," she declared, face twisted with fury. I held on to my clipboard as the examination tent vibrated with her power. "I am the destroyer!"

I nodded. Some patients took longer than others to adjust, but it didn't change the fact. "You're also pregnant."

"Impossible," she spat, even though we both knew that wasn't true.

I made a few notes in my chart while she threw her head back and let out a screech that shook the tent.

Ouch. I tried not to wince.

In my professional opinion, screaming often did help.

"Doctor," she hissed, smoke curling from her nose. For a moment, she was unable to form the question. Her perfectly sculpted brows knit as she brushed a hand through the wild mane of snakes on her head. "How?"

I gave her my most reassuring smile. "The old-fashioned way, I assume."

She should know. The Gorgon was nearly three thousand years old. And from what I'd seen of the ancient Greeks, they certainly knew how to party.

She drew her hands slowly, almost reverently, down her green-scaled torso to the perfectly flat stomach under her examination gown. "I'm cursed," she hissed. "I'm barren. My body is poison!"

"Don't be so hard on yourself." Sure, my fingers went a bit numb when I was checking her blood pressure, but all in all she was far less dangerous than the ancient Norse dragon in need of an enema this morning.

That had taken us two doctors, three orderlies, a set of ambulance drivers, and Jeffe the guard sphinx. Although to be frank, all Jeffe did was warn us not to set the motor pool on fire.

I whipped out form 3871-K, which was actually a little slide wheel designed to help me calculate the Gorgon pregnancy cycle. "I'd estimate you're fifty-three days along, which is seven weeks and three days pregnant. Your gestation time is slightly shorter than the average human, longer than the average goddess." I slipped the chart back into the pocket of my white coat. "Still, I don't think we need to see you again until the end of your first trimester."

I opened a drawer in the medical cart next to the examination table where we kept basics, including samples of prenatal vitamins. “Because you’re over thirty-five years old,” I said, handing her a pack, “we’ll want to do an ultrasound at your next appointment, along with a few other routine tests.”

The pale skin on her neck and arms flushed as she took it all in. She growled low. “My parents are going to kill me.”

Well, I couldn’t offer her any advice on ancient marine deities. Besides, the grin tickling at the sides of her mouth told me more than I needed to know. Once she recovered from the surprise, she’d be tickled pink. Or at least a light green.

“It’s just that”—her gaze wandered as she nibbled on a talon—“I haven’t talked to my mother since I turned her lover to stone.”

“About that,” I said, setting her chart on top of the medical cart. “You’re going to want to try to control your temper. Stress isn’t good for the baby.”

Medusa snarled at me, then caught herself. “I’ll try,” she muttered.

“Do,” I told her.

Ever since the cease-fire in the war of the gods, we’d converted our MASH unit into one of the premier (and only) supernatural clinics in the area. That was saying something, considering we were located in Limbo, just north of a major hell vent.

We were known for taking in all patients regardless of their origins or ability to pay. Which was the way it should be. It was also why we got a few of the interesting cases.

“Go ahead and get dressed. I’ll see you in five weeks,” I told the Gorgon. “The nurse out front will set your appointment.”

I ducked out of the examination room and handed the chart to our charge nurse, Holly, who was one of the only full humans in our unit.

She tilted her head, flipping her blond ponytail to one side. She'd gone from red streaks in her hair to pink. I liked it. It softened her up.

"Rough one, Dr. Robichaud?" she asked.

"Nah, everything's going to be fine," I replied. "Even so, you'll want to keep your eyes averted when our patient comes out," I warned her. Just in case.

Flesh-to-stone injuries were painful and time consuming to treat. We needed Holly on her feet.

I followed her to the front, where she had her desk.

We'd converted the front half of the surgery recovery tent into a makeshift clinic, with an intake area and curtained rooms—eight on each side. At the front sat the nurses' station, which was basically a red metal desk with a portable file cabinet behind it.

"It's quiet around here," Holly said, slipping behind the desk and starting a new file for Medusa.

"I like quiet. Quiet is good."

Peace had broken out exactly three weeks, one day, and six hours ago. It was an uneasy truce. We all knew it wouldn't last. Still, at the MASH 3063rd , we were going to take what we could get.

The younger gods had revolted against the older gods right around the time Troy had fallen. Before this month, neither side had even called for so much as a cease-fire in the last seven hundred years.

A lot of them didn't want peace now, but my hot Greek boyfriend and I had fulfilled a prophecy and forced their hand.

Thinking about that—and him—made me smile.

Holly had refilled her M&M jar, the foul temptress. I stole a handful.

The prophecies came in sets of three, and shockingly enough, they were about a healer who could see the dead. Me.

They gave nebulous warnings about disasters and opportunities, sending me scrambling as fate came crashing down. If I passed the test, we were spared. For a while. If I failed, well, let's just say it hadn't happened. Yet.

To make things worse, my involvement had to be kept secret from everyone, including my closest friends and colleagues. The gods had outlawed my particular gift. Exposing myself would mean a slow, painful death. If I was lucky. More likely, I would be tortured eternally by something creative and mythical, like being tied to a rock while a python devoured my small intestine or set on fire upside down while spiders nested under my toenails.

Still, I was glad I'd taken the latest risk and bought us a little peace. At the moment, patients were living instead of dying.

If they survived their injuries, immortals healed fast. The last of our soldiers in recovery had gone back to their units a week after the cease-fire began.

So we'd adapted. We'd changed. Now we were treating real problems instead of endless battle injuries. We were making our patients' lives better. As far as I was concerned, that was the way things were supposed to work.

Of course, there was no telling when the gods would start up again, or who would fire first. I leaned against the edge of the desk, finishing off my M&M's.

Holly eyed me, as if she knew what I was thinking. "The colonel has us stocking up on everything."

"Good." We'd kept our heads on our shoulders this long by being prepared, fast, and more than a little lucky.

Unfortunately, luck can only get you so far.

* * *

Once Medusa had made her way out, with her vitamins and all of her questions answered, I signed out of the clinic. Technically, I'd been coming off duty when I'd grabbed her chart. Still, it seemed like the Gorgon had needed a friendly female ear. Or at the very least, someone who wasn't squeamish around snakes.

I banged out the door and into the heart of the MASH 3063rd. I'd gotten into medicine to make a difference, to treat the creatures that others couldn't—or wouldn't.

Then representatives from the New God Army had shown up at my door. I'd been drafted, forced to leave my practice in New Orleans, for this.

It was hard to believe sometimes that it had been only seven years ago. Most days, it seemed like a lifetime.

The suns set low over the Limbo landscape, throwing off brilliant oranges and purples. A wide desert stretched beyond our MASH unit.

Underfoot, and as far as the eye could see, rock littered the barren red landscape.

It was how I'd pictured Mars as a kid.

The entire place was flat save for the cemetery. We had a hard time digging into the Limbo rock, so it was more efficient to make a dirt hill for the bodies.

"Hold up!" I heard from two buildings down. Shirley was stubbing out a cigarette in front of Colonel Kosta's office. She worked as the commander's private secretary. "Have you heard?" she asked, red hair sticking every which way out of her bun as she jogged toward me.

"What? That the USO is sending us a Sycion lyre quartet?" I'd heard. "I wish the gods would appoint somebody new to the entertainment committee." I'd settle for anybody whose idea of a good time went beyond lutes, fire eating, and ancient plays. My life was already a Greek tragedy.

"No." She stopped in front of me, her eyes swimming with sympathy. "Galen just got called back."

Cold apprehension seized me. I knew this was coming someday, but that didn't stop my stomach from turning to lead. Galen of Delphi was the commander of the Green Hawk Special Forces team and, well, let's just say we'd been enjoying the break in the fighting a little more than most. He was on leave from his unit, due to a paperwork mistake that I'd hoped it would take the army a long, long time to rectify.

My throat felt tight. "Where is he?"

She glanced toward the shadows past the cemetery. "I think he went out to Father McArio's."

Father McArio was our unit chaplain. "Okay, thanks." I headed straight across the common area. Father lived past the graveyard and through the junk depot, in a little hutch on the very outskirts of camp. He claimed to enjoy the solitude. I suspected he was secretly ministering to the lost souls of Limbo.

I scrambled up the rise toward the cemetery, almost thankful for the energy burn. My mind raced. It was too soon to lose Galen. We'd barely dated. I didn't know where this was going.

Wooden grave markers of all shapes and sizes stood at attention. These were the doctors and the nurses, the mechanics and the clerks. People like me, who would never make it out of Limbo. Not unless the war ended for good.

"Petra," Galen called, emerging from behind a tangle of burned-out Jeeps. He strode toward me, and I took off in a run.

He wore black combat fatigues with a Ken rune etched in red on his left shoulder. It was the symbol of flame, action, and heroism, and the man had it all in spades.

"I just heard," I said, dodging graves, rushing into his

arms. He held me tight and squeezed. God, I was going to miss him. I closed my eyes. "When do you leave?"

"In an hour."

My eyes flew open. "What?"

That was ridiculous. He had to pack, prepare. We had to say goodbye.

He stood in front of me, all brute force and power. He was built for combat, but he couldn't fight this. "You know the army."

Did I ever. I understood it the moment I'd sat in my little paranormal clinic in New Orleans and opened the New God Army draft notice.

My dad couldn't even see me off as they led me out into the depths of the bayou to a portal that hung like a misty cloud amid a tangle of cypress trees. Before I could say *bad idea*, I was in the flat red wastelands of Limbo.

Still, Galen should have been different. He was with an elite unit that took on the most important, and deadly, missions. In the past, he'd been given special consideration. He was one of them—the immortals—until a risk he took for me drew the ire of the gods.

They'd stripped him of his immortality. Now the demigod was as good as human, and he was leaving to fight immortals.

I might never see him again.

"It's too soon," I said, running my hands down his uniform. I wished there was something I could do to stop this, to buy more time.

He lowered his mouth to mine for a sweet, soulful kiss that was like coming home. I needed this. I needed more time.

He was set up in the VIP tent, which was a slice of heaven. We'd spent most of my off-hours laughing and talking and feeding each other fruit from the incredible daily ration they gave him. He had to keep up his strength, after all.

He drew a breath. "Gods, you're beautiful." He leaned his forehead against mine. "I could stay here for eternity and still never get enough of you."

"I like the staying-for-eternity part."

"I know."

We rested for a moment. There were no right words. Nothing either of us could say would make this better.

He drew me close and stared out over the darkening cemetery.

I traced my fingers along his bicep, a few inches below his unit patch. There was a scar there, crisscrossing over to his chest. I couldn't see it, but I knew it was there. I knew every inch of him. "It's going to be okay," I said.

"No, it's not," he said into my hair. His posture was stiff. As he pulled back, his face was a mask of pain and regret. "Petra." The agony was clear in his voice. "We can't see each other anymore."

For a split second, I didn't understand what he said. "What?" He hesitated for a moment, and I knew. I *knew*. My ears buzzed and my brain threatened to explode. "You're breaking up with me?"

He winced as if I'd slapped him. "I don't want to." He took me by the shoulders, as if he could somehow will me to understand. "I received my orders this morning. What I'm going to do—" He stopped and shook his head. "What I *must* do could expose you and your secret. I'm not going to take that chance."

Expose me? "What's going on?"

He stiffened and dropped his hands. "It's classified."

"Oh, no. Do not pull that on me." He could at least give me the facts so that we could argue about them.

His jaw was tight, his expression guarded, and I realized I was talking to Galen the warrior instead of Galen the man. "If there was another way, I'd find it. You know I'd fight for you. I'd do anything to be with you. But I'm not going to lose you. I'm not going to be the one who unleashes the gods on you." He spoke as if he were in physical pain. "We have to cut it off. Now."

"Just tell me what changed." I needed to understand. "And why is this your decision?" He had to throw me a bone. I was stronger than I looked. "Tell me what's going on, and we can fight this." Whatever this was, we could face it together.

He bristled. "This isn't up for debate. I'm not going to let you do anything stupid that could get you killed."

Oh, sure. Fine. "But it's okay for you to die."

He cleared his throat, and suddenly I felt horribly guilty. There was a real chance I would never see him again, even if he wasn't being an idiot and breaking up with me.

He said the words slowly, as if he'd gone over them so many times in his mind that they were permanently fixed. "We knew when I lost my powers that eventually it could end badly," he said. "Please. Don't let this be the way we say goodbye."

I planted my hands on my hips and stared him right in the baby blues. Too bad for him I was terrible at letting things die. "I'm sorry to screw up your noble moment here, but this is war. We're soldiers. We fight. And I'm going to be with you until the end whether you like it or not."

"You are in danger," he said, his words clipped. "Every second I stay here in this camp with you, you are at risk."

"Maybe this is how it's supposed to be." He'd known from the start I was the loyal type. The prophecies had worked in strange ways last time, but we'd made it precisely because we'd stuck together. "Why don't you let me choose whether or not I want to risk it?" I'd been through enough already. This was war. I'd lost my first love, Marc, to the senseless violence. I never regretted sticking with him until the end, and I wasn't about to abandon Galen, either.

He glared at me. At least he wasn't arguing anymore.

"So it's a risk," I prodded. "What kind of risk?" I'd chanced the wrath of the gods themselves last month. I could handle whatever Galen had to face. I could see him working to close himself off.

He scrubbed a hand over his face. "I shouldn't have even told you that much."

"But you did," I pointed out. We didn't have secrets. "You've let me in on things before."

He broke. "Not this time," he thundered.

Why did I go for the stubborn ones? "You said you loved me," I pointed out.

He cursed under his breath. "I do," he stated flatly.

"Boy, every girl dreams of a guy saying it that way," I mused.

He reached out slowly, deliberately, and tucked a stray lock of hair behind my ear.

"I want you to be happy," he said simply.

"Then don't be an asshat." If I had to get out the hand puppets, I would.

Galen ran a hand through his short, clipped hair. His jaw ground tight. "If I somehow make it back in five, ten, fifty years and you're still here and still available—then it's fate. But if I come back and find you happy, I'm okay with that, too." He was intense, almost pleading. I'd never seen him like that before.

"Galen—"

His eyes glittered. "If I die, I don't want to go knowing this time we had only caused you misery in the end."

Well, then he was doing a crummy job of it. "You realize you're making me miserable right now."

His expression softened. "Don't hold back your life the way you did before I met you. You were only existing." His fingers skimmed my cheek. “More than anything, I want you to live, even if I can’t be there with you.”

I didn’t know what to say.

He brushed his lips against my forehead. “Goodbye, Petra,” he said before he walked out of my life.

CHAPTER TWO

So this was it.

"Un-fricking believable!" I kicked a tombstone, which was a really bad idea. It hurt like a mother. "Son of a..." Tears stung the back of my eyes.

I liked the pain. I liked being ticked. Otherwise, I was going to curl up on the ground and cry like a baby.

Galen had no right, no business deciding anything for me. I didn't care if he was protecting my secret or if he was shielding me from some other abomination of the gods. We'd tackled both of those things on our first adventure —together.

We'd won, too.

I didn't see why it couldn't be the same now. And I wouldn't know because he'd shut me out. Cut me off. He'd ended our partnership in the cruelest way possible, because he refused to even tell me *why*.

He'd decided for me, for us. Now he had peace. He had resolution, and I had a gaping hole where my life used to be.

"I've got to get out of here," I mumbled to myself,

weaving through the tombstones, kicking up a small cloud of dust and decay. I ignored my aching right toe. It would heal.

As for the rest of me?

I wasn't so sure.

I had to move, think. Get away.

I couldn't imagine what kind of military order Galen could get that would make him destroy me, end *us*.

Unless he really didn't want to be with me. The horrifying notion settled in my stomach like an ugly black rock.

Maybe I'd been just a fun diversion, something pleasant to pass the time while he was stuck here, a trophy to be won.

I barreled onto the main path and almost ran into a supply clerk. She reached out to steady me. "Hey," she said, "sorry to hear about Galen."

"You and me both," I said, stepping around her, the apology dying on my lips as I wondered how she knew. She had to be talking about the transfer, not the way Galen had just ripped my heart out. Still. Did the whole camp know?

The petite blonde lingered. "He'll be fine."

"Right," I said, taking off for my hutch.

A cold wind whipped in from the desert. Daytime was stifling hot, but we had to fire up the heaters at night. I wrapped my physician's coat around my body and hugged my arms tight as another gust of wind blew straight through me.

"Petra." A few of the nurses clustered outside the officers' club, waving at me to get my attention.

I took the long way around. I didn't want to talk.

Galen had left me. Just like Marc. Only Marc had had an excuse—he was dead.

It was full darkness by now, which was good. I wanted to hide.

Torches lined the walk, casting scattered pools of light.

We'd talked the new gods into a generator for the hospital, but otherwise they insisted we go old school with lanterns and anything else we could set on fire. And we were supposed to be on the progressive side. Ha.

I trudged past the OR and the recovery tent. A few soldiers crouched outside the enlisted quarters, laughing as they raced baby swamp monsters and did shots of Hell's Rain.

The laughter died down as I passed. Holy Hades. I was a walking party killer.

"Gentlemen." I nodded to them as I passed.

I probably should have warned them that Colonel Kosta would skewer them for harboring illegal creatures, or that as a doctor I didn't recommend drinking the 180 proof precipitation that fell from the Limbo sky. But that would mean talking to them.

Yes, Galen is gone.

Yes, he left me to pick up the pieces.

Yes, I've been through it before.

I made my way to the officers' quarters and banged into the hutch I shared with a moody vampire and an overemotional werewolf. Luckily for me, the werewolf was home on leave. The vampire was another story.

Marius stood preening in front of a mirror we'd tacked up to one of the main hutch poles. He'd lit every lantern in the place.

He wore a black leather jacket, black leather pants, and knee-high swashbuckler boots. His blond hair draped roguishly over one eye, and he gave himself a smoldering look before frowning at me. "I'm sorry to hear about Galen."

"Does the whole camp know?" I asked, thumping down on my bed.

"Yes."

"He also broke up with me," I said, pulling a blanket up to my chin. It was rough and scratchy. I hated it. Maybe I could sleep for a year.

The vampire tucked a six-pack of Oreos next to me.

"Where'd you get these?" I grudgingly inspected the pack. They certainly weren't from his private stash. Marius didn't eat. And the PX never had chocolate anything.

He showed his fangs. "I threatened to devour Phineus, the deliveryman."

"You don't even like werewolves," I said, sitting up.

"Phineus doesn't know that."

I sampled a cookie while Marius opened a bottle of red wine and poured us both a glass. "Drink," he said, handing it to me. "Doctor's orders."

I tried to give him a grin and failed.

Marius took a seat on his footlocker, and we drank in silence. The wine was good, smooth. Very Marius.

He didn't ask questions or try to talk to me, which was a relief. We just sat and listened to the tar swamp bubble out back. If he'd been on his way out the door before, he didn't let on.

I swirled the liquid in my glass. "Men suck."

Marius held up his glass in a mock toast. "Yes, they do."

* * *

Shirley rapped on my door early the next morning. "Did you hear?"

I rolled over in bed. "I don't want to know."

She let herself in. Shirley wore her red hair in pigtails today. It was very...Heidi. "The armies are gearing up again," she said. "It's all over the news. They say there's going to be a new prophecy."

"Lordy." My head felt like it was filled with cotton, but I sat up anyway.

I ground my fingers over my eyes.

"Come on," Shirley said, inspecting one of the wineglasses from last night. "The prophecies are exciting."

I stood slowly. “Not the word I’d use.”

It was quite a trick—trying to save the world while being sneaky about it.

But eventually, it was said that the prophecies would bring lasting peace. I had to cling to that.

In the meantime...

“I need a shower,” I told her, using my foot to dig the caddy out from under my cot.

My towel hung on the clothesline strung across our hutch. I was tired of blood and guts and war. Now Galen had skipped out, the armies were gearing up, and I’d bet my last Oreo that the oracles were going to give us a prediction that would cost a lot of soldiers their lives.

I managed to make it in and out of the shower tent without anyone giving me any sympathetic clucking about Galen. Probably because everyone was in the mess tent, watching the Paranormal News Network. PNN was our answer to CNN. It was *Immortality’s never-ending news source.* Or so they said. I supposed we mortals would simply have to take their word for it.

We owned one television for the entire camp, an ugly, 1970s cabinet model with the carved wood and the curved gray screen.

We loved it.

A few of the mechanics had it bolted to a makeshift stand on the far right wall of the mess tent. Today the place was packed. It seemed like everyone who wasn’t on shift was sitting on one of the long cafeteria tables or in one of the chairs clustered up front. An undercurrent of fear whispered through the room.

Shirley and I wound through the crowd as we worked toward one of the back tables.

“Petra.” Holly waved from the front. “Come on up.”

People scooted aside as Shirley and I slid in next to her. I was surprised at the way people let us through. PNN watching was usually a full-contact sport.

"We heard about Galen," Holly said, commiserating.

Ah, so this was a pity seat.

I could feel people watching me. I lowered my head and scooted in. "I don't want to talk about it."

"We all liked him," said someone behind me.

Yeah, me too.

"Here. You need this more than I do," said a round-faced nurse in front of me as she turned and handed me a Bloody Mary with a limp celery stick.

"Thanks," I said, trying not to knock the bendy straw. I wasn't about to turn down liquid fortification.

Her lips pursed. "If there's anything I can do..."

"This is plenty," I said, pulling out the celery stick. Any more of this sympathy and I was going to jam it in my eye.

PNN came off commercial break, and everybody cheered. It was like feeding time at the zoo. The picture started skipping, and an orderly sitting on a stool next to the television stood up and pounded on the side of the set a few times.

A skinny young reporter huddled under an umbrella next to a sheer cliff face. I could tell he was new, and slightly terrified. Volcanic ash and bits of glowing embers rained down, but he pasted on a newsy smile in spite of it. Scalding winds whipped at his bright yellow lava-coat, and he gave a slight cringe as the ground under him vibrated.

"I'm Fletcher Turley reporting live from the Oracle of the Gods, where the sky is purple and the lava is flowing," he said breathlessly. "My sources tell me we haven't had a magma shower like this since they buried Pompeii." He braced himself as the wind nearly blew him sideways. "PNN was the first on the scene then, just as we are now as the oracles get ready to reveal the next chapter in the war of the gods."

The news anchor's voice boomed from the studio. "Can we get a close-up on that lava shower, Fletcher?"

"Sure, Stone," he said, microphone shaking. The camera panned down to the glowing embers bouncing off his polished brown dress shoes.

I knew what fiery stone looked like. I was more interested in how young Fletcher was going to make it out of that lava field.

The wind buffeted his umbrella and blew his hair sideways as he held out against the storm. "The crowds are growing out on the water, even though Lemuria is a lost continent," he hollered, voice rising above the fracas as the camera panned out. Everything from barges to sailboats to kayaks bobbed out on the water. "Officials are warning that observers not use wooden boats, as they are flammable."

The camera cut back to the PNN studio, where a slickly coiffed, overly tanned werewolf sat behind a news desk. "Thanks, Fletcher. You're doing a fine job out there," he said in perfect news monotone. "As you can see, we have some severe eruptions in the south. Let's check in with PNN Weather for the update."

The camera cut to a skinny redhead in front of a radar screen. "Thanks, Stone. We have a severe eruption warning from Lemuria all the way to the Atlantean islands." She flipped back her hair as she posed in front of a map of the lost islands dotting the Indian Ocean. "We're getting reports of falling lava rocks the size of golf balls. PNN Lava Radar shows continuing storms for the next two days, suggesting that the oracles will indeed be shaking things up for a while longer."

I turned to Shirley. "I don't want to wait a few more days." Then again, maybe I did. Who knew what disaster they were going to predict?

Shirley chewed her lip as the reporter droned on.

"The heat index in the impact zone is one eighteen. But where we are, Stone, you're looking at a breezy seventy-five."

A restless stir wound through me. I needed to know what might happen next. It might even give me some clue as to what was going on with Galen.

The newsman smiled, his teeth blazingly white. "Thanks so much. This is Stone McKay, and you're watching PNN twenty-four-hour live coverage of Oracle Watch 2021. More after this break."

They cut to a commercial for Fang-zite. The all-natural male fang enhancer. A handsome vampire held up a bottle and winked at the camera. "Show her you've got a little something extra...with Fang-zite."

Ew. I slid off the table. "I need to move."

Shirley caught my sleeve. "Are you sure you want to be alone right now?"

I glanced at half a dozen pairs of sympathetic eyes. "I'm sure."

There were no secrets around this camp, which meant I'd be hearing about the prophecy about a minute after Fletcher Turley, junior reporter.

The last batch of oracles had threatened my life and my sanity. Maybe this time, they'd go easier.

And maybe I'd grow wings and fly.

The TV blared behind me. "Tune in tonight, when we take a special look at supernatural hoarders. We'll visit a voodoo queen buried in bones. A vampire who can barely fit into his coffin. And a pet-hoarding MASH surgeon. The doctor is in, but she can't even get into her hutch!"

I winced. Would they quit it with the reruns? My roommate had accidentally bred a gaggle of swamp creatures, and in doing so scored the only successful prank ever pulled on our camp commander. Rodger snagged the prize—three weeks' leave. I'd gotten cleanup duty, and a reputation.

My dingbat colleagues could never resist a practical joke. When PNN showed up, my friends made me out to be some crazy cat lady of the swamp. I was both impressed and horrified.

Add that to the footage PNN shot of me wrangling the beasts and *Supernatural Hoarders* had their best ratings in years.

I had to believe they'd stop running it. Eventually.

Ever since peace broke out, PNN seemed to be having trouble filling the twenty-four-hour news cycle. There was no slow period for them, no downtime. Not with vampires, werebats, and other nocturnal creatures in the audience.

Maybe they'd have more to report on after the prophecy.

What an unpleasant thought.

Luckily for me, the clinic was busy. I spent the next several days focusing on my patients rather than dwelling on gods, newsmen, or my less-than-stellar personal life.

Just as bad as Galen leaving me was my complete inability to understand what had made him do it. We'd faced down the prophecies before—what made this any different? I turned it over and over in my mind until I was sick.

Those weeks with him had made me feel more alive than I had been in the ten years since Marc's death. I didn't want to go back to that. It hurt too much.

How was I supposed to simply move on?

I treated a werehyena with a bad lung infection and one of our motor pool mechanics for a broken arm. I also saw a fury with a heart condition. Heart issues were common in the more high-strung of the supernatural races, which was no excuse, really. This was where preventive medicine really paid off.

As the days wore on, my colleagues bugged me less and less about how I was feeling. It didn't stop me from hoping that Galen would come back safe and that somehow, someday, we could put this war behind us forever.

Marius burst into the recovery tent as I walked a demigod up the aisle between beds.

Dang, the sun was down already?

My patient was moving slower than I liked. I shook my head. "That's it. I'm keeping you overnight."

The wiry young soldier held up his hands, his Celtic war braid winding over one shoulder. "Lay off, Doc. I'm fine."

He was in pain, the dufus. I didn't care how fast demigods healed. He needed a twenty-four-hour stay. It was my personal minimum after doing this type of hernia surgery. But the New God Army hadn't come out with non-combat surgical guidelines yet, and of course this yahoo was in a rush to get back to his unit. I couldn't force him back to bed.

"No heavy lifting," I warned him.

He puffed out his cheeks at me.

"Petra." Marius stood behind me.

I held up a finger. "Just a sec," I said, focusing on the demigod. "I'm not the one who tried to impress a girl by lifting a manticore."

The soldier crossed his powerful tattooed arms over his chest, looking everywhere but at me. "I feel fine, Doc."

"You come right back in if you detect any tenderness or swelling," I said, handing over his release forms. Just like that, he was out the door, letting in a gust of warm air. "You're welcome," I hollered after him.

Antiseptic and desert dust. This place always smelled the same.

Marius stood watching me. "We've got a prophecy."

"Oh wow." My stomach sank. He didn't look happy. "Were you there?"

He kept his eyes on me. "Yes," he said, leaning against the nurses' desk.

"So what'd they say?" I adjusted the stethoscope on my neck, trying to keep my breath steady.

"*The peacekeeper will find love*," Marius began.

I blinked twice. Okay, that was good. Hope surged. Maybe Galen would come back.

"*As*," he continued, "*a hideous new weapon is born*."

He had to be kidding me. "We don't need any more weapons." The old-fashioned swords and cannon fire were destructive enough.

"You can't beat love," Marius said simply.

Did he suspect?

I'd deny it like my life depended on it—which it did.

Still, I could understand his interest. The prophecies predicted an eventual end to the war—if they all came true. Marius had a bigger stake in that than anyone.

Every last one of us was enlisted in the army until the end of the conflict. Since I was a half fairy, I'd be here for about 150 years. Our werewolf roommate, Rodger, had the least amount of time. He'd grow old and die like a human. But Marius was immortal. He was here for eternity.

* * *

Long after lights out that night, I lay awake and thought about it.

The peacekeeper will find love.

I'd found it already. Twice. And both men had left me. Marc I couldn't fault. Galen was another story.

Still, I couldn't help but wonder. Maybe this meant Galen had misinterpreted his orders, or that he'd have a short mission. Maybe he'd be back. He could be sorry for how he'd ended things.

He should be.

I woke the next morning still thinking about it.

What would I do if he did come back?

Marius had gone into his death sleep, either in his footlocker or—more likely—in the makeshift lair we'd cobbled together out by the tar swamps. I glanced that way, watching firebirds as they soared and dove for bog beetles. I sat up and saw a note fluttering on the outside of our door.

If it was another sympathy note, I was going to scream.

I took it off the door on the way to the showers.

Meet me by the burned-out officers' showers.

My heart squeezed. "No way." I had to read it twice.

Galen had always found it amusing the way we tended to go through officers' showers. It wasn't my fault, though. They seemed to get caught up in a lot of practical jokes.

I read the note again and then shoved it into the pocket of my robe. You'd think he'd come into camp if he could. He was sure popular around here. Unless he couldn't show himself. Had Galen left his unit? I cringed to think of him going against orders again, especially when the consequences had been so severe the last time.

The gods had punished his insolence by stripping him of his immortality. It was basically a death sentence. When the war started up again, Galen would be pitted against immortal demigod warriors over and over again. Until...

I didn't want to think about it.

Instead, I took the fastest shower in history and changed into a fresh set of scrubs. I could roll with this. I combed my fingers through my wet hair. If he'd come back, we could at least talk. We could set things right before he headed off to war again.

I barged out of the showers and ran straight into Holly.

"You're not on shift today, are you?" she asked, righting herself.

"No," I said, already halfway past her. "Sorry. I'm meeting a friend in the minefield."

"Way to rebound." She gave me a mock salute.

"It's not like that," I said, walking backward, eager to be on my way.

We called the unit junk depot "the minefield" only because the field beyond the cemetery was so full of broken-down vehicles, half-wrecked buildings, and machinery parts that the bored among us had seen fit to rig it with practical jokes. It was pointless and immature, but that was why we liked it.

You'd think that people would avoid the place, but you had to go through the minefield in order to make it to the prime make-out spot—the only place you could really count on being alone—the rocks.

I'd never been to the rocks. Scratch that. I'd been there once with Galen. And it had been amazing. But most of the time, I went into the minefield to see Father McArio or to work in the makeshift lab I'd set up out there.

But it never failed. If you braved the minefield, people always assumed you had a date on the other side.

If I remembered correctly, the burned-out officers' showers should be about halfway through the maze of junk, right after the mangled helicopter.

I rushed through the city of scraps faster than I should have. Hulking skeletons of half-rotted bed frames and Jeeps lay rusting on either side of the rock-strewn path. I ducked past leaning heaps of particleboard and a mashed-up refrigeration unit, breathing in the tinge of rust and dirt. A slight left after the gutted ambulance took me past my workshop and almost to the officers' showers.

The Limbo suns beat down. I stripped off my scrub shirt, glad to have a tank top underneath.

A low peeping made me stop. Dukkies. They were tiny red birds with black horns and sharp little beaks.

In the egg stage, you could eat them. In the adult stage, they might try to nest in your shoes. But in the just-hatched baby stage, they'd bond with you like you were a mother duck.

I lifted my foot and searched for trip wires. Two steps ahead, I spotted them half buried in the dirt. They led to an innocent-looking box.

Ouch. I'd be sure to tell Father McArio. He worked with a group of nuns who did creature rescue. In the meantime, I stepped over the wires and continued on my way.

Just past it, I spotted the burned-out showers. The door stood ajar.

"Galen?" I called, walking carefully, keeping an eye out for any more dukkie-style traps.

I could see a shadow moving inside. The two front stalls had been ripped out, leaving one main tent support.

Maybe Galen was trying to be subtle. Yeah, well, subtle didn't work on me.

"Did you miss me?" I barged in the door and nearly fell over.

The shower-turned-shack was small and dim, smelling of charred wood and rotting canvas. Light filtered from loose boards in the ceiling.

And there, right in front of me, stood Marc.

My pulse pounded and my head swam. I hadn't seen him since New Orleans.

He loomed larger than I remembered, harder, with slashing green eyes that made him look like he wanted to eat me alive. I could feel the heat of them through my thin tank top.

His blond hair had been shorn hard, so that it spiked at

odd angles as it grew out. He needed a cut, but I doubted he cared. Marc was never one for rules that didn't suit him.

He'd been drafted ten years ago into the Old God Army. He'd been killed ten years ago. And while I had a special talent for seeing the dead, I could tell right away that Marc was very much alive.

Sweet heaven. I'd sat in his mother's living room and grieved with her. I'd helped bury an empty casket.

"Marc?" I choked.

His face was unreadable. At least I had no reference for it. Not anymore. He wore the tan fatigues of the enemy, with a green ankh emblazoned on the sleeve. I shook my head. Of course. He was with the medical corps. They'd taken him from Tulane Hospital on a cold day in February. We'd eaten cookies for breakfast that morning in the hospital cafeteria. That was the last time I'd seen him.

Until now.

I opened my mouth, but nothing came out. What do you say to a dead man?

He took a measured step closer. "It's been a long time, Petra." The light fell on him, and I saw a jagged scar along his neck.

He'd suffered.

Hadn't we all?

A chill skittered up my spine. "You're alive." All those years, I thought he was gone. I mourned him. I missed him.

He took another step closer, and I caught my breath. If I could have ever imagined having this kind of second chance, I would have thought I'd rush into his arms, or wax poetic. Or at least have something interesting to say. But I couldn't even bring myself to move.

He looked older. Leaner. There was an unfamiliar hardness about him.

He shook his head ruefully, the same way I'd seen him do

it a hundred times. Only he looked different doing it now. He'd changed.

So had I.

He began to reach out to me, then stopped, swearing under his breath. "It's good to see you."

It was all so surreal. "What happened to you?"

He glanced toward the door. "I don't even know how—" he began, his words heavy with regret. "First, I need to ask you something, and I don't have much time."

"No kidding." He was in an enemy camp.

He blew out a breath, as if he'd read my mind. "I can't believe you're here." A trace of light skittered across his features.

"Why are you?" I asked, standing opposite him, as if we were separated by a great divide instead of two feet of dirt.

Frustration stirred in my gut. He was no better than Galen. Scratch that. Marc was worse. He hadn't even had the decency to tell me he was alive.

He clenched his jaw, determined. "I need someone I can trust."

CHAPTER THREE

"Trust?" The man wanted to talk trust? For as much as I wanted to feel relief and joy, all I could comprehend was stark white shock.

He'd abandoned me. He'd lied. For ten straight years. "We thought you were dead," I said, body shaking. "We buried you." I'd gone with his mother every Sunday to place lilies on his grave.

My head felt like it was going to float away. I stood stock-still, trying to get a grip. "Now you're back. Not because you're sorry or because you miss me, but because you *trust* me." It hurt more than I would ever admit. And at that moment, a secret awful part of me wished he'd stayed dead.

His voice grew husky. "The army made a mistake." He stared at me hard, as if he could make me understand by force of will alone.

My stomach hollowed. "You did, too." He'd had ten years to correct the error, and he didn't.

He reached for me. "Listen, I know—"

I held out a hand to block him. "Why'd you do it? What happened?" How had this gotten so messed up? "No more lies," or wishing things were different. He'd had his chance, and he blew it.

He scraped a hand through his hair, making it spike up even worse. He was shaking. "Our unit was too close to the front," he said. "We had to retreat. But I'd just done an arterial reconstruction. There was no way we could move that patient for at least twenty-four hours."

I crossed my arms over my chest. "So you stayed." I'd heard this part before.

"Yes." He was tense, his muscles drawn painfully tight. "It was the only thing to do."

I knew that. "I never blamed you." His father hadn't understood. His mother had been so angry. But I knew he didn't have a choice. I would have done the same thing.

A muscle twitched over his cheekbone. "The camp was overrun, and the New God Army was ordered to take no prisoners."

My stomach dropped. It was as good as an order of execution. "My side did that?" The shock of it loosened me. I stepped backward, hand on my hip, trying to make sense of it. We didn't order killings. We were the enlightened ones.

Marc's voice tightened. "My patient was given to the Shrouds."

"No," I said, the word tumbling out of me.

The enemy—their side—they were the ones who used the cursed creatures who fed on life like parasites. Shrouds moved like silvery shadows, sucking the life and souls from humans and endlessly torturing immortals to the brink of death.

Marc had confessed it without malice. He hadn't asked for pity. He was telling me the plain truth. He'd accepted it. I couldn't even fathom it.

His eyes held mine. "One of their special ops officers was supposed to take me out back and slit my throat. Only he pulled his punch. Left it to the fates. Said if I was supposed to live, I would." The pain of it crossed his face. "I lived. I made it back to our lines." He cast me a guilty look. "By then I'd been reported dead for a month. They'd shipped my personal effects back home. The funeral was over."

I couldn't imagine going through something so horrific, so wrong. Still... "You didn't feel the need to tell us you were alive?"

Part of me died when I lost him. He'd been my entire world. I didn't have anything else besides Marc and my studies at Tulane. He'd stayed and done his fellowship there so that we could be together. He was the one person who was never going to leave me.

I didn't know what was worse: That he'd let me grieve. That he'd torn a hole in his own family when they lost him. Or that he couldn't seem to comprehend just how much he'd meant to us.

He swallowed hard. "I knew I was never coming home. Sure, I could have given you false hope. I could have written you letters. But it was killing Mom." He cast me a miserable look, as if daring me to deny it. "She wasn't sleeping. She wasn't eating. She was afraid to live, because what if she so much as cracked a smile while I was dying somewhere? You know it's true," he said, noting my surprise. "She told me."

My throat tightened. Of course it was true. "She loved you." How could he expect his own mother to let go? How could any of us ask that?

As far as I was concerned, the family Marc had left behind was a gift. They truly loved one another. And me. Yes, we'd suffered together because of it, but I wouldn't have wanted it any other way.

He grimaced. "You weren't moving on," he said, as if it cost him to utter each word.

I shrugged, helpless. "I couldn't."

The air around us thickened. "I know," he said simply. "I never planned to let any of you go." He cleared his throat.

He reached out for me and then changed his mind. I felt it like a slap. "It was better to let you have closure," he said.

Of all the... "Do you honestly believe that?" I demanded. Did he have any clue how much it hurt to know that the man I loved was dead?

I closed the distance between us, wanting to at least hug him, hating myself that I refused to do it. I wanted to punch Marc and Galen and every man in the history of time who'd tried to be noble. "It doesn't work that way. You can't manipulate people like that. You have to live your life as it comes." No apologies. No sugarcoating it.

We stood inches apart, unmoving. He didn't back down. Neither did I.

He was so mad, spots of color streaked his cheeks and forehead. "I didn't want you living your life for a day that would never come," he ground out. "I didn't want to hold you back. I was never going to make it home. You still had a life. I wanted you to move on, get married, have babies."

"I thought you loved me."

"I do love you!" he snapped.

I stepped back. "Well, then you've got a screwed-up way of showing it."

He shook his head slowly. "Maybe I do." He dropped his chin for a moment. When he faced me again, the pain of it was staggering. "I'd have done anything—even let someone else have you—if it meant you'd be happy again."

What? Did I have *move on while I go die nobly* printed on my forehead?

I twisted my lips into a mock smile. "That was your mistake." I'd never cared about anyone else. Not until Galen.

And look how that had turned out.

"Petra." His take-charge bravado slipped, and I saw the

Marc I remembered, the man who felt too much. The pain in his eyes seared me to the core. "I didn't want you to suffer."

Too late.

I let out a breath. This was so messed up. I leaned my back against the rough wooden tent pole. "It would have been nice to know you were down here when I got conscripted." I could have used the support.

He dug a hand through his hair. "We're on opposite sides."

"Right." He was the enemy.

A loud crash sounded outside. Quickly, Marc and I ducked back into the dusty shadows behind the last wooden shower stall. He drew me close, and for a moment I held my breath for an entirely different reason. I remembered the warm steady feel of him, the way his fingers gripped when he held me.

The heat of him seeped through my clothes as his body pressed against me. We used to wake up that way, his lips brushing my cheek.

I closed my eyes as his breath warmed my ear. His chest rose and fell against me. I felt myself soften. It was my body's natural response to being held, nothing else. I didn't want this. I didn't want to remember. I tried to draw away, but he held me close. He even smelled the same. Under the sweat and dirt, I detected the warm, spicy scent of him that used to make me feel safe and loved.

Two men outside cursed loudly. Dukkies quacked up a storm.

Fear pricked along my spine. Our patrols didn't usually monitor the minefield unless they suspected a threat had made it past our defenses.

Their voices calmed, and once again, we heard them speaking low to each other as they approached. My heart sped up. The air inside the showers hung heavy and hot. A drop of perspiration slid down my chest. I couldn't make out the words the guards spoke, but I knew these two weren't out to party in the minefield—or at the rocks.

Seven hells. I was hiding out with the enemy.

I wondered what they'd do to him if they caught him here. I pressed closer to Marc without even thinking about it. His arm tightened around me. The last time, our side had tried to execute him.

"Hey now," I heard a familiar voice say. It was Father McArio. He was usually in camp during the day.

"Have you seen any suspicious activity?" one of the men grunted.

"Yes," Father said with conviction, and my heart sank. "Out by my hutch. I was just coming to find you."

Thank heaven. I about collapsed against Marc as Father McArio led the men away.

I caught myself and drew back, bracing my hands against his chest. Desert dirt dusted the stiff, rough material of his field jacket. He'd always been lean, but now he was coarser, harder.

His gaze raked over me. His fingers traced me like he was trying to memorize every breath, every touch, every nuance of my expression as I watched him. I should have stepped back, but I didn't.

"I can't believe you just waltzed into my camp," I whispered.

Marc drew a hand down my arm, as if any moment I'd bolt. A wry smile twisted his lips. "I didn't think they'd forward a letter."

Most people I knew grew more cautious with war. Marc had grown more reckless. And while I'd never been a big believer in the rules, I knew which ones to follow in order to stay alive.

I shook my head. He was nuts to try to find me. It was too cocky, too bold. "Can you at least try to be practical?"

The corner of his mouth tipped into a grin. "I am. This was the best way to find you."

I snorted. "You still haven't told me what you want."

His humor fled. "It's complicated."

I'd figured.

He checked his watch. "I need to get back soon. I'm with the MASH-19X. We're set up about thirty miles away on the other side of the Great Divide."

That was even crazier. "How'd you make it over?" The Great Divide was the line of demarcation for the immortal armies.

He shrugged a powerful shoulder. "I flew out just before dawn."

I gaped at him. Sure, he was a shapeshifting dragon, but you couldn't just breeze over hostile territory.

"I had help," he said, drawing me into the light. "This is important. I've been working on a big project with Dr. Keller."

He had to be kidding me. "Dr. Keller from Loyola?" He'd been Marc's mentor and one of my professors, too. Keller was tough but good.

Marc nodded. "We were conscripted at the same time. Last winter, he called on me to help him develop a new medicine. Supposedly." He frowned. "Research is overseeing it."

"Interesting." The gods tended to shun new technology, thinking the old ways were superior. Any new medicines were usually the result of little labs like mine.

The light played off Marc's face. "We were only given one part of the project. That alone is unusual. But there's also something off in the chemical structure. I don't think it is what they say it is. It could be dangerous."

"This is war," I reminded him. Heck, I'd already blown up my lab once trying to come up with a simple anesthetic that worked on immortals.

His eyes narrowed slightly. "Believe me, nobody's ever seen anything like this. I covered for Keller while he ran some special experiments," he said, his tone grim. "Off the books."

"That sounds like Keller." And Marc.

"Until the night I was on call in the OR. He stayed in the lab. He was on the verge of a big breakthrough. I hadn't seen him that excited in months." He paused, his lips pressed together. "Then he disappeared."

My stomach twisted. I'd heard about how people disappeared in the Old God Army. "Maybe he was transferred," I said. It could happen.

Marc shook his head. "We both know that's not true." He drew in a breath. "Now there's a ghost in the lab. It's destroying everything, and I don't know why."

My heart squeezed a little. "You think it's him."

He gave a long sigh. "No one has been able to get close, but I'm pretty sure it's Dr. Keller."

Marc was the only other person besides Father McArio and Galen who knew my secret. And while Father McArio would take it to his grave, and Galen had sacrificed to hide me, Marc's intentions were suspect. "You want to expose me."

"No," he said, hard, unrepentant. "I only want you to talk to my ghost."

"To a murdered soul," I whispered under my breath.

"In all likelihood, yes," he admitted. "But I'll stand with you," he promised. "I'll do anything you need to keep you safe."

But he wouldn't see what I saw. The souls couldn't touch him.

The men who died in battle rose up, noble, their missions complete. Murdered dead were traumatized by the sins of their killers. They were unpredictable, angry. If they moved on, they could be restored. Until then, they were lost in darkness. Their rage gave them wild and unpredictable powers.

"I told you about the spirit of the murdered girl in Laveal Swamp," I said. I'd steered my boat out to her. She'd dived straight for me, burrowing into my skin, greedy to get inside me. For a brief moment, she'd possessed me.

I'd blacked out, lost myself, and felt only the sheer, startling pain of her tortured soul crushing me.

Not only did murdered souls become mindless and vicious, they became obsessed with the desire to live again. They'd do anything to find an easy host—me.

"I know what I'm asking," Marc said, his words low and unapologetic. "I've thought long and hard about this. You're not a teenager anymore. And I wouldn't ask this if it weren't important." He fixed his gaze on me. "Can you talk to him?"

My mouth went dry.

It was very likely that Keller had been slaughtered just so he couldn't talk.

I drew a hand over my eyes. It might be too late anyway. "How long has he been gone?"

"Two nights ago," Marc said, regret coloring his words.

Dang it. There was a good chance he'd be around. Spirits often lingered where they died, especially in the cases of violent death.

"In your lab. In an enemy camp," I said, trying to wrap my head around it.

He looked at me steadily, willing me to say yes. "I can get you in."

It was nuts. "I'm not even sure how you got out."

"Look here," he said, drawing a small military map out of his back pocket. He unfolded it over his leg. "The armies are dug in at the edge of the fourth quadrant, both in a U-shaped pattern."

He traced a blunt finger over the sandy beige topographic map. In red, he'd scrawled the long front lines of the armies, with their backup forces pulled in on either side.

"How am I supposed to get around that?"

That much power in one place could literally make the battlefield vibrate. The energy on the ground would be astronomical. It would fry me in a second.

Marc glanced up. "I've got a person working on it."

I studied him. "Do you really think I'm crazy enough to go with you?" Even I had my limits.

A dull suspicion spiraled in the pit of my stomach. "Wait. Are you trying to use this to somehow try to reunite?" Because it wouldn't work. "I can't handle that." I was done getting yanked around.

He didn't budge, but his eyes betrayed the depth of his hurt. "I've known about you for weeks."

"Oh," I said, stung. He certainly hadn't rushed to my side.

Guilt flashed across his features. "PNN."

The hoarders. Great.

He looked me square in the eye. "I'm not going to lie to you."

I nodded, not sure if I appreciated that or not. There's nothing like knowing your ex truly didn't miss you.

Stamping down the hurt, I offered a tremulous smile. This wasn't about love or loss. The practical, bold, take-no-prisoners Marc hadn't been hell-bent to see me. He was risking his skin in order to talk to our dead ex-professor. And this really was about a reckless field trip to an enemy camp.

I pushed back a layer of hair that had fallen over my eyes. "I don't even know how I'd get there." He could shift and fly, but I was stuck on the ground within the strict confines of camp.

We kept our borders protected for a reason. Imps roamed the Limbo landscape. And if they didn't get you, you were just as likely to be swallowed by a bottomless sinkhole or attacked by a rogue demon.

Not to mention the punishment I'd face if the New God Army discovered I'd gone AWOL.

If the army went easy on me, I'd face execution. If they wanted to make an example out of me, I could be looking at eternal torture.

Still, I couldn't help but think about the prophecy, about the new weapon.

Marc's eyes searched mine. "I know it's too much, but do this for me. With me."

Even though I don't want anything to do with you.

Merde. Was he trying to shove a knife in my chest?

Or make me want to shove one into his?

He stood before me, ready to lead the charge, curse the consequences. It was as if he could change things through sheer force of will. I drew a hand over my eyes. "You're certifiable."

He seemed to take that as a compliment. "And you're stronger than you think."

I sighed, torn. "I don't know how to do this."

"It has to be under the cover of night." He glanced out of the tent. "I came in by the priest's hutch, but that's too dangerous now with the patrols out."

"Don't tell me you were going to rope Father McArio into this." The realization dawned on me. "You already did." That was why the padre drew the patrol away. That was why he was wandering around the minefield.

Father McArio was sixty-five if he was a day. He should be starting to think about retirement. Instead, he'd volunteered for an assignment in Limbo, a life sentence. He was my mentor and my friend, and as far as I was concerned, he took too many risks already.

He was going to get himself killed one of these days, and I didn't want it to be because he was helping me.

Marc cast me a rueful look. "I met Father McArio while

scouting the camp. Great guy. Before I knew it, I was telling him who I was."

Father had a way of making people do that.

"He delivered the note to your door. He told me where we should meet."

I groaned out loud. They were two peas in a pod. The old Jesuit never could leave well enough alone, but this was too big—even for him. I shot him a look. "No more talking to Father McArio."

"You're right," he said, completely nonplussed. "It's a risk to both of us at this point." He thought for a moment. "When I was flying in, I saw a maze of gas tanks at the rear of the helipad. Go there. I'll get you transportation. I'll get you one of our uniforms as well."

As if all we needed was a Jeep and a new plan. "You're asking me to go AWOL. To hide out in an enemy camp. To seek out a murdered soul. To spy on a top-secret project."

He stood tall, unapologetic. "That about sums it up."

"You're not worried about me?" Galen would never let me take this kind of risk.

"You're not a kid anymore," Marc said. "You're a strong, smart woman. I need you on my side."

He didn't say it, but I knew. He wanted me as an equal.

I glanced up at him. "You think it's that important?"

"I know it is," he said with utter conviction. No sugar-coating it, no backing down. He was a soldier, the same as if he carried a sword into battle.

"Then I'll do it." I'd been in the clinic for two weeks straight. I could take a few days off. "Give me a few hours to pack. I'll be at the helipad when the suns set."

CHAPTER FOUR

I'D LEFT Marc with a handshake, as if we were passing acquaintances or business associates who'd met for a chat over coffee.

This was so screwed up. I didn't know what to think or feel, much less what to do around that man. But I'd felt the urge to reach out to him in some manner, so I did. In the lamest way possible.

It was an uncomfortable end to a gut-wrenching meeting. I could hardly believe he was alive, or that I'd agreed to help him.

I made my way down the busy walkways of our small tent city, one hand stuffed in my pocket, holding the note that had started this whole thing, running my fingers over the paper as if I needed to make sure it had even happened.

A group of nurses passed me going the other way, and I nodded to them, or at least I thought about it. I glanced back at the rise that led to the minefield. I just hoped Marc had gotten out before that patrol came back around.

He'd asked the impossible. I had every right to be ticked at him for that. I was.

But like a fool, I'd taken him up on it. It was a terrible risk, one I'd never planned to take.

Aside from the demonic creatures that would delight in eating me whole, there were hell vents, bottomless sand traps, not to mention the stark dry desert itself. That was before I arrived at the Great Divide.

Immortal armies built up incredible amounts of energy. It was a side effect of the enormous power of these demigods. It could melt engines, jam guns, short out modern weapons systems. Colonel Kosta told me once that walking the front lines could actually make an immortal's hair stand on end. Which was pretty funny at the time because Kosta was stone-cold bald.

The current wouldn't be as powerful with the armies standing down, but it wasn't like I could skip through the middle of the Great Divide. Marc was a silver dragon. He'd shifted and flown. I'd have to find another way.

When I reached the hutch, I saw my werewolf roommate's bags stacked outside, along with half a dozen crates of *Star Trek* figurines.

"Really, Rodger?" I said, opening the flimsy wooden door and banging inside. "You could have brought back Girl Scout cookies. New sheets, pillows, blankets. Instead we have plastic Captain Picards."

My auburn-haired, barrel-chested roommate turned from his suitcase on the back cot. "They're called action figures," he said, as if I were the one being ridiculous. He gave me a half hug and a clap on the back. "Besides, you should know by now that I only collect classic *Star Trek*."

"Of course. Nothing but the best." They all looked the same to me.

"These are really valuable down here," he insisted.

Right. "I didn't think I'd see you for another two days."

He shrugged. "They offered me a deal. Come back early and take four days at Christmas."

I had to grin. "No kidding. Christmas with the family."

"It's a dream come true," he said, returning to his unpacking.

I hoped Rodger had made them specify which Christmas. Unlike the gods, we didn't live forever. But if he hadn't thought of that, telling him now would only depress him.

"Dang, you've gotten tan," I told him—or at least more red. Rodger's fair skin didn't do well in the sun. His hair was wilder than ever, approaching Einstein proportions. It seemed he hadn't had time for a stop at the barbershop. "Did they say why they wanted you back?" I asked, taking a seat on Marius's footlocker. My roommates occupied the two cots on the far wall, overlooking the tar pits. "We still have a cease-fire." As of this morning, anyway.

He shoveled a stack of sweaters into the dresser next to his bed. Mary Ann sure liked to knit. "Something's going down."

That was what I was afraid of. "Did they say what?"

"Of course not." He slammed his suitcase closed. "I suppose we'll find out soon enough."

Didn't I know it. "You look like you've been in the desert for a month."

He grinned at that. "Try the pool with the kids."

For Rodger, there was no better place to be. "How's Mary Ann?"

Rodger's expression went goofy at the sound of his wife's name. "She's fantastic. I'm so lucky." He headed for the door. "Before I forget—" He ducked outside and returned with a stack of *Star Trek* junk, with a Macy's shirt box on top. "She sent you this."

I took the Macy's box and opened the lid on a batch of Cajun ginger cookies. They were small and perfectly rounded with thick, glistening sugar sprinkles on top. I bit into one and could taste the fresh spice and molasses, not to mention the cayenne bite.

"Stephen helps her bake now," Rodger said, heading outside for another load. "His favorite shows are *SpongeBob* and *Cake Wars*."

"I think I've found my dream man."

"Speaking of which," he said, easing another load inside, "how's Galen?"

My heart twisted. "Gone."

"Aw, geez." He set his boxes down on the floor.

Rodger had lived through the first set of prophecies with me. So far, I'd managed to avoid telling my closest friend I could see the dead. For all he knew, my involvement was a freak accident. It sure felt that way sometimes.

"It gets worse." I told Rodger what had happened with Galen.

He planted himself on the edge of his cot, elbows on his knees. "But why?" he asked, just like I had. "Why wouldn't he let you in on this?"

I shrugged. I'd run the question over in my mind so much I was exhausted with it. "And in case you thought my love life wasn't screwed up enough—" I sighed, hardly believing it "—Marc's back."

His brows shot up. "No way."

I dug my hands through my hair, as if that would help me make sense of it. "He's still on the other side. But that didn't keep him from tracking me down. In our camp."

Rodger's eyes bugged out.

"He thinks one of our old professors got caught up in something dangerous. He wants me to take a look."

"You?" my roommate repeated as the absurdity of it sank in. I knew the feeling.

My head hurt thinking about it. "He said they were

working on a medicine, but with the prophecy talking about a weapon, and seeing as how we never luck out when it comes to these things..."

"That's nuts," said Rodger, openly staring at me.

"I know." I hated to assume the worst, but—

"You've got to do it."

"Excuse me?"

Me saying I was going to do it and Rodger saying it were two different things. I found myself resisting, even though I knew I didn't have much of a choice.

"Have you even been outside camp?" I asked him. I'd bet anything he'd just gone through a portal to go back to the UK.

Rodger leaned back on his elbows. "I went out once, about two years ago. Remember that case at the medevac?"

Now that he mentioned it, yes. "Still, that was you, two other docs, and the MPs. This is me taking off across the desert toward the Great Divide. Even if I can figure out how to cross the lines, I'll be sneaking into an enemy unit, spying on their new technology. Is any of this scaring you yet?"

"Of course," he said.

This wasn't a *Star Trek* episode, for heaven's sake. "I could be executed."

"Or worse," he said solemnly.

Still, I couldn't get the second half of the prophecy out of my head. *A horrible new weapon is born.*

There was no way to know what it was. Unless, maybe, if I went and took a look at this thing...

"You want me to go with you?" Rodger asked.

"No," I said quickly. There was no way I'd let anyone except Marc see me talk to the dead doctor. Besides, I didn't want to be responsible for Rodger's life, especially when he had a family to think about.

"Good," he said, "because I'd probably wet my pants halfway to the Great Divide."

I buried my head in my hands. "I'm in too deep."

"What else is new?"

I looked at him. "I'd miss at least two shifts at the hospital."

"Not if I cover for you. I'll take your schedule. Heck, I owe it to you anyway." The cot dipped as he sat next to me. "I checked on the way in. I'm not even on this week's docket."

It could work, but... "What if someone comes looking for me?"

He thought for a moment. "I'll diagnose you with a nasty case of the imp flu. Nobody will want to come near this place for a week. We may even get to fumigate my footlocker."

It could use it.

I stared at the red dirt floor of our hutch. "You make it sound so easy."

"It's not. But I do think we can pull it off, at least from this end."

"I'd be AWOL."

Rodger nudged me with his shoulder. "It's always been your dream to run away."

I smirked. "Only this time, I have to come back."

"No escape is perfect." He grew serious. "Look, Petra. I don't know why this is happening or why you're in the middle of it." He stopped to consider. "You're always in the middle of it, aren't you?"

"Lately," I said, giving nothing away.

Rodger watched me as if he was trying to put the pieces together.

Nothing to see here.

I let out a breath when he let it drop. "If it does have something to do with the prophecies, you have to do it," he said. Avoiding fate could spell disaster. "My pack leader always used to say things happen for a reason." Rodger shook his head. "I mean, here I am."

It was eerily unsettling how Rodger had arrived home early. As if even before I'd seen Marc, events had been set in motion that would allow me to get out of camp and confront the murdered Dr. Keller. If I actually had the guts to do it.

"It's the little things, remember?" he said, repeating my words back to me. The last prophecies came true because of seemly inconsequential decisions.

How could I forget it? "Still, this decision is hardly free of consequences."

"If you don't go, what if you miss changing that one thing that could make the difference?" Rodger cocked his head. "What it boils down to is that I don't think you have a choice."

The truth of his words settled low in my stomach. "That's what I was afraid of."

CHAPTER FIVE

"TAKE THIS," Rodger said, tossing his army field jacket my way. It missed my cot by three feet and smacked against the canvas wall of the hutch.

"It's at least three sizes too big," I said, turning back to my duffel. I'd stowed a flashlight, extra batteries, and six of the energy bars Rodger had brought from home. Plus the cookies.

I swallowed, my mouth too dry to even contemplate eating one.

"What?" he asked, leaning up against the hutch pole. "Did you actually replace your uniform coat?"

"Of course not." I'd lost my field jacket the last time I was crazy enough to try to leave camp. But I didn't want to swim around in my buddy's. "Marc said he'd leave me a uniform."

Rodger's eyes widened. "That's the easiest way to be shot as a traitor."

"Thanks for the pep talk." I said, turning back to my duffel. "If you can tell me another way to sneak into an enemy camp, I'm all ears." Fingers trembling, I searched the nightstand next to my cot for a notebook. I tore out some pages, folded them down, and stuffed them into my boot, along with a pen. There they rested, a comforting weight against my ankle. "I won't change until I'm past the Great Divide."

Rodger harrumphed. "Speaking of which, do you have a plan for that?"

"Marc gave me a map of the armies," I said, feeling for it in my back pocket. That was treason right there. I shoved it into my other boot. It wasn't like I'd be changing my shoes.

I glanced behind me. Rodger stood in the same spot, eyeing me like a disapproving father. Tell me about it. I tried to give him a smile and failed.

"He's leaving transportation," I said, "most likely a Jeep, outside camp."

"Did he say a Jeep?"

"No," I groused, the realization prickling at me. Yeah, okay, this really was insane.

I rubbed my temples and wondered if James Bond ever got a stress headache before a mission.

Whatever Marc left for me, it had better be fast. I had to outrun imps before I could even think about crossing the Great Divide or sneaking into the enemy camp.

No telling what else was out there, either.

"Remember what I said about this being a good idea?" Rodger asked.

I searched under my cot for a weapon of some kind. All I had were shower supplies and my dress uniform, still in the box.

He stood next to me. "I changed my mind."

Yeah, well, it was too late for that. Besides, I didn't have to be a conventional soldier to pull this off. Lots of people made do. "My cousin Regis used to hunt alligators in the swamp with just a hook and a bang stick."

"What? You think self-defense is genetic?"

Sitting back on my haunches, I made a quick search of my pockets. Maybe I could stab an attacker with my penlight.

I gave a shuddering sigh. "I can't back out." Despite the fact that I was no warrior, and certainly no James Bond, we had to know what was going on in that other camp. If Dr. Keller had discovered a weapon of some kind, I could bring back photos and information. Maybe Colonel Kosta would know what to do about it. Then I really would be a spy.

Seven hells.

I stood, nudging Rodger out of my way as I tossed the penlight into my bag. Couldn't hurt, right?

"What do you think the catch is?" Rodger asked. "You know how the prophecies can be twisty and not one hundred percent literal."

I didn't even want to imagine. "Can I borrow your camera?" I asked. I hadn't bothered to bring one down here. But Rodger took pictures to send to his kids.

"Don't break it." he said, as if that was our biggest problem.

As dusk fell, I zipped up my dark blue New Orleans Zephyrs jacket. It was the best camouflage I was going to get.

Rodger stood behind me. "I still think—" He stopped himself. "Never mind."

I patted him on the shoulder. "Thanks, buddy."

The footlocker behind him rattled, and we both jumped, our nerves getting the better of us.

Marius shoved open the lid and flipped his longish blond hair out of his eyes. It fell in stylish layers that framed his face.

My stomach crumpled.

"Stay right there, missy," he said, his limbs stiff and awkward as he climbed out of the cramped space.

Yikes. "I assumed you were in your lair." And not listening in.

"I'm having new mirrors installed," he said, brushing imaginary lint from his black silk smoking jacket. Marius squinted against the lingering orange rays in the sky.

Worry stabbed at me. "I'm going whether you approve or not." I just hoped he wouldn't tell. I had to think that even if he wouldn't outright lie for me, he wouldn't turn me in.

"What you do with your short life is none of my business," he said, "but going out there without a weapon is patently ludicrous."

"Thanks for the insight," Rodger remarked.

Marius ignored him.

He turned his back on us both and began working an ornate, blood-red chest from under his cot.

"I've never seen that before," Rodger said.

"Me neither." Despite Marius's claims, we didn't really bother his stuff. Unless it was already out. And at that point, he was just asking for it.

Marius lifted the lid. Inside lay an assortment of weapons the likes of which I'd never seen. He had curved swords and jewel-handled daggers, gleaming Chinese throwing stars, and what looked to be a Regency-era dueling set.

Rodger whistled. "What are you doing with all that?"

The vampire stiffened. "I used to display them in my home. I find them quite stimulating. Here, they're just going to waste."

He had a point. Nothing could improve this dump.

Marius reached for the pistol set, and I thought he was going to give me one of them. Granted, they only had one shot each—not very useful against a pack of imps—but it was something.

Instead, he reached for a velvet sack underneath and produced a strange-looking silver-and-bronze pistol, with a snub nose and rounded handle. There was a knob on the side in an exotic spiderweb design, as if the gun could be cranked up or down. It almost looked like a toy or a weapon carried around by a crazed Victorian inventor.

"Keep this in your pocket," Marius instructed, handing it to me.

It was...interesting. "How do I load it?" I asked, turning it to the side, inspecting the scrollwork, trying to find where the bullets would even go.

"It doesn't take ammunition," he said. "It acts as an energy disruptor. I'd give you a demonstration, but you seem to have a soft spot for Rodger, as well as the swamp creatures out back. Besides, it's extremely bright when it goes off. Take your sunglasses."

I didn't know if I should be glad or worried. "Thanks," I said, touching the knob.

Marius hovered at my side like an overprotective mother. "Keep that on the lowest setting."

"No kidding? Why?" I asked. It really was a gorgeous weapon.

"Or else I'm not responsible for your scrawny hide," Marius said. "Here's the safety." He touched a long manicured finger to a lever next to the handle. "Keep that on until you're ready to use it."

"Thanks," I said, reaching sideways to give him an awkward hug.

He stood unresponsive, and I felt him stiffen under my arm. "Yes, well, if someone has to go, I'm glad it's you."

"I'll take that as a compliment," I said, easing my duffel over my right shoulder. Night had fallen. It was time to leave.

"Other side," Marius instructed. "You want to leave your firing hand free."

I opened my mouth to protest because, really, who was going to shoot at me in the middle of camp? But then I shut it. Marius was right. I needed to stay in a position to defend myself, if only because I needed to get in the habit.

"Do you know how to use all those?" I asked him as he returned the weapons chest to its place.

"I wouldn't have them if I didn't," he said, his back to me.

Rodger and I exchanged a glance.

"Be careful," Rodger said, closing in to smother me with a bear hug.

"Piece of cake," I lied before heading out into the night.

* * *

Flickering torchlight bathed the red dirt path as I made my way silently across camp.

There weren't a lot of people out, and I thanked my lucky stars I'd managed to hit the lull between dinner and late-night debauchery. Most of the people out were either returning from shifts that ran late, or catching up with a friend before heading out to the club or home for the night.

I nodded to a pair of nurses going the opposite way, my hand sweating against the canvas strap of my bag, the gun in my pocket bumping against my leg with every step.

Don't mind me. I'm just going AWOL.

Lord help me. I hadn't even snuck out of the house as a never-wild and anti-rebellious teenager. The consequences, namely disappointing my father, had seemed too high. So why not make a go of it when I was only risking my medical career and my life?

My heart pounded, and I was tempted to turn back, go home, forget I'd even run into Marc. I'd gone ten years without him. Why not another ten? Or twenty for that matter?

But I had to figure out what was happening over at the MASH-19X. I tightened my grip, straightened my back. I was the only one who could.

The oracle had predicted a hideous new weapon. It was

bad enough that the war would start up again soon. If I could learn what was happening, if I could prevent some of the horrific injuries, some of the senseless death, it would be worth it.

Please let it be worth it.

The helipad was set up on a hill overlooking the surgery tent. I ducked into the shadows between surgery and recovery and tried to stay as inconspicuous as I could. I was a shadow. Alone.

Breathe in, breathe out, I reminded myself as I made a dash for the unlit side of the hill. I didn't dare take the main path. It blazed with torches, and I wouldn't have been too surprised to run into a few guards as well. We kept some of the helicopter fleet gassed up and ready to go at a moment's notice. This was a strategic place in more ways than one.

I battled up the rocky ground, bracing my hand against the sharp stones when I felt myself slipping. There was no way to do this quietly. The rock crunched like glass under my feet.

This was one of the few natural rises on the Limbo plain. Chances were, they'd located our MASH unit here to take advantage.

There was a road off the back side—probably where I'd find my Jeep—but I wasn't about to snake around the base of the hill in the dark. There were shallow caves back there. No telling what liked to nest in them.

Besides, I had somewhat of an excuse to be on the helipad, more than I did wandering the cave openings below.

If any guards spotted me, I'd tell them I'd lost my ID.

And pray they didn't search my boots.

At last I reached the top and stepped up onto the smooth, flat dirt of the helipad. I didn't see any guards, at least not yet.

Fiery torches outlined landing zones Alpha, Beta, and

Gamma. Each pad was marked with a Greek letter and the ankh, an ancient symbol for life. It resembled a cross with a loop at the top.

That same ankh was emblazoned in red on my scrubs and on the roofs of our medical tents. It was our version of the red cross.

Beyond the landing pads, I caught a glimpse of movement in the shadows. My breath caught. It could be a guard or a creature of the night. Or my ride.

I closed a hand over the gun in my pocket, praying I didn't need to use it.

Wait. I yanked my hand back. Of course I couldn't use it —not on my own people. My head pounded. I was too keyed up.

Relax. *Breathe.*

Easier said than done.

There was no way to make it across the helipad unseen. Heart hammering, I inched along the side, making my way for the hulking machine on Gamma pad. If I could keep it between me and whatever was out there, I'd at least have some protection.

I stayed to the shadows, moving in silence.

My hand touched the cool metal of Gamma pad's chopper.

"Hurry," a familiar voice ground out.

Recognition whooshed through me. Marc. "Where are you?"

He stepped from the shadows. He'd stayed. I wasn't alone. "Thank God. I could kiss you."

His smooth facade faltered. "You don't mean that."

"No," I said automatically.

I actually didn't.

He stood with his flak jacket open and nothing underneath. Firelight flickered over the wide expanse of his chest.

"The patrol should be back in five minutes or less," he said, shrugging off the jacket completely.

Wait. "What are you doing here?" He should have been back at his own camp by now. He'd be missed. Discovered.

"You need a ride," he said, matter-of-fact.

"Right." Of course he'd stayed for me. It was Marc.

Yes, I was still mad at him, but the clenched fist inside me loosened. There was some justice in the world. One good man survived, when so often many did not.

His hands went to his waist, unhitching his belt. Firelight illuminated the curve of muscle at his hip.

Wait. I saw where this was going. A Jeep was bad enough, but if he thought I was going to ride over the Great Divide on dragonback...

He dropped his pants.

"Do you mind?" I asked, glancing behind us as he shucked his boots. Yes, I'd seen it all before, but not for the last decade. And besides, I was still angry with him. And I kind of hated him, and here he was stripping, and Harry Potter on a pogo stick, I'd forgotten how good his backside looked.

"No out-of-uniform jokes, okay?" he said, his voice betraying a smile.

Yeah, yeah. He could still get to me. I was glad one of us was amused.

"It's nothing I haven't seen before, soldier," I said, trying to keep it light, trying not to stare—and failing miserably.

He was lithe, with the build of an athlete. My tongue stuck to the roof of my mouth as I stared at the dip of muscle just below his left hip. There he wore the mark of the silver dragons. It was circular, with the head of a dragon swallowing its tail. It was supposed to symbolize never-ending loyalty to the clan. I used to play with it while we lounged in bed on our days off.

"Keep an eye out," he said, lowering his head to shift.

He was at his most vulnerable during the change. I scanned the area in front and behind us as he bent, the muscles in his back expanding, his bones re-forming. His neck grew long, and scales sprouted along his back. The air around him glittered as his hands and feet morphed into talons, and he grew to the size of a large horse. I'd seen it a hundred times, and I'd still never seen anything like it.

Spikes framed his long face, curving downward toward the hard white plates of his underbelly. Dorsal spines inched down his neck, as hard as his thick armored hide. He pawed at the ground with four-clawed talons. Legend said the claws symbolized earth, fire, air, and water. Marc was an elemental dragon of the air. Immense wings unfurled from his back.

Marc was a born dragon, silver and beautiful.

He crouched before me, rumbling low in his throat, and when he caught my eye, he blasted my leg with a shot of cold air.

"Cut it out," I said, gathering up his clothes. Teasing would not make me relax. Escaping here in one piece would.

Maybe. At least it was a start.

His clothes smelled like him, spicy and warm. I cradled them under my arm. "This is insane," I muttered, climbing onto his back.

I wound my fingers around a wide dorsal spike at the base of his neck. Its blunt tip curved upward like a saddle horn.

He snorted, his warm breath washing over my stiff fingers. For this one night, this one mission, we'd come together. So I braced myself as he shuddered and leapt off the helipad.

CHAPTER SIX

WE HUNG in midair for a split second before he dove low. My stomach jolted at the sudden drop. Show-off. It reminded me of the times I'd flown with him back home.

He had no fear, which was good, because I had plenty for both of us.

Back in the day, we'd take long hot baths after flying. Marc had never been a big tub guy until I showed him just how fun it could be if he had company.

I zapped the memory before I could dwell on it too much. I didn't need to be thinking of Marc that way. He was my past. And he was on the other side. Permanently.

Tonight was just a fluke—a brief moment in time. We were together to investigate the circumstances behind Dr. Keller's disappearance. Nothing more.

Knees tight against Marc's flanks, I clutched the thick spike at the back of his neck with one hand. The other, I used to cradle his clothes to my chest. I should have stuffed them into the duffel bag strapped over my shoulder. I would have if I hadn't been so distracted by him in the first place.

Wind tore through my ponytail as he skirted the rocky

plain beyond the helipad. We flew so low that I could make out the shadows of rocks in the moonlight.

It wasn't my worst night in Limbo.

I was just glad he'd waited for me. It was the least he could do, considering I still didn't know how we were going to survive once we hit the Great Divide. Or how I was going to face a murdered soul without it trying to kill me, possess me, or worse.

I focused on the dark desert and the bright moon. Wind buffeted my legs as his body flexed under me, his wings beating in a comforting rhythm.

I'd forgotten just how tight and powerful he was. Many of the doctors I'd known had let their bodies go, even in medical school. Marc had been a swimmer and it showed.

He'd been my first love, ever since he was my head resident and sent one of the techs to the lab to get fallopian tubes. His joke had flopped when the tech started thinking about it halfway to the lab, but it didn't matter. I'd fallen hard and fast.

I glanced behind us at the endless wasteland stretching out into the darkness.

I romanced him by having his least favorite orderly transport a body to the morgue, a body that then came blood-chillingly back to life and had the orderly screaming through the hospital and out into the parking lot. I'd never seen that woman move so fast in her life. Of course, there were no real zombies in New Orleans, none that I'd ever met, anyway.

Still, with the right makeup, I could be quite convincing.

Marc wised up and took me out for a round of oysters at Cooter Brown's. I took him home to meet my family. I was never one to play games, and I knew I wanted to be with him. He'd wanted to be with me.

Until he'd been dropped straight into Limbo.

An unearthly screech echoed across the desert, and I felt

Marc tense. I turned toward the sound and saw a pack of dark creatures barreling straight for us.

Marc growled, and I left my stomach somewhere on the ground as we rocketed straight up into the night. "Wait!" I felt like I was hanging in midair, my legs losing their grip on his back.

Sweet mother.

I grabbed him with both hands, clinging to the back of his neck. Hard curved spikes pressed against my chest as I willed myself to hold on. He wouldn't drop me. I couldn't fall.

We leveled off and spun straight for the pack of large flying *things*. They almost looked like giant vultures, slick and spindly in the moonlight.

Marc roared, icy air blasting out of his mouth, and I saw the creatures for what they were—flying imps.

I slammed my forehead into the cool scales of his neck. I didn't even know imps could fly. We were heading straight for them. Marc tensed under me as screeches filled the air. Leathery wings beat at my back. I braced against the sharp clawing of talons, waiting for them to try to rip me off Marc's back and make me fall.

But I only felt Marc's strong body underneath me, his breath raw and ragged.

Gasping, I raised my head to see past Marc's long curved neck. I saw empty sky and the full moon beyond.

"Where'd they go?" I whipped around to look over my shoulder.

The whole pack of them trailed us about fifty feet back. They flew close and disorganized, snapping at one another as their wings collided. But they didn't attack. Not yet, at least.

Marc dove close to the ground again, keeping a firm driving pace. No question he knew they were right on our tail, but he didn't charge them again. We kept flying, straight and low.

It seemed that speed was more important than victory over the wildlife of Limbo.

"Okay." A shudder ran through me. If they could attack me, if they could swoop in and snatch me, I had to think he'd take them down, or at least try. I wound my fingers more tightly around the blunt spike at the back of his neck. "We'll get through this," I told myself.

I almost believed it.

But here I was, whole and uninjured and, I realized with a start, gripping Marc with both hands. "Oh no." I'd dropped his uniform somewhere over the desert.

I rolled my left shoulder and felt the pull of the strap and the weight of the duffel resting on my back. Marius's gun lay heavy in my pocket. This was going to be fun to explain. I had my things. Marc was the only one who was going to have to walk around in the altogether.

Maybe I could lend him my Zephyrs jacket. He could wrap it around his waist à la Tarzan.

Heat blasted us from below. Squinting, I saw lava tracing across the desert floor like an insidious growth. It glowed orange hot against the blackness. My legs and feet warmed as if I were standing too close to a BBQ grill.

Keep that thought. BBQ grill. Not hot lava.

Energy crackled in the air. It weighed hard on my chest. With every breath, I could sense us drawing closer to the armies.

Sweat trickled down my back. It felt like the moment before a violent storm, when every living thing, on the most primitive level, knows to run, to hide, to seek shelter before the onslaught. Instead I held on with all my strength as we advanced.

With every beat of Marc's wings, I could feel the energy thicken. It wound low in my belly and tingled along my spine. I felt rough, wild.

Flames from the soldiers' camps burned hot on the horizon. The Great Divide stood dark and menacing between them, a no-man's-land, crackling with power. It reached out to me like a living, breathing thing.

Marc beat his wings harder, raising us higher. Soon I saw why. Giant tubes scattered across the desert floor. They glowed red against the rivers of molten rock. With great, snuffling pops, they sent lava flying into the air like mini geysers.

I could feel the heat of each burst through my combat boots.

Merde. Was this what our evac people saw every day? No wonder they didn't like to send mortal doctors too close to the front.

Dotted among the flaming geysers, large flat rocks reminded me of giant cave formations.

The energy was palpable now, a slow steady pounding that thundered through my veins and slid with an aching familiarity over my skin.

We'd lost the imps, which was as frightening as it was a relief. If minions of the devil didn't want to be here, what business did we have?

Shoulders hunched, I hugged my knees and my thighs closer to Marc as he circled one of the flat rocks. I couldn't believe he was actually getting closer to the ground and the geysers.

I felt the heat on my face, then a lurch as his talons hit the surface and we came to a shuddering stop.

"Here?" I asked.

He grunted, as if I were the crazy one.

"Okay, dragon boy. Don't get huffy," I said as steadily as I could. With a snort, I remembered how that used to drive him crazy back in New Orleans. He'd shift and then I'd start telling him how the Zephyrs were way better than the Saints (his favorite) or how I was going to paint his apartment pink (the most un-Marc-like color in existence).

It wasn't like I was razzing him on purpose this time.

I pried my stiff fingers from their grip on Marc's back and eased onto the ground, hoping my legs would hold me.

Landing hard, I let the weight of my duffel slide off my shoulder and down onto the ground. "Nice meet-up you've got going here"—a flat rock in the middle of nowhere. My skin flushed, my body trembling.

Get a grip.

I squinted as my eyes adjusted to the brightness of the lava bursts below us against the darkness of the night. I trusted Marc with everything I had. At the same time, I hoped he knew what he was doing.

At any rate, I gave him his privacy as he shifted behind me.

Hands unsteady, I rifled through my duffel. "Hey! Lookie here." Part of Marc's wardrobe had made it into my bag. I pulled out one very large, war-roughened combat boot.

Lovely.

I kept hold of the boot and drew my hair out of my eyes as I straightened.

The barrenness of this place was overwhelming. The heat of it wound through me. I stared out at the blistering wasteland, at the distant battle lines of two massive armies.

Trembling, I checked for any sign of the imps. The air burned to breathe.

"What are we doing here?" I winced. I felt like we'd been dropped into a churning firestorm.

"We can't cross the Great Divide without burning up." His voice resonated low in my stomach. "We can't skirt it without getting shot down."

"Well, then." I flexed my free hand, refusing to look back at him. Marc was naked, I knew it. I didn't need to be looking at that right now. My face heated even more. “What if we go really far out of our way?” Preferably now. We’d probably run into imps again, but... “We still have plenty of night.”

“Both sides have patrols and skirmishers,” he said, moving to stand next to me. “I don’t know how far out. They’ve also set up charges at the edges of their lines. If we don’t get arrested, we’ll be incinerated. The safest way is to go straight through the Old God Army lines.”

“Naturally.” That was about as suicidal as coming here with him in the first place.

“We’re meeting my contact here.” I glanced up at him to find him watching me. “So if you don’t mind, I’d like to get dressed.”

“About that...” I tried to think of a suave way to put it. “I dropped your uniform—” I winced, giving myself a mental shake “—except for this.” I handed him the boot.

The skin at his forehead crinkled. “Well, I suppose this is better than nothing.”

I didn’t see how.

“Step back,” he said, moving me aside as lava pooled near one of my feet.

“Holy—” I leapt straight at him, colliding with warm skin and muscle.

“This way.” He drew a hand around my waist as we both took several steps back. If I’d thought he looked good from a distance, it was nothing like up close. He was leaner than I remembered. Harder. I took in the sculpted planes of his chest, the pure natural strength of him.

I froze and he guided me back two more steps.

“Come on. We don’t want you to get incinerated because you had to see me naked.”

I flushed straight down to my toes. “I wasn’t—” Oh, what the heck. “I don’t know what got into me.”

“It’s this place,” he said, his voice deepening. “It magnifies whatever you're feeling. With the armies, it's usually battle rage. With us, it seems to be..."

Attraction. He didn't have to say it.

I struggled to untangle myself from him. "I'm not starting this again," I said quickly.

"I know," he rushed, his voice raw. Suddenly impatient, he brushed past me, focusing on the lava finger. "I'm not a masochist. Why do you think I stayed away from you before?"

I'd assumed it was because he didn't want me. Now?

I was almost glad for small homicidal lava creatures.

The line of magma seeped from the underside of the rock, straight for me. My duffel sat a few feet away, near the edge, untouched. Most of the rock remained clear, in fact. "What is it doing? Following us?"

"In a manner of speaking." He slipped a hand inside his boot and pounded the hard sole onto the ground. "They like organic creatures." The lava shrank back like a frightened animal. "These are treated," he said, matter-of-fact, showing me the red underside of the boot.

"How does it not freak you out?" It wasn't like the lava was fast, but it would have been on me before I realized it. And then what? How do you shake off molten rock?

"You don't get lava fingers in your camp?" he asked, somewhat surprised. "We must be closer to the front."

Another reason to avoid MASH-19X.

My eyes darted over his body again. I couldn't help it. He was sleek, gorgeous.

His chest shone with a thin sheen of sweat.

Get a grip. This was not a sexy place, and Marc was not even mine anymore. Besides, if I was going to have any sexy thoughts at all, they should be about Galen—whom I would never see again.

Merde.

"Tell me again why I agreed to do this," I said, watching Marc flip the lava finger off the rock like a hairy spider.

"Because you always do the right thing." He dropped the boot and closed the distance between us. The corner of his mouth tipped up as he drew me into his arms, "Even if you have second thoughts about it. Or third."

"Or fourth." It was too much. Being here. With him. I felt like we were on some demented outdoor camping trip, only we were on a life-and-death mission, and we couldn't afford to get distracted.

I ran my hands along his shoulders, up his neck. "So this," I said, to be clear, "this is just the Great Divide?"

"Definitely." He brushed his lips over mine once, twice. "Maybe."

"Don't say maybe," I ordered. If anything, I needed the excuse.

Then he really kissed me, and any second thoughts I had went flying out the window. It was so achingly familiar, like coming home.

He deepened the kiss. Or maybe that was me.

This was the man I'd fallen for all those years ago. He was straightforward and brave, vibrant and alive.

He drew back, his breath heavy and harsh against my cheek. "Sorry. I just had to..."

"I know."

This wasn't just the lava or the energy or the Great Divide. This was me and I knew it.

"Marc." I pulled away from him. "You realize this is a bad idea."

"Yeah," he said, letting me go. He took a few steps toward the edge of the rock and thwacked a lava finger with his boot. "We gotta keep an eye on these buggers."

"Not what I meant."

I didn't need to be getting involved with Marc. There was no future for us anymore.

He returned to me, dropping the boot at my feet. "Remember my three-story walk-up near Snug Harbor?"

It was a dump, and the air-conditioning hardly worked. "It's one of my favorite places on Earth."

We'd sneak up to the roof on steamy summer nights and listen to the sound of jazz in the distance while we made out like bunnies in heat.

But that was a different time, and we were different people back then.

I was just about to tell him that when he stiffened. "Petra." He stepped in front of me as rocks tumbled across the ground at our feet. "Stay back," he said as we faced one of the largest men I'd seen in my life.

His eyes were fiery, wild. He was at least seven feet tall if he was an inch, with leather armor studded with animal teeth. His mustache was long and curled at the ends, and he wore mounds of colorful beaded jewelry. He looked like he'd been out riding with Genghis Khan.

"Oghul," Marc said. He drew an arm around me while staying half a step in front of me. "This is the man who's going to get us across the divide."

I wasn't so sure about the *man* part. Marc refused to budge, so I reached around him, holding out a hand. "I'm—"

"No names," Oghul said, whipping up an enormous curved sword.

Marc seized the barbarian's wrist. "Point it down," he ordered.

The Mongolian's eyes were crazy, wild.

"Oghul," Marc said, a clear warning in his tone.

The brute grunted and lowered his weapon.

Sure. This was just the guy we wanted to sneak us through an enemy camp.

Marc must have read my mind. "You don't want to startle a berserker," he said low in his throat.

"I'll keep that in mind," I said, noticing Marc hadn't taken his eyes off the wild man since he'd gotten here.

Oghul shrugged off his pack and began tossing uniform clothes at me. A tan medical officer's shirt landed at my feet, a pair of pants sailed over my head, and Marc caught both my socks.

He'd also brought a spare uniform for Marc, which proved the Mongolian was way better at this spy business than I was.

Marc was dressed in no time. I tried to convince myself I was glad for him.

What was I saying? I *was* glad. I drew a shuddering breath. As far as I was concerned, I'd dodged a bullet.

"Are you ready for this?" he asked. I still held the enemy uniform in my arms.

"Yes." We'd come this far. There was no backing down now. "I'm just not one for the uniform. That's all." I was a doctor, not a soldier, and I avoided combat fatigues whenever I could.

"Stay in front of me," I told Marc, although it didn't look like Oghul was paying much attention. He stood at the edge of the rock, sniffing the air.

"Don't look," I said as I slipped my shirt off.

Oghul didn't seem to have heard, but Marc took me at my word. He stood facing the Great Divide as I lost my scrubs and slipped on the old army tan.

My throat tightened, and I told myself it was just me getting used to the stiff, thick material of the pants and flak jacket. And not that I could be shot for wearing them.

"All set," I said.

At least, I was as ready as I could be to head out into the superheated wasteland.

"Let's do this," Marc said, turning to me. His uniform fit to his wide shoulders and trim hips, and he was barefoot.

"You still need boots," I said as his gaze followed mine to his feet.

Oghul grunted, shucking off his. He had the widest, hairiest feet I'd ever seen.

"Thanks, buddy." Marc patted him on the arm and slid his feet into the boots.

"Now your friend is going to stand out," I said, as if the pointy-tooth jacket and wild jewelry weren't enough. He even had hoops in his ears.

"He's fine." Marc said, tying the laces tight. "Nobody likes to question the berserkers. Besides, it's obvious he belongs here."

Wait. "We don't have any berserkers in the new army?"

"No," Oghul barked.

The barbarian was going to have to chill out. He was giving me heart palpitations and we hadn't even gotten off this rock.

I straightened my Old God Army uniform and faced the burning fires of the enemy line. "Do you really think we have a shot at sneaking through?"

Oghul snarled at me, showing sharpened yellow teeth.

"No offense," I added. The guy needed to stop growling.

Marc ignored him. "I made it once before," he said, hoisting my duffel over his shoulder.

"When you were flying," I said, following him to the edge. "And crossing your own lines."

Oghul had driven a spike into the rock. A rope hung from it down to the lava fields. The barbarian took the cord in both hands, turned his back to the desert, and rappelled down the rock like he was born to it.

I stared down. It had to be at least a ten-foot drop. Not awful, but enough to break my neck.

"Hey, we'll get through this," Marc said. "Think whatever else you want about me, but know I'll do anything to keep you safe."

"I trust you." I did. "Now let me go first," I said, getting into position. No way was I going to be the last one off that rock.

"Do you know how to rappel?" he asked, his hands closing over mine, readjusting my uncertain grip on the rope.

"Sure," I said. "Why not? Basic training prepared me for this kind of thing."

He raised his brows. "You had basic?"

"No. I was making a bad joke," I said, teetering on the edge of the rock. I'd been dropped straight into the medical corps, same as Marc. "I haven't even read the handbook."

"Yeah, me neither," he said as I stepped off the edge.

It wasn't quick and it wasn't pretty, but I made it down the rock.

Marc brought up the rear, with more athletic skill than I'd managed. But hey, all three of us were down.

It was even hotter on the ground, the energy more intense.

We walked the last hundred yards through the fire spurts, dodging the lava that only seemed to follow me. Or maybe I just took those little buggers personally.

Still, it was the most bizarre feeling in the world, like walking through the gates of hell.

Marc stayed close. "Oghul is going to escort us through." He shot the berserker a cool, confident grin. "Right, buddy?"

Oghul eyed me as we neared the sentries at the edge of the enemy lines. "You look straight ahead. You don't speak. You follow me."

The *or else* was implied.

He didn't need to worry, though. I was too shocked to speak when I saw what waited inside the gate.

The Old God Army had cornered the market on nightmares.

There was no fence, no minefield, no line of troops to defend the enemy camp. Every fifty feet, for as far as I could see, battered guard stations held soulless, merciless Shrouds.

CHAPTER SEVEN

The Shrouds rustled behind dingy glass, watching, waiting.

A burly-looking sentry stood outside each outpost, no doubt bearing an amulet that controlled the monsters. I sucked in a breath, my throat tight from apprehension. I wasn't one for mass executions, but if the army put it in their minds to annihilate those creatures, I'd applaud it.

I felt my muscles stiffen with disgust as we approached. "What is it with your side and the Shrouds?" I muttered.

Marc eyed me, the light from the fires casting his face in shadows. "Your side uses them, too."

That was a fine accusation. "And you know?"

"Personally."

Dang it. "That's right," I said, the fight draining out of me. He'd lost a patient to those soul suckers. I knew that. I should have remembered. What was this place doing to me?

I opened my mouth to apologize when Marc shot me a tense look. "Keep quiet."

Of course. We had to blend. This was not the time to screw up.

We approached a pair of demigods outside the main guardhouse. They wore the red scythe on their sleeves, which I found eerily appropriate. The guard on the left wore an amulet. He held a sword at the ready, watching us. The other held a clipboard. “State your business.”

Oghul shook out his long hair, the beads at the ends clacking together. “Medical personnel transfer,” he grunted. “I take them to MASH-19X.”

The man’s brows furrowed. “On foot?” He looked us over. He knew. “Where’s your transport?”

Uh-oh.

“I do not have one,” Oghul shot back, blocking the guard’s view.

I kept my face and my emotions in check. Still, my mind raced. There had to be something about me, something in the way I looked, talked, moved, breathed.

“Regulations say—” the soldier began.

“I do not care,” Oghul snapped.

The guard raised his voice to be heard over the stomping Mongol. “—that you must have approved transportation in order to transfer—”

“I do not have a Jeep,” Oghul said. “I will not have a Jeep. I crashed it into a hell vent because this one pissed me off.” He pointed a thick, knobby finger directly at my nose. I stared at it, shocked.

The guard looked from me to the berserker and back again. “Well, why didn’t you say so?”

“Humans,” Oghul muttered, rolling his eyes.

Not technically.

“Tell me about it,” the guard said as the berserker dug papers out from under his body armor. They were crumpled and folded too many times to count.

“Please. We can’t even carry our own orders?” I muttered to Marc.

He gave me a look like *you've got to be kidding me*, which was appropriate, I supposed, given the fact that I'd momentarily forgotten I didn't have any kind of orders, not from the Old God Army at least.

The guard narrowed his eyes at me. "I can see why you drove into the hell vent," he said to Oghul.

The berserker grunted. "Too bad I had to drag them out, eh?"

They shared a chuckle at the completely unfunny joke while I harbored a particularly graphic fantasy about those orders and the Mongol's rather large nostrils.

"Everything's in order," the guard said, returning the paperwork to Oghul, who shoved it back into his sweaty breastplate. "You can continue the transport."

Oghul nodded and started walking. Marc nudged me and I followed. He didn't have to tell me twice.

We moved swiftly past the Shrouds and made our way into camp.

Jeeps bounced over the uneven ground. Low-slung hutches rose on either side of us, with MPs posted at their battered wooden doors.

The energy was even thicker here. It crackled along my skin and made my head pound.

"She's half human, Oghul," Marc said, stopping us to check my pupils.

"This is the easiest way." The berserker's stale breath blasted against me as he tilted his head sideways and made his own inspection. "The quickest way."

"Doesn't matter." Marc leaned closer, resting a hand on my shoulder. "Can you hear me?"

I swallowed and nodded.

The berserker stood fuming, shifting from one foot to the other as Marc wrapped an arm around me. "Come on. We'll get you farther back from the front."

I stumbled along next to him, unable to speak.

"Sure, sure." I could practically feel the ground vibrating behind us as the berserker followed. "Let's let her walk all over camp. We never said we'd take her into camp."

Marc gave a sharp glance back. "And I never thought I'd be holding your intestines together at Kamar Ridge."

The Mongolian fell in behind us, mumbling. It was just as well, because I was about to fall over. Marc braced me against his shoulder as I concentrated on putting one foot in front of the other.

Marc pressed me close, as if I could somehow draw on his strength. "She's not a spy."

Oghul harrumphed. "So you say."

The road was heavily pitted and filled every so often with sanded-over holes. It almost looked like they'd dug out the fire tubes. I tried to avoid them, but it was impossible in my current state. My feet twisted, my ankles ached. Wherever there wasn't a sinkhole, crystalline rocks dug into the soles of my boots.

I cleared my throat, about to try to ask if we could sit down for a minute, when a terrified shriek cut the night air. Some creature was injured, dying. A plume of black smoke jetted from around the corner ahead.

We had to try to help. Head swimming, I braced a hand against Marc's chest. I coughed. "Sounds like a—"

"Dragon," he finished, jaw tight.

Both sides used dragon conscripts for aerial battles as well as scouts. They were seen as tools of war—expendable. This one bellowed in pain.

We turned the corner and saw a black dragon the size of an SUV. It moaned and growled as half a dozen animal wranglers held it with iron chains around its neck, legs, and tail.

The poor thing was frightened and in pain.

"Do not be rash," Oghul ground out.

Marc didn't speak for a moment. I watched as outrage warred with determination.

I pulled away from him, feeling steadier on my feet since we'd moved farther from the Great Divide. "I'm okay." I swallowed. "If you need to do something..."

"No," Marc said. "Oghul's right."

"Yes, I am," the berserker said, taking my arm and trying to lead me back the way we came.

Marc shoved the berserker away and took my hand. "This way," he said, leading me into a maze of closely spaced tents.

We were in a housing unit now, not unlike the one at the MASH 3063rd. I could hear the sounds of camp life behind the canvas walls.

Marc glanced behind us. "They never let them shift back. It's like they aren't even human anymore."

"Are they all humans?" I asked, remembering the ancient Norse dragon I'd helped at the clinic. Some dragons really were just dragons.

"These are," he said, his face grim. "There are no pure black dragons in nature. Those are shifters."

My heart clenched for him, and for every person forced to fight this unholy war.

When would it end?

And how many of us would have to die before that happened?

"Have you seen any silver dragons?" I asked, almost afraid to know. Marc's clan came from the southern United States—Louisiana and Florida mostly. But most silver dragons still lived in northern Canada, Iceland, and the Scandinavian countries.

"Not in this camp. Yet," he said. "But yes. They have my people, too."

His eyes hardened, and I knew what he was thinking. He'd been spared. He'd kept his humanity simply because he happened to have a skill that the army needed more than they needed his ability to fight.

Marc could heal the injured and send them back to the front.

"Hold up," he said as we came to the end of the path. It opened into what looked to be an archaeological excavation or maybe a mining operation. Strange. A few moments ago, we were waist-deep in troop housing.

"What are they digging for?" We should be passing more tents or maybe the supply depots.

Not this.

Oghul's eyes darted around. "We go back," he ordered. "We take our original route near the Great Divide."

I balked. "Over my dead body." No way was I ready for that kind of head-clanging experience. "I'll stop asking questions." We'd make it through camp. "I don't even care what you have going on," I added.

It wasn't necessarily true, but I'd tell the Mongolian anything at this point.

"We are helping you." Oghul shoved a meaty finger into my shoulder. "You don't spy."

"First of all, ow," I said, slapping his finger away. "Second, Marc brought me here. I'm not snooping. I'm trying to make it through this place alive and relatively"—I ducked another poke—"unharmed."

"Stop it." Marc stepped in between us. "Both of you," he said, that last comment aimed at me. As if I'd started it.

Marc turned his back to argue with Oghul, and I took the opportunity to get a decent look at what was happening. In all fairness, I couldn't see much, just a covered tent with lots of workers underneath. They were dressed in white and shoveling out some kind of crystal.

It appeared to be a large version of the crystals that littered the ground. I reached down and pocketed one.

It was clear the old army was using the cease-fire to find something. Exactly what was anyone's guess.

I picked up another rock and examined it closely. It reminded me of clear quartz.

"Don't look at that," Marc said, plucking it out of my hand.

"Hey," I protested as he tossed it onto the ground. Jerk. "I wasn't going to take it."

I'd already taken one.

Good thing Marc hadn't noticed, or I doubted I'd get to keep the one I had.

"You need to listen to me," he ground out. "I'm trying to get you through here in one piece."

That was beside the point. "Does your side need to stay here?" I asked under my breath. "Is that why they stopped fighting?"

He knew something. Or at least he suspected. I could see it in his face. "You're here to find out what happened to Dr. Keller," he reminded me, "nothing else."

Since when had I ever been able to keep my nose in my own business? When had Marc, for that matter?

"You have to admit," I said, baiting him, "it makes you curious."

His mouth twisted into a wry grimace, and I knew at that moment that I had him. "I don't know what you're talking about," he said, leading me away from the dig. "Now wipe that grin off your face. You're in the old army now."

CHAPTER EIGHT

"We just need to hitch a ride," Marc said when we'd made it as far as the motor pool.

"You have paperwork?" I asked, surprised he'd want to go on record as being here.

"That's the catch, isn't it?" he asked.

Indeed.

We walked several yards behind Oghul, who was in animated negotiations with a supply clerk. The suns rose over the rows of dusty Jeeps, troop trucks, and bronze cannons on elaborate artillery carts.

At least we were far enough from the Great Divide for machinery to work. The entire area was roped off and ringed with fuel tanks and oil drums.

I glanced into the rear of a parked Jeep and jumped back as a two-headed bulldog leapt up, snarling.

Marc gritted his teeth. "I need you to focus," he said, leading me away.

"I didn't start that one." It was the dog.

"We have a mission. We don't want you doing anything to compromise it."

"Excuse me, Rambo." Since when had he gone military? I glanced behind us to make sure we wouldn't be overheard, then clutched his arm and leaned in close. "Your side has some kind of hideous new weapon going." He stiffened, but I plowed ahead. "There's an entire prophecy about it."

A sheen of sweat coated his brow. "Now isn't the time," he said, his words stiff. "We have one goal—to get you out of here and to my unit. Now behave."

"Says the man who brought a berserker into this."

"I need him to play good cop, bad cop," Marc said, glancing at his highly animated buddy in front of us.

I arched a brow. "You've done things like this before?"

"Once or twice." Marc tried to hide his amusement as the Mongolian snapped the clerk's clipboard in half.

Ah, well, as long as we had a plan.

The clerk rushed to speak with a second worker near the back of the motor pool. Oghul followed and promptly began arguing with them both.

I almost felt sorry for the old army clerks as Oghul made it to the line of Hummers and Jeeps and was stomping and waving his hands. I mean, yes, they could have had us arrested and killed, but I'd worked retail and knew what it was like to deal with a jerk.

"Showtime," Marc muttered. He strolled up to Oghul, eased him aside, and began talking to the motor pool staff in muted, reasonable tones about how we should ignore protocol, bend a few rules, and just get the crazy berserker a ride. Worry about the paperwork later.

I didn't see how it could possibly work. No one was that smooth.

Two minutes later we had a hard-top Jeep with a harpoon sticking out the back, not that I knew how to shoot it.

The private pulled it up for us and left the driver's side door open. "It's filled with gas," he said.

Marc opened the passenger door for me. "And it's krilon-coated?"

The clerk nodded. "She won't get sick."

I was about to ask him what he was talking about until I sat down on the worn leather seat. The tension whooshed out of me and my head cleared. I didn't even realize how much the energy of the Great Divide weighed down on me until the pressure lifted. "This is fantastic."

"And rare," Marc said, sliding into the driver's seat and closing the door.

The Mongolian stood frowning as Marc shifted the Jeep into gear and we started off toward the back gate.

I watched the berserker fade into the distance. "Why isn't he coming with us?"

Marc had both hands on the wheel as we bounced over the rocky ground. "He has a few more things to work out for me."

No kidding? "Like what?"

Marc pulled out the back gate and into the bleak desert landscape beyond. "I'd rather not dump you into the middle of it."

"Too late," I said as I spotted the outer guard posts.

I'd say one thing for my ex. He had interesting friends.

This time, the sentries merely waved as we passed. It seemed it was much easier to get out than to get in. Go figure.

"It's a straight shot from here," he said.

There were no fire-spurting tubes out here, no lava fingers, just miles and miles of parched soil.

"So you weren't surprised when I mentioned a weapon back there," I said. "What's that about?"

Marc glanced at me. "You think we don't get PNN?"

Fair enough. "I'm wondering if the dig we saw back there has something to do with it."

He kept his features even, but I saw how he gritted his jaw. "How do you know it's not your side that's developing the weapon?"

Well...I didn't. And I was ashamed to realize I hadn't even thought of it.

Sure, Marc's side had a dead doctor, but our side had just sent Galen off on some supersecret mission. And they'd been willing to sacrifice us before.

Okay. We had to think about this. "The prophecy talks about a massive weapon."

His grip on the wheel tightened. "Listen to me. We can't do anything about whatever weapon the gods are developing. We have a big enough job to do already."

I could see his point, but, "We can't just let this go."

Marc kept his eyes trained on the desert in front of us. "I'm just saying we can't get sidetracked by some smoke-and-mirrors prophecy."

Wait. "You don't believe in the prophecies?"

He snorted. "They're vague and they won't tell us who—or what—killed Dr. Keller."

I grabbed the door as we bounced over a particularly jarring rock. "They're going to bring about peace."

He glanced at me. "Words can't do that, Petra."

Um-hum. Man of action. "These predictions are more powerful than you know."

"Are you serious?" he asked. "You don't even believe in reading your horoscope."

All the men in New Orleans and I'd had to pick the one with the steel-trap memory. "It's not the same. Look," I said, shifting in my seat to face him, "you said you've been bending the rules a little? Well, so have I." And a recent adventure had changed my mind. For good. "What if I told you the prophecies are about me?"

Ha. At last I'd surprised him.

"It started with a healer who could see the dead," I said, ready to lay it all out.

He wanted to deny it. I watched him try to absorb it. "That's impossible," he said, steering us past a distant hell vent.

I gripped the dash in front of us as we bounced over a rough patch of ground.

"Is it?" I should have stopped using the word *impossible* the second I landed in Limbo.

He refused to look at me. "It doesn't mean that it's you."

All that gorgeousness and he was as stubborn as a goat.

"Then explain this: I received a bronze dagger, just like the prophecies predicted," I said, ticking off the first of the old prophecies on my fingers. "Then, prophecy number two: I used that dagger to arrest the forces of the damned." That got his attention. Yes, well, I couldn't wait to tell him that story. "And then for number three: I found peace while this guy I fell for found death." Or at least he'd lost his immortality.

Marc's nostrils flared. "You dated someone?"

Leave it to a guy to pick up on that detail.

I dropped my hands to my sides, ignoring a tendril of guilt. This was ridiculous. I had nothing to be sorry about.

In fact, he should be glad.

He knew we had no future together. We'd both moved on. He'd lied about his death, devastated me in order to force me to get over him.

And so I had.

Marc sat ramrod stiff with the rising suns behind him. Fine. We might as well get it all out onto the table.

"Yes. I fell for someone else," I said.

A muscle in his jaw tensed.

Well, too bad. I didn't start this. "He broke my heart and now he's gone. Are you happy?"

"No," he said simply.

Why did he even care? It wasn't like he'd been there for me. He'd cast me aside.

But I knew I'd hurt him and it stung.

I wanted to say something to make it right, but I didn't know how. Or if it was even a smart idea. Distance was a positive thing. We needed to remember where we stood. I folded my arms over my chest and stared out my window at the endless desert.

"Look," Marc said, breaking the silence. "I shouldn't be surprised you were with someone else. I'm not," he corrected himself. "I wasn't there for you."

"You lied about being dead." And it had nearly killed me.

I was still raw with what we had lost. I always would be.

"I'm sorry," he said. I turned and saw the contrition on his face, the regret that went far beyond words.

"I don't want to talk about it anymore." There was nothing else to say, no words that would make me feel better, or fix what had gone wrong between us.

We just had to live with it, and without each other.

I settled back against my seat and tried to convince myself it was better this way. It wasn't. But there wasn't a thing I could do about it.

Marc glanced at me from time to time. The hopelessness of the situation hung like a dark cloud over our heads. He kept to himself, and I pretended to be deep in thought, eyes fixed on the journey ahead.

In less than an hour, MASH-19X appeared on the horizon.

I shaded my eyes against the growing glare of the morning sun. Nineteen-X was bigger than the 3063rd. Definitely as dusty. We drove along a dirt road, a flat piece of nothing, distinguished only by the relative lack of rock and debris. Low-slung tents and hutch buildings formed a miniature city.

This was it. I steeled myself.

Sneaking through the lines was bad enough. My stomach tightened. Here, I would have to blend in while talking to a murdered soul.

I blew out a breath. *Shake it off.*

Marc caught me out of the corner of his eye. "I've got you covered. Try to relax."

Easier said than done. I realized I was shaking out my hands and stopped, forcing myself to fold them neatly, tightly in my lap. I had to look at ease, like I belonged there.

Then I had to do my job and hope I could escape.

We pulled in right near the main hospital building. It was a red tent with a gold ankh emblazoned on the side, probably on the roof as well. I shoved my back hard against the seat behind me. I was easygoing. I was calm.

Marc rolled his window down and waved to a group of nurses as we bumped down the main drag toward the motor pool.

I couldn't believe he was being so bold. "What are you doing just driving through camp?" I hissed.

He took a particularly sharp curve past the main bulletin board. "What did you want to do? Park in those trees over there and sneak in?"

"You have trees?" I asked, trying to see.

"They're dead," he said, giving me a sideways glance. "I don't want to draw any attention." He steered us past the officers' club. "I'm going to introduce you as a visiting doctor, and by the time your paperwork doesn't come through, you'll be gone."

That was actually a good plan. I tried to unclench my shoulders.

Marc glanced back over at me. "Seriously. You look like you have a mouth full of my mom's broccoli casserole."

I'd never been one for green vegetables. "She never would have figured out I didn't like it if Romper hadn't thrown up."

"Sure. Blame it on the dog."

Who named a dog Romper anyway? And how was I supposed to know his dog had a weak stomach?

I eased my hand from the door and tried to take a better look at the MASH-19X.

They had the same torch posts we did, the same type of helipad on a hill past the hospital. I noticed long black poles situated along what appeared to be the edges of camp. "What are those?"

"They're the new 'redline' devices. They make the camp invisible to enemy radar."

Oh. "We don't have them."

He kept his eyes on the motor pool ahead. "I know."

At that moment, it really hit me. "You truly are putting your side at risk by having me here."

He shot me a look. "You're not a spy."

No, but I'd be telling Kosta about this new radar blocker.

Wait. How would I tell Kosta without letting him know I'd left?

Marc steered the Jeep into the motor pool. "Chances are, your side already knows our capabilities. We know yours."

Peachy. "Why do you have to keep reminding me we're on opposite sides of this thing?"

"Same reason you do." He pulled into the nearest empty slot and shoved the Jeep into gear. "I don't want to forget."

* * *

We turned the Jeep in at the motor pool and began trekking back the same way we'd come. I couldn't believe I was just strolling through an enemy MASH unit. Their recovery room stood next to the hospital, same as ours.

Next came the medical supply tents and the admin offices. I even smelled the familiar combination of antiseptic and dirt.

The red dirt of Limbo never changed.

In fact, save for their tricked-out radar, I didn't see anything here that we didn't have back home.

Except... I leaned close to Marc. "I can't believe you have a research facility in camp."

"Later," he said close to my ear as he waved to a group of doctors.

I craned my neck to see them after they passed. "Do you have to be so friendly?"

Marc shoved his hands into his pockets as we came up on the residential tents. "Count yourself lucky they're on the way to morning rounds, or you'd be playing visiting doctor. Your name is Kate Gordon, by the way."

"I won't forget."

"It's on your uniform in case you do."

I smoothed out the pocket, and sure enough, *Gordon* was sewn onto a patch.

"You thought of everything, didn't you?"

"I sure hope so." He drew a hand around my waist. His grip felt warm and sure as he led me down a side path. Just as quickly, he let his hand drop, as if I'd burned him.

We made our way past the enlisted hutches, dodging ropes and poles. They were packed in a lot tighter than I was used to.

"It will be safer to accomplish our job if we wait until nightfall," Marc said, guarding his words. "In the meantime, you can stay at my place."

I tried not to trip over my feet as dread warred with anticipation. No way, no how had his place been part of the bargain.

Besides, it could be dangerous. "What are we going to tell

your roommates? I'm assuming visiting doctors don't shack up on the first day."

I could see his fists tighten in his pockets. "I live alone."

No wonder the hutches were so tightly spaced.

He snorted. "Here in the old army, the men live in huts, with the women serving."

I looked up at him, shocked. "That's the dumbest thing I've ever heard. You have women doctors, don't you?"

He nodded. "They live in two big barracks, and they serve the men in their spare time."

"I can't believe they put up with that." Then again, it didn't seem like they had a choice.

"The old gods like to cling to what they can," he said humorlessly.

"Wait. So you have a woman serving you?" I was still trying to get my head around it. "Getting your coffee, rubbing your feet?" As if Marc didn't already have an ego. I couldn't believe he was about to toss me into the middle of that.

At least he looked as disgusted as I was by the thought. "I don't make anyone serve me. I never wanted that. But plenty of the guys do it, especially the immortals. They're not big on change."

"No kidding," I muttered under my breath.

He cleared his throat. "I can't send you to the women's barracks, or someone else might call you for 'service,' so to speak."

"That's nuts." On about ten different levels.

He didn't argue.

"Okay, so we're going to your hutch." All the same, "Nothing is going to happen there," I warned. It was bad enough I'd gotten too close to him on the rock. "I'm not going to use you to get over Galen."

He didn't look too happy about that. "So that's his name."

He glanced away. "Don't worry. I know how to keep my distance."

"You do," I said. "After all, you were the one who ended it."

After the enlisted area, we reached the officers' hutches. They were spaced just as close together, but seemed to have a little more room inside.

"Here," Marc said, leading me through the maze and to a wooden door that looked like all the rest.

I stepped inside.

Soothing green draping hung along the walls, held in place with ornately wound rope. He had a bed, a real bed, which must have cost a fortune to get through the portal. A homemade quilt lay over it—one I recognized from his grandmother's house. It had been one of her favorites, displayed proudly in her guest room before she passed away.

A small desk stood near the door, crowded with pictures of Marc and his family. Marc and me. There were Christmases and birthdays and picnics and parties.

"I can't believe you still have all of this." It was both heartwarming and heartbreaking, remembering all we'd left behind.

"My mom put together a mean care package," he said as the door snicked closed behind us.

"But they shipped your things back to your family," I protested. I'd seen the boxes.

"Not all of it," he said. "Or even most of it," he added. "The shipping around here is as slow as the paperwork."

"Of course it is."

The floor was covered in carpets I recognized from his apartment, a green and gold woven one in particular that I used to lay on in front of the fireplace.

I stood with my hands on my hips and tried to take it all

in. It was like he was trying to torture me with everything that had been stolen from us.

Keep it light.

I only needed to survive until nightfall. "No offense, but it almost feels like your mother decorated this place."

He smiled despite himself, and I could tell I'd hit a nerve. "I told her I didn't want anything new. I wanted things from home."

I itched to remind him that he still had a place to go back to. He had a home, if he wanted it, and people who loved him. But it wasn't my business. It wasn't my fight.

Against my better judgment, I picked up the picture of us at Sally's Donut Shop. We were obviously pulling an all-nighter. I didn't even remember that picture being taken.

Had I ever been that young? That happy?

Marc drew close and I felt myself soften.

I hated that he made me feel this.

No matter how hard I tried to forget, I missed my old life and everyone in it, including Marc. And if I was truly honest with myself, I missed my old life because of Marc.

I set the photo back down on the desk, harder than I'd intended. He'd made a decision for all of us—me, his mom, his family. He'd "sacrificed" without even thinking about what it cost the rest of us. "What are you going to tell them if the war ever does end?"

He let out a sad, strangled sigh. "You know that's not going to happen."

"It could." It might.

He remained silent, and for a moment, it seemed he almost wanted to hope. Then he slammed into clinical mode. "Don't get your hopes up, Petra."

I hadn't been the type before.

But was I now? Maybe.

Yes, we were enemies in an eternal war. But I had to think

the fact that we were standing here, as unimaginable as it was, meant something.

"I know I was never a big believer," I said. All science, no art.

How ironic that I was now in Galen's old role as the one who wanted to have faith in something larger than myself. But I'd seen firsthand how it worked. I'd been changed.

Marc drew closer. "I don't believe in fate. I only believe in what I can see, what I can touch." His fingers seemed to move of their own volition as he reached to brush the hair at the nape of my neck. "I missed you."

My breath hitched. I tried to ignore the way his fingers traced the sensitive skin at the back of my neck.

I pulled away.

"You need to get some rest," he said, struggling to find that stoic mask that we'd both worked so hard to perfect. "Take my bed," he said, retreating.

No. I wasn't going to steal his bed. "I'll take the chair."

He stood, arms crossed. "Fine. I'll sleep on the rug."

"You don't always have to be the one to make the sacrifice, you know."

He pulled the chair away from his desk and dragged it in front of the only door. "We've been going all night. You skirted the Great Divide. Don't tell me you're not exhausted."

Yes. I was completely fried, but that didn't mean I wanted to lie down on his bed, on his grandmother's quilt.

"It's okay, Petra," he said, taking a seat in front of the door.

"No," I said, forcing myself to sit, "it's about as strange as it gets." He stood and unfolded a knitted afghan at the foot of the bed. "Sleep," he said, easing it over me.

I watched him retreat. "What about you?"

He returned to his post at the door and dropped into the chair. "I'll be all right."

I lay stiff and uncomfortable. "You're not going to watch me sleep, are you?"

"As long as you don't watch me read," he said, picking up a book from the desk. I couldn't see what it was. Probably one of those thrillers he liked so much.

It wasn't my problem. *He* wasn't my problem. "Good night, Marc."

I settled into his bed, pulling the soft afghan up to my chin. It smelled like him, and of home. My body sank into the comfort as my mind scrambled to find a way to process it all.

Sleep was smart. It would help me be alert and ready tonight. This was about the mission, not about me snuggled up in his bed, surrounded by his things.

I'd lived without him and without any of this and I'd been perfectly fine.

The light-blocking shades were down. He extinguished the lamp on his desk, and the room darkened.

I was helping him for one night only. We'd get into the lab, see what Dr. Keller had to say, and then get out. No complications. No strings. No more Marc.

He'd clipped a book light onto his paperback. He sat with his book open, but he wasn't turning the pages.

"I missed you," he said softly.

My blood felt heavy as it pulsed through me. I watched him through half-lidded eyes. "I missed you, too."

I didn't even remember falling asleep, until a sharp pounding at the door jolted me awake.

"Belanger," a male voice called. The pounding grew more insistent. "Belanger!"

Marc stood, his chair scattering as he held the door closed.

I sat up, half dizzy with a head full of cotton.

"I know you're in there." The door vibrated. "Open up," the man ordered.

There was nowhere to go. Panic shot up my throat as I scrambled off the bed, fighting the afghan. What was my spy name again?

Marc held the door closed with the entire weight of his body. "I can't do that, sir."

"Belanger!"

"Colonel," Marc gritted out, "trust me. You don't want to do this."

I scrambled for my white doctor jacket. "Kate Gordon," I murmured frantically to myself. I was Kate Gordon.

The man outside cursed.

It would be better if I wasn't caught at all.

I searched frantically in the dark for a place to hide, but I knew I was trapped.

"Don't make this difficult," the man threatened.

Maybe I could pry my way out the back.

My fingers ached as I tried to wrest the canvas bottom away from the ground. Maybe I could crawl out.

But it was tied down tight.

"Belanger," the voice bellowed, "now!"

CHAPTER NINE

I STOOD and faced the music with my back straight and shoulders held back. I could do this.

We hoped.

The pounding stopped. "You have a girl in there, Belanger?"

He winced as he flipped on the lights. "Yes."

His cool gaze caught my wide-eyed stare. He'd still kept a hand braced against the door, but at that point, he might as well have swung it open wide.

I was new to this whole pseudo-spy business, but I was pretty sure giving up one's partner was a big no-no.

The man outside chuckled. "She has a pretty voice."

And what did that guy outside have? Super hearing?

It wasn't exactly rare in the supernatural community.

I retreated a step and felt the canvas wall at my back. Marc had admitted I was here. Mister Mouse Ears out there had heard me. I didn't know what to do. The primitive, panicked side of me still wanted to hide.

"She smells nice, too," Marc's superior officer commented.

"He can smell me?" I hissed.

Marc placed a finger to his lips. "So now you know," he said to the man outside.

He motioned for me to come up and stand next to him. I did, because, truly, I had nothing else to lose.

"I'll be damned—" the voice lightened—"that's the first girl you've had in what? Ten years? How long you been here anyway?"

My breath caught as Marc slid an arm around me.

He hadn't wanted to see anyone else in all that time?

I took in my silent, sexy ex. A small, angry part of me was glad he'd suffered. He'd brought this down on us. He'd chosen to cut me out of his life.

Now it seemed like he'd been just as paralyzed by it as I had. I wasn't sure what to do with that.

He moved the window shade aside just enough for a fat-nosed, red-faced man outside to see me.

The stranger chucked and gave us the thumbs-up.

I forced myself to raise a hand and wave. I was both sad and weak with relief. If they were going to be sexist pigs, at least it worked in my favor.

"Come see me later," the colonel said, "when you're not so busy," he added with a chuckle.

"Will do, sir." Marc dropped the shade closed as we watched the officer's retreating form.

"Come on," he said, "let's get you away from the window."

As we stepped back, I almost tripped over a book on the floor. "You were still reading?" I wished he'd tried to sleep. I didn't know how long I was out, but my head had cleared and I felt better for it.

"I got distracted," he said, blocking me as I reached down for the blue binder-style book. This wasn't the thriller he'd picked up before. If I wasn't mistaken, it was something I'd made for him.

I ran my fingers along the worn cover.

It was.

He cursed under his breath. "I haven't gotten that out in a long time," he said as I carried it to the bed.

"Why now?" I asked, sitting down.

"Because I'm a masochist."

It was missing the photo I'd glued to the front, but I would have recognized it anywhere. I'd made this for him on our second anniversary.

It had been a hellish year. Well, before I'd realized what that truly meant.

I was in my third year of residency and he was in his doctoral fellowship. We didn't have time to see each other as much. So I'd put together a memory book of ticket stubs, greeting cards, the stupid poem he'd written me on a Sam & Ace's bar napkin.

I intended to find that epic bar napkin, but instead opened the book on a torn notebook page he'd left on my door.

Roses are red
Violets are blue
Don't freak out
I'm in your bed

P.S. I have chocolate sauce.

I broke out in a smile. "You're quite the poet."

"You think that's bad." The bed dipped as he sat down next to me. He flipped a few more pages. They were soft-edged and worn.

I knew it as soon as I saw it. "The bounce house!" I'd forgotten we had a picture. Well, it wasn't of us. It was of the goofy, multicolored blow-up contraption with eighteen kids running around it. But still...

He'd gone with me to my cousin's fifth birthday party, and my aunt had rented it. The kids had jumped and ricocheted off the walls like Tasmanian devils and then run off somewhere—probably for cake and ice cream.

Marc and I bounced until we were dizzy and then hung out on the air-mattress bottom and talked about the future—how we wanted a house in the Garden District, four kids, and a black lab who would eat his mother's broccoli casserole.

When the kids wanted their place back, we'd stuck around for cake, then headed off for a hike together. We'd found a small field by a stream and spent the rest of the day tossing wildflowers at each other, talking and laughing.

My heart clenched.

Despite my better judgment, I looked up at him. His face mirrored what I felt, bittersweet longing and regret.

I swallowed hard. "I thought you were trying to forget," I said.

He gazed at me for a long moment. "I am."

CHAPTER TEN

WE SPENT the rest of the afternoon sitting on his bed, talking. And as we reminisced about all we'd left behind, it was almost easy to forget where we were—when we were. I'd give anything for the last ten years to be one long, bloody, awful dream.

How many times had we just hung out like this back at my little bungalow on Camp Street?

My stomach clenched. *Merde*. I was asking for it. He'd crushed me when he left for the war. It had almost killed me when word came that he was dead. It had taken years to get over this man. And now I was signing up for it again.

Beyond this brief oasis, the menace of the Limbo desert hung like the blade of a guillotine.

This wasn't New Orleans, and Marc wasn't my soon-to-be fiancé. We were five klicks off a hell vent. I was in enemy territory, taking a stupid crazy risk just so that I could stick my neck out even farther and confront a murdered soul.

It would be time to leave soon.

Before I could remind Marc of that fact, the hutch door rattled.

"Stay there," he said, launching himself out of bed as the chair that was still halfway blocking the threshold pitched forward and fell.

My heart skipped a beat as the door crashed open and a looming shadow filled the entryway. "What is this?"

"A rude awakening," Marc said, moving to block the intruder. Moonlight filtered in behind the hulking form.

I brought a hand to my chest as Marc lit the lantern. It was Oghul. If I'd been any more relieved, I would have hugged the hairy battering ram.

The door smacked closed behind him as he strolled into the tent. "It is time," he said, firelight playing off the individual plates on his chest armor.

"Wait." I sat up straight. "We need a berserker with us to sneak into the lab?"

"We do." Marc nodded. Then, ignoring my discomfort, he added to Oghul, "Give us a minute."

Oghul's expression clouded. "There will be talk of me outside your tent. I do not blend well."

"Act natural," Marc said, leading him the rest of the way.

The Mongol looked a bit like a scared puppy as Marc slammed the door on him.

"Act natural?" I asked, scrambling off the bed. "A berserker?"

"At least nobody will mess with him." Marc sat down next to me as I pulled on my boots. "I just wanted a minute to say thank you." He sighed. "I know you didn't have to do this. You didn't have to trust me."

I'd always trust him.

When it came down to it, I might as well admit to myself that I'd always love him.

"It was a nice interlude," I said, yanking my laces.

"Why are you shutting down on me?"

"Because there's nothing else to say." We were going on our mission, and then I might never see him again.

I needed him to stop talking. I needed to stop thinking about him, us—everything.

He sighed. "I'm going to talk to Oghul. Don't be long."

What did he think this was? The senior prom?

Next to the desk, I found the duffel I'd brought.

Rodger and I had packed a flashlight and extra batteries. I stuffed them into my pants pocket. That left the other pocket for Marius's tricked-out silver-and-bronze snub-nose pistol. I studied the exotic spiderweb-looking knob on the side. He'd called it an energy disruptor. I cranked it all the way up and slipped it into my pocket.

There was no telling what we'd find in the lab.

I left the rest of it behind.

It was a dark, starless night. The torches lit both sides of the path.

A chill bit the air. Oghul and Marc stood in the shadows between the tents, speaking in low, urgent tones.

When Oghul saw me, he straightened. "It must be tonight," he said to both of us.

"I know that," Marc said, scowling. "Let's go." He wrapped an arm around me as we headed for the main part of camp.

I shook him off.

"Are you annoyed with me or the situation?" he asked.

"There was never any problem between me and you," I informed him. We just couldn't catch a break.

But I couldn't dwell on that right now. I had to stay focused, to feel my fear at what we were about to do, and the pain of what we'd left behind. I needed it. Anger was about the only thing that kept me from cracking wide open.

"I had Oghul do some advance work for us," he said,

walking next to me. "It seems the emergency exit, which never has a guard, now has three."

Yikes. "Do they know we're coming?"

"I don't know," Marc said. It was plain that he was worried. "It may be new since the murder. It may be that they're watching us."

My heart sped up.

Nights in the desert were cool, but nevertheless, I was beginning to sweat. The torches lining the path cast eerie shadows.

It would be easy for Old God Army security forces to hide in the darkness and watch. I could be caught and executed as a spy before I even had a chance to snoop. "What are we going to do?"

He kept his eyes on the path ahead of us. "We have a backup plan to bypass the guards."

"Something you've done before?" I asked.

"No." Marc was strung tight. "One step at a time," he said, his voice low. "For now, I'll be happy if we make it to the main path."

I gave him my best what-the-hey.

His eyes darted over the shadowy road ahead. "If they know something, they'll arrest us right away."

Well now, that was a comforting thought.

"Almost there," Oghul gritted out behind us.

I could see the lights up ahead. I looked over my shoulder at Oghul and the inky darkness behind us. Just a little bit longer. I returned my focus to the light. We could do this.

A pair of soldiers stepped out from a side path. "Hey, you!"

My heart leapt to my throat. No. We were so close. These were cyclops guards, MPs.

Marc gripped my arm protectively. His other hand went down to his side, and I was suddenly terrified that he had a weapon. Cyclopes weren't immortal, but they were extremely hard to kill. Especially in the middle of a MASH camp.

They stopped in the path in front of us, blocking us.

The one on the right looked me up and down. "By the blood of Cerberus," he snarled then chuckled low in his throat. "You finally took a slave girl."

For Pete's sake.

"I can smell you all over her." The bald one on the left grinned, openly leering. "It's about time. Where did you come from, sweetheart?"

"New Orleans," I answered.

The guard on the right barked out a laugh. "I think I need to visit."

His buddy nodded. "When you retire."

"What do you have left, Barak?" Marc asked.

"Only eight years." The cyclops grinned, showing a set of stubby gray teeth.

Cyclops MPs were forced to retire when they turned six hundred. Lucky ducks.

I stiffened as an entire squad of elite troops marched down the main path ahead of us. "What are they doing out so late?"

"Is one man not enough?" Old Baldy leered a bulging, bloodshot eye, and his buddy joined right in.

Marc's grip on my arm tightened. "Too bad for you I don't share."

"Gotta go," I added as he ushered me past the guards.

When we were out of earshot, Marc leaned back toward Oghul. "That isn't normal. The troops on the road."

"No." The Mongol breathed heavily behind us as we made it onto the main path. "Still. If they knew, they'd arrest us."

"Ah, well, there you go," I said, practically jogging to keep pace with them. "No problem, then."

"This way," Oghul said, leading us across the center courtyard. With a glance back, we ducked into the shadows next to the main supply tent.

Oghul kept on, going past the tent and behind a small storage shed near the cemetery. I could see wooden tombstones leaning awkwardly up the hill.

Marc pulled out a flashlight and so did I. Mine came from Rodger's care packages. I couldn't believe Marc had one, too.

"Where did you get that?" I asked.

"My mom sent it," he said, aiming it at the ground.

"You really need to write her."

"Not now," he said under his breath. The ground dipped as he led us over to a decrepit hutch.

"This is your lab?" I'd have thought it was nicer from the way he'd talked about it.

Although who was I to judge? I'd cobbled my lab together with discarded junk from the minefield.

"It's underground," Marc said, shining his light on a circular grate.

What the—? "Really?" I tried to see down the darkened grate. "And this is how you get there?" Somehow, I didn't see Dr. Keller commuting to work down a grate.

Oghul stood over us, breathing hard out of his mouth. "They will not let you in the front. The back is guarded."

Okay, that made more sense. Still... "What is this? Some kind of exhaust vent?"

Apprehension crawled up my spine when I saw the ground around it lay charred and black. They had some caustic experiments going on down there.

Marc crouched in front of the grate and aimed his light down as far as he could. The piping was made of smooth metal. "We work with toxic chemicals. There are vents all over camp."

It smelled like burned hair. "It's just like the old army to take care of its people," I muttered, feeling the bitter air in the back of my throat. No telling what toxic debris they were blowing right into camp. The immortals didn't mind. They didn't get cancer.

Marc's expression was grim. "They have my protest on file." He turned his head and coughed into his sleeve. "This vent leads straight to the main research room."

I hunkered next to him. "Where Dr. Keller died," I murmured.

Marc nodded. "It's where he is now at least," he said low, under his breath.

Probably where he was murdered too. A lot of ghosts had a thing about the place where they'd died.

I straightened and double-checked my gun. I really didn't like this vent idea, but it didn't look like we had much choice.

Oghul turned his attention to the shadows behind us. "Hurry."

Right. We were sitting ducks out here.

Marc stood next to me. "Go for it, Oghul."

The berserker bent over the hole and seized the bars blocking it. He twisted his face, grunting as the bars groaned apart.

Marc dug in his pack and handed me the most bizarre-looking thing I'd seen in a while. It was a gas mask. Only this one looked like it had been issued in the early 1900s.

The seeing apparatus resembled two large bug eyes. A round breathing hole was capped with a red grille. A bendable rubber tube like an old vacuum hose ran from under the breathing hole down to a small square pack designed to strap onto the back.

"You don't have anything from this century?" I asked.

"You know the old gods," Marc said.

Actually, I didn't.

"This is only until you make it through the vent," he continued. "I'll go first."

I was amazed he even had a working gas mask. I took it and strapped the pack to my back.

We were here. We had one shot, and I couldn't chicken out now.

Oghul gripped Marc's shoulder as my ex swung his feet into the opening. "Do not be irrational."

Marc pointed his flashlight down the hole. "This coming from the berserker."

"You don't have a mask." It was the first time I'd seen the Mongolian worried.

My stomach hollowed. "This is the only one."

"Army regulations," he said, shoving the flashlight into his pocket.

Of course they only issued one.

Marc grabbed a pistol out of the bag and shoved a magazine into it.

"They do not issue masks to my kind," Oghul said. "I'm not going down there."

"Then you can't go, either," I told Marc. I could handle this. "We don't need you breathing whatever turned the ground black."

"I'm not going to argue with you, Petra," he said, then slipped down into the blackness.

He *didn't.* I rushed to the hole. He did! The jerk was already in there. And he'd gone down fast.

What was with him? Thinking he could risk himself like that. There was bravery and then there was driving the people who loved you nuts.

I shoved the gas mask on, breathing in the stale rubber air, making sure the filter was secured on my back. I had no peripheral vision from the eyeholes. I could barely look down. Oghul had to help me as I stumbled to the edge of the vent.

"You find him at the bottom," he ordered, his voice muffled by my mask.

I slid down into the vent, feet first. My light bounced off the walls as I careened down about five feet and stopped. My vision was all screwed up. I could barely look down. My feet had gotten hung up on a twist in the pipe.

"Of all the—" My voice choked.

That's right. Stay mad. Because if I really thought about what I was doing, I was going to freak out.

I eased around the curve in the vent, forcing myself downward as it leveled off.

My chest tightened. I was closed in, trapped, the gray walls pressing down on me, inches from my nose.

My breath came hot and wet against the mask. Stifling. I wanted to rip it off. I wanted to yank off the filter pressing into my back, jamming me into this narrowing network of pipes.

The tunnel narrowed. I could feel the walls closing in.

I swallowed, tasting blood in the back of my throat.

Get a grip.

I wouldn't get stuck. I couldn't.

Marc had made it. He was down there somewhere.

I refused to let myself think he could be hurt, gasping for breath, because if I did, I really was going to panic.

Sweating, chest heaving, I inched forward.

I could make it. I could do it. I wasn't going to die down here, stuffed into a pipe, trapped underground.

Alone.

I listened for Marc, for any sound beyond that of my own labored breathing.

As I pressed on, the pipe began to widen. Or maybe it was just my imagination. I didn't know, didn't care as I scooted forward more rapidly. I was just starting to think I might make it when I began sliding.

"No, no..." I gripped the sides, my sweaty palms sliding over the smooth metal. I could do this. I could make this.

The vent made a sudden, terrifying drop.

A wild cry caught in my throat as I hurtled down into the blackness.

CHAPTER ELEVEN

I FELL for what seemed like an eternity.

It had to be only a few seconds because I was still holding back my scream as I slammed sideways onto the floor of the research room with a bone-rattling crunch.

My hip ached. Everything throbbed. My hands burned. I cradled my arm to my chest as I rolled onto my back.

"Petra." Marc helped me sit up. Glass littered the floor. "Where does it hurt?"

"Everywhere." Heaving, I peeled off the gas mask and immediately regretted it. The place smelled like melted plastic and fifty kinds of chemicals. My eyes began to water. "Are you okay?" I asked, trying to adjust.

He handed me a detox wipe for my hands. "I've been better, but yes," he said as I got my first decent look at the lab.

We'd crash-landed straight into a nightmare.

The place was trashed. Light fixtures hung by wires. Test tubes and broken bottles were strewn over the lab tables and the floors. The fume hood had been ripped off its hinges.

My throat was raw. I'd never seen a murdered soul go on such a violent rampage. "Dr. Keller did this?"

"I'm counting on you to tell me." Marc gave me a hand as I stood. "But right now, we need to hide."

"Why?" My knees were like rubber, and my nose was starting to run.

"You screamed."

"No, I didn't." I'd held it back.

"Well, there was definitely a short screech followed by a hard landing."

"Dang." I winced.

Aside from the insane murdered ghost, we still had to worry about live guards with swords. I stiffened as soldiers' footsteps pounded down the hallway outside.

What I'd give for a get-out-of-jail-free card.

The chains around the lab entrance rattled. "You sure we want to go in there?" asked a soldier on the outside.

"Unlock it," another replied.

Marc and I exchanged a glance as the chain dropped to the floor.

"This way," he said against my ear. Broken glass crunched under our boots as he led me to a cabinet with a bright yellow warning label displaying a black biohazard symbol. Underneath, it read:

Caution

Fatally toxic to mortals and immortals.

Open only with proper equipment.

I stared at my gorgeous, but clearly deranged ex. "You've got to be kidding me."

The cabinet was sealed with what looked to be a complex enchanted lock. It was boxy, bronze, and emblazoned with protective runes. Marc placed his thumb in the center and inserted a key into the bottom.

I searched for the gas mask and realized it had cracked right between the eyes.

It wouldn't have been enough anyway.

My pulse thudded in my ears as Marc popped open the lock to the biohazard cabinet.

I wasn't going in there. Better to get arrested than eaten alive by toxic chemicals.

"Trust me," he said, swinging the door open just far enough for us to slip inside.

I did. I heaved my aching body into the closet. Marc followed and swiftly closed the door.

Now we just had to hope we survived our hiding place.

I pressed tightly against him in the dark. His roughened cheek scraped against mine. The soldiers were already in the lab. Steel slid against scabbards as they drew their blades.

If they saw us duck in here, we were dead meat.

"Up there," one of them said.

We must have broken the vent on the way down. I pressed my forehead into Marc's shoulder.

"Is that new?" a guard asked.

"Since last night? Yes."

What—were they keeping track of the destruction? They'd better not see the gas mask I'd dropped. The issue number would lead them straight back to Marc.

Sweat trickled down my back. We were going to get caught. There was no way not to get caught.

He shifted against me, his entire body flexing against mine. I curled my fingers against his chest.

One of the guards whistled under his breath. He was far too close to our hiding spot. "They need to get an exorcist down here."

"That would mean admitting they have a ghost," his partner replied.

They were almost on top of us.

I wound my fingers into his uniform, grabbing him, holding him, seeking comfort the best way I knew.

The guards were methodical, precise. I could almost taste the palpable fear. They were too well trained to act on it.

No doubt they'd be more than happy to find a human source of this horror and skewer it. Marc's body felt hot under my hands as I listened to the footsteps of the guards, the steady brush of cloth, the click of metal against metal.

"Papadakos, find where that vent leads and send a unit up. The last thing we need is a rampaging poltergeist in camp."

I hoped Oghul was smart enough to have found a place to hide.

The lab grew eerily silent, as if they were listening for our breath.

Marc held still, his arm curled around me, supporting me. I could feel the thud of his heart under my palm, the tug as his chest rose and fell.

My mouth was dry, my head light. Please let it be from fear and not from some twisted chemical compound.

This was so screwed up. I should have stayed home, not gotten involved. What did I think I was? Some kind of super spy? I didn't have any business traipsing around haunted underground labs. Or hiding in a biohazard cabinet. I mean, who does that?

Truly?

I was terrified of a vent, much less this.

I froze as footsteps echoed just outside the flimsy metal doors.

This was it. The end of the road. There was nowhere else to hide, no way to fight.

Nothing else we could do.

Heart hammering, I squeezed my eyes shut.

Please let them keep going.

They stopped.

I found Marc's hand and squeezed it tight. Fiercely, silently, he pulled me into a tight bear hug. I clung to his warm body, his flak jacket rough against my cheek. This was it. He cradled my head protectively with his hand and rested his lips on the top of my head as we waited for the end.

At least we were in it together.

Static broke through as the soldier hit his radio button. "The lab is clear."

I gripped Marc tighter.

Footsteps echoed outside. "What about the closet?" a soldier asked.

"I took care of it personally," the guard responded.

A beep sounded from the radio. "Understood. Seal it back up."

"Head out," our guy said to the room at large. "We've done our spook check for the night."

I pulled away from Marc, shaky, never so relieved in all my life. He stood at my back as I pressed my hands against the cool metal of the doors and listened to the soldiers lock us back into the lab.

"Easy." Marc's voice tickled my ear, and I realized my hand had wandered down to the door handle.

I knew. We had to play this right. But I couldn't wait to get out of the toxic storage vault.

Yes, I was glad Marc had saved us. I was relieved and grateful and fall-down ecstatic not to be caught in the web of old army justice.

But at what cost?

We waited three full minutes—exactly 180 seconds—after the last soldier left.

At last, we popped the door.

I staggered out as fast as my bruised body would allow. Marc caught me around the shoulders. "I've got you," he whispered as I lurched sideways.

The lab lay dark except for dim security lights on the tables. I checked my arms, my legs. "What was in that closet?" I hissed.

"Nothing." He gripped my good shoulder as he smoothed the hair out of my eyes with his other hand. "I'm sorry I scared you. There wasn't time to explain."

"I don't get it." Just past him, I could see the toxic storage vault.

My mouth fell open.

Empty.

"What was it?" I whispered. "Some kind of radioactive isotope?"

"Dr. Keller and I put up that warning to keep the old army out of our paperwork. As much as we could, at least."

I blinked, trying to absorb it all. "So we weren't getting eaten alive in there?"

He held me steady. "No."

I grabbed him, hugged him, so glad to be whole and healthy, even if we were locked in a secret lab with a poltergeist.

"That guard," I said, glancing at the sealed door to the lab, "was he a friend of yours?"

"No," Marc said, "just someone smart enough to be afraid of biohazard signs."

I grinned despite myself.

"Okay, hotshot," I said, wiping my nose, trying to recover, "let's get down to business."

Marc was all too happy to oblige. "Keller is here somewhere," he said low, scanning the room as if he had a chance of seeing the ghost.

"Dr. Keller?" I murmured, starting down the first of two rows of lab tables.

Wonder upon wonders, there was still some equipment intact. Glass cases with specimen samples lined the tables. I took it slow, my knees and hips aching with every step. The samples glowed green in the dim light of the room.

Bulky thermal generators and other lab equipment crowded the tables along the walls, casting eerie shadows. Most of it had been torn apart.

Marc lingered a step behind, watching as if he expected the ghost of Dr. Keller to pop out of nowhere. Then again, maybe it might.

"When was the last time you called a spirit?"

I started down the second row. "Never." I usually tried to avoid them.

I focused my mind on Dr. Keller with his round spectacles and easy manner. We'd thought he was so old, but the last time I saw him, he had to be only in his mid-forties.

He was quick to laugh, a vegan who rode his bike to work every day.

"We know you're here," I whispered, focusing my thoughts out into the room.

Worry churned in my gut. We needed to talk to Keller and then run like blazes.

Of course, I had no idea how we'd make it out of the locked compound. We were underground, and there was no way we were going to be able to go the other way up that vent.

I rubbed my temples.

"What are you picking up?" Marc asked.

Other than the fact that this was a bad idea? "Nothing," I said, starting down the dimly lit row of lab tables again. "It's not like I can pick up my phone and call a ghost." I didn't even have a phone down here. My gaze darted across the room for some trace of a sign, but I saw only darkness and shadows. "Is there anything else that would catch his attention on this floor?"

"Only 18F," he said, "but there's never been a disturbance there."

I touched my fingers to the cool metal of a smashed optic microscope. "What's in 18F?"

"Live testing," Marc said, his voice full of contempt.

I stopped. "You use animals?"

"I don't," he said, his expression grim. "The old army does. Hell, they use people."

I gaped at him, knowing instantly that he wasn't kidding.

"We have to stop this war," I told him. Somehow. Some way. This had to end.

"I'd give my life if we could," he vowed.

I would too. Still... "Let's hope it doesn't come to that."

I focused once again on the young professor. "Dr. Keller," I said under my breath, "it's Petra Robichaud. You remember me." He had to remember me. "We can talk if you show yourself."

"Talk?" a voice echoed as the temperature in the room plummeted. "I don't have time to talk." A frigid wind burst through the lab, scattering what was left on the tables.

"Jesus," Marc muttered under his breath.

My heart skipped a beat as the ghost of Dr. Keller materialized at his desk, directly behind us. He rooted through file cabinets that had already been spilling their guts.

"You see this?" He fisted a wad of papers. His chest had been torn open. I could see his rib bones working as he shredded the paper with his bare hands, desperate and shaking. "All of this has to go."

"Why, Dr. Keller?" I asked, voice even, approaching him slowly. He was older than I remembered. His face had taken on hard angles on the cheeks and softened in the jaw. He was thinner than before, skeletal. Goose bumps trickled down my arms. "Tell me what you have to hide. I can help you."

He rushed me. Before I had time to react, he was on me. "Do you have matches?" he asked, his face inches from mine.

"No," I said, the hair on the back of my neck standing on end. He hovered parallel to the floor.

His eyes narrowed, and the temperature of the room iced to a bone-chilling freeze. I could see my breath puff between us as he stared me down.

He whipped around and toppled the lab table next to me. Glass and petri dishes flew in a hundred different directions. "They took mine!" He threw his hands up in the air. "They stole my matches. Heat kills it."

"Heat kills what?" I asked, keeping my voice steady, trying to stand straight when every instinct screamed for me to duck. "Teach me," I said. He was an academic. And he certainly had my full attention.

"Take these," he said, handing me a sample tray with two dozen test tubes filled with glowing green liquid. "Destroy them."

I exchanged glances with Marc. "Do you have a neutralizing station?"

"Here. Like this." Dr. Keller grabbed a test tube and shattered it on the floor. Then another. And another.

Marc recoiled with every shot. "What are you doing?"

Hurling toxic chemicals. What did it look like?

I had to gain Keller's trust, get him talking. "Here," I said to the ghost, fingers shaking as I smashed the tubes, one by one. "I'm doing it. I'm helping."

Marc watched, wide-eyed. "And you call me crazy."

"Good. Good!" Keller reached for another tray. That one was empty, but he didn't seem to notice. "We must destroy the compound and every shred of research. It's not a medicine," he said, the fear plain on his face. "It's a biological weapon. One hundred percent fatal to humans."

I froze. "This?"

"Yes. They're working on a pathway. They haven't found it yet. We must be faster!"

"This could kill me," I said, voice cracking. Marc grabbed the tray from my hands.

Dr. Keller didn't even notice. "It will kill you only if it is airborne," he lectured. "And it has a one hundred percent kill rate."

"They're going for one hundred percent casualties?" I could hardly believe it. "But they're still working on the pathway," I said, just to be clear. I rubbed my hands on my pants as I watched Marc slide the tray into a biohazard can. "Are you sure?"

"Yes. Yes!" Dr. Keller was growing frantic again.

"Okay," I said, my mind racing. It was something.

A pathway basically offered the means for a bioweapon to enter the human system. If they hadn't finalized a way to get it to the general population, then we still had time.

"You see why we must destroy the lab," Dr. Keller insisted.

I hated to break it to him, but there were a lot of other labs.

"It's a biological weapon," Marc said, shocked. He stood about two feet from the ghost of Dr. Keller. "Ask him why they need one hundred percent casualties."

"Because they're twisted," I said. But he had a point. If we knew why, maybe we'd find a how. "Why everyone?" I asked the ghost. It didn't make sense for them to wipe out the human race. We worked for them. We lived among their soldiers.

Dr. Keller shrank down upon himself, his eyes glazed with abject horror. "They want to eliminate the competition," he said simply. "The New God Army has more humans in it. Kill them and you cripple the enemy."

He began to cry. "Kill the humans on Earth and that way, the gods have more room to play. It's a win-win for them. Besides, they said the humans suffer too much anyway. They believe this weapon is the humane solution." Tears rolled freely down his cheeks now. "My wife is topside. My kids. They don't deserve this."

"None one does." Heaven almighty. How were we going to fix this?

CHAPTER TWELVE

THE FIRST THING we needed to do was get out of there.

The lower half of Dr. Keller's body faded in and out as he rooted through the debris on the nearest lab table. "I need a working burner plate," he said, eyes wild. He found two flat, analog hot plates and sent them tumbling across the table. "These won't plug in."

Yes, they would. The ghost just couldn't grip them. He could only shove them.

Marc and I stood on the other side of the table, which was covered in yellowish sand that reeked of garlic. The doctor had mixed a metallic powder in there, too.

Keller was too far gone. It was clear I couldn't help the doctor, or save the human race, while trapped down here in a busted-up lab.

But there was nowhere to go. Our only way out was locked and chained, courtesy of the Old God Army.

Marc and I exchanged a glance. "Please tell me you have a brilliant idea."

Dr. Keller swiped at the fluorescent lights above us, sending them crashing to the floor. Bulbs exploded around us.

Marc examined the doors. Chains rattled on the other side. "We can't make it out this way."

A frigid wind tore at us, toppling the lab table. "You will not leave. You will stay and work for me!"

In a forbidden lab where we couldn't make a difference.

"We need to go, Dr. Keller," I hollered over the wind. "Marc and I need to go topside and try to fix this!"

"No!" the ghost hurled a test tube at my head. I ducked it. He was a good man, but his desperation was taking over. We needed to calm him down while we worked on a way to get out of here.

"We brought scientists," Marc hollered over the gale. "They're right outside. We can work together."

My hair whipped my face. What was he, nuts? A poltergeist could kill you. You didn't want to lie and tick him off.

The ghost ripped the doors open. "Where?" he demanded.

"Now." Marc grabbed my hand and we took off in a dead run past the ghost and out the door.

Holy mother. We were so dead.

We dashed down a narrow cinderblock hallway, the ghost bellowing in outrage behind us.

The lights from the lab surged and crackled, illuminating the path ahead like lightning strikes. The rest of the doors along the hallway lay dark—abandoned, or at least closed for the night.

"Wait," Marc said. We skidded to a stop as the hallway cornered off. He planted his back to the wall and snuck a glance ahead. I looked behind.

An electric storm poured from Dr. Keller's lab. The doors hung drunkenly off their frames as the good doctor's howl echoed off the cinderblock prison. But he hadn't pursued us. Maybe he still had enough of his humanity left.

Maybe he didn't know he could leave.

It was a wonder we didn't have an entire squad on top of us. Then again, I wasn't so sure I'd be running toward this place if I were in charge of security.

A purple cloud poured from the lab.

"Okay, let's go," Marc said.

We took a hard right around the corner and faced an even narrower hallway. Gaslights flickered above.

My stomach fluttered. I could get lost in here so easily. "How do we get out?"

"Quietly," he said, our footsteps a whisper as we hurried down the corridor.

My breath sounded loud in my ears. Shadows danced off the walls. I tried to forget that we were underground.

It felt like some kind of macabre dungeon. "This place had to be creepy before the ghost."

Marc huffed. "Welcome to my world. We're on the lowest level. Three stories underground."

Anxiety wormed through me. I felt both exposed and trapped at the same time. We could be discovered at any moment, yet we had no choice but to follow the elaborate underground network of tunnels.

We hurried past a series of gray painted doors with the word *Containment* written in red block letters.

I stiffened as I heard shuffling on the other side.

Marc walked at my side, his hand on his gun. "They're locked," he said, as if that was supposed to make me feel better. "Almost everyone on this floor has gone home for the night."

My palms began to sweat. "What about the other floors?"

He looked as uneasy as I felt. "We'll have to play it by ear."

He stopped in front of an unmarked gray door at the end of the hall. "Do you have a flashlight?"

I patted down my pants and jacket. "I think I dropped it."

Marc cursed under his breath. "Mine's gone, too." He propped the door open, and I entered before him. Narrow industrial stairs circled up into the abyss.

The door closed behind us, leaving us in pitch blackness.

"At least we'll know if someone's coming," he said, voice low.

"But you know where we are." I felt for the metal banister, desperate for a little good news.

"Yes."

We wound our way up in the darkness. One floor. Two.

Shouts echoed from another space—muffled, yet eerily close.

Marc exhaled, warming my neck. "They're sending troops down the other staircase."

And suddenly, the acuteness of our situation hit me once more. "They could have just as easily used this one."

"We had a fifty-fifty shot."

If they'd taken this one, we'd be dead. I tightened my grip on the banister and forced myself upward.

I was scared and tired. My body still ached from the fall down the vent, and I was starting to get out of breath from the stairs.

His hand closed over mine on the banister. "I never should have gotten you into this."

"Don't start," I said, pulling my hand from under his. I didn't need regrets. Not about this, anyway.

We strained to see any light or movement above us, although I had no idea how we'd hide if a door suddenly opened or a lantern flipped on.

I might have been able to pass for a visiting doctor at the start of the night, but not after a trip through the vent, or after Dr. Keller's smash-'em-up at the lab. I probably looked more like a berserker than a scientist.

"Stop," Marc said.

We'd reached a landing. My hand closed around a smooth, cool door handle. No way would I open it without having some idea what was on the other side, but nevertheless I clung to it. It was as if I needed to know there was a way out of this.

Of course, even if we did make it back to solid ground, they still had a bioweapon that could wipe out the human race.

I remembered the prophecy. *The peacekeeper will find love as a hideous new weapon is born.*

Marc rested a hand on my back. "There are going to be guards along the main hallway. We can't risk it. When I open the door, I'm going to make an immediate left into the clinic. Follow me."

He opened the door slowly, and I squinted against the bright light pouring in. Dirt smeared Marc's cheeks and neck, and his hair spiked in all directions.

"Are we clear?" I asked.

He had his eyes on the hallway. "For now."

"Then here." I reached up to smooth his hair back.

With the corner of my sleeve, I wiped the dirt from his face. He closed his eyes as I brought the cloth to his chin and rubbed the indent below his cheek.

"Petra—" he began.

My heart squeezed. What began as a defensive measure turned into a surprisingly intimate gesture.

"You want to fit in," I said gently. His uniform still looked good. More than good, in fact.

He looked at me for a long moment. There was so much we would never be able to say. "Petra—" he began again. He paused, considered. And the moment was gone. "Keep your head down," he told me.

"I will," I promised.

We exited into what could almost pass for a hospital hallway. With Marc in the lead, we hung a sharp left and passed through a set of double doors.

A nurse at the check-in desk stood. "Dr. Belanger, thank the gods." From her pointed ears and silvery complexion, I could tell she was more than half fae. "We have a situation."

She scooted out from behind our desk and followed us as Marc headed into some sort of underground ER. "There was a mining explosion on the front lines," she said, chart in hand, "twenty-five casualties. Four immortal. Twenty-one mortal. They breathed in what we believe to be a toxic dust."

It was like flipping a switch. I immediately channeled my fear and slammed into clinical mode.

"Let me see," I said, grabbing for the chart.

"Who is this?" She yanked it back, as if she were noticing me for the first time.

"Kate Gordon," I said quickly.

"Visiting from HQ," Marc added.

"Sorry, Kate," she said, the smooth skin between her eyebrows puckering as she took in my disheveled state. "This is classified. You'll have to go back up top."

"Right." Back up top.

"Where you just were," Marc added.

I had to admit the proposition was attractive.

"Security," the nurse called. I reached for my gun and saw Marc do the same as two elite guard troops rushed me.

They wore the scythe insignia of Cronus the Titan. These were high-level guards, not lab lackeys. I wondered just what they were doing in a secret underground clinic.

"Escort her out," the nurse ordered.

"Wait. I'd like to confer with Dr. Gordon on this." Marc reached into a med cart and pulled on a pair of gloves. "Where are we on those patients?"

"The mortals are dead. The immortals are in surgery."

He slowly removed the gloves. "So you don't need me immediately."

She flipped her blond hair from her shoulder. "I'd like to go over their charts," she said defensively.

He tossed the gloves into the trash, not at all amused. "I intend to do just that. But first, I'll escort my colleague out."

The nurse frowned. "Just don't escort her back to the woods," she said under her breath.

"What?" I asked as Marc led me farther down the hallway. It looked like any other ER, except for the guards posted outside each room. And the two following us.

"The woods are a local hookup spot," Marc gritted out.

Ah, so it seemed the nurse mistook my messy appearance.

At least she knew I had good taste.

We hit the guard station outside the clinic. We were almost out. Which was usually when it all went sideways...

Four guards blocked the double doors. Two manned the desk. Our escorts stopped behind us as we approached what looked like an airport metal detector.

"You first," the guard at the other side said to me.

Great.

I didn't know what they were testing for. Weapons? Had one. Toxic chemicals? Take your pick. Illegal items? I had a map of the armies tucked into my boot.

The vast desert night lay just outside. I braced myself and stepped across the threshold.

An alarm blared.

"Stop." The guard drew his sword.

I yanked Marius's gun from my pocket, fell to my knees, and fired.

A blinding light shot out of the gun. Spots danced in front of my eyes, and the energy aftershock knocked me to the ground. The guard in front of me fell, along with the four behind him.

Marc dove next to me as I rolled, closed my eyes, and fired behind us.

The second shock hit, this one worse than the last as the energy bounced back at us. I buried my head against my shoulder, tasting metal and smoke.

"What the hell is that?" Marc barked, cringing at Marius's funny little spiderweb gun.

"No clue." My eyes stung and I forced myself to see beyond the spots dancing in my vision as Marc and I scrambled to stand.

"This way." We stumbled past the six unconscious guards before Marc opened the sliding steel door that led out into the cemetery. "Go."

"Wait," I said as the frigid desert air whipped inside. "You're not coming?"

He glanced back into the compound. "I can't."

"Do not start this sacrificial BS again." His life might not mean anything to him, but it did to me. "I'm tired of it."

His green eyes bored into me. "Petra, I'm compromised."

He was right. Numbness gripped me. "I should have taken out the security cameras."

His jaw was tight. "This is the old army," he said, resigned. "They don't have any. But they know I was with you." He gripped me by the shoulders, willed me to focus. "You're going to have to shoot me."

"What?" He was crazy. "I have no idea what this thing does." Marius had said it was a disruptor, but I didn't know if it left people wounded or dead or worse.

"Hurry," he said, not giving me an inch. "The guards are starting to come around."

That was actually good. I didn't want this weapon to kill, not if I was going to shoot Marc. I clutched the disruptor, unsure. "The guards are demigods." What if they could survive and Marc couldn't? Even if I shot him in the leg, he'd get the full burst of energy.

"Petra." His face was grave. "I'm dead if you don't do this."

I didn't know if I could do it. I'd thought he was dead for the last ten years. It had nearly killed me, and I hadn't even been the one to pull the trigger.

My mind raced, desperate for a different way out of this. "They don't know that you know that I'm a spy."

"This is the old army," he said, resigned. "They'd kill me just to be sure."

"We'll find another way." I'd think of something. If only we hadn't triggered the alarm.

He softened. "I'm glad I got to see you," he said, touching the back of my neck. "I'm glad I got to spend a day with you, even if I should have just let you go."

He kissed me. It was hard and desperate and full of the things we had never said. That we'd never have a chance to share.

I clung to him, not wanting this, wishing I could erase all of it.

He stepped away, looking more handsome and strong and determined than I'd ever seen him before. "Do it."

It was wrong. I was so sick of him being the one to take the fall.

I drew back as far as I dared, to the edge of the doors, until I stepped out to where the path outside met the coarse dirt of the cemetery.

Marc's eyes never left me. "Now, Petra."

I pulled the trigger.

The blast of light hit him straight in the chest. Horrified, I watched him topple forward and fall to the floor.

CHAPTER THIRTEEN

MARIUS'S GUN felt hot in my hand. I'd shot him. I'd shot Marc. I'd never forgive myself if I killed him.

Run.

I stood. The electric aftershocks clung to my arms.

Run.

I couldn't move. Every medical instinct I had screamed *Stay, help, see if he's breathing, for God's sake.*

But even as I stared at his crumpled body, willing with every fiber of my being for him to cough, twitch, blink, I knew I had to go. Marc needed me to be the security risk, the bad guy—the one who got away.

"Goodbye," I whispered, turning and fleeing into the cemetery. The night was cold and unforgiving. My breath hitched as I stumbled among the graves, crouching low.

I'd never intended for things to get this out of hand.

I tripped, sending up a plume of desert rock and slamming my elbow into a headstone. I welcomed the pain. I'd earned it. And on some level, I felt I deserved it.

A scraggly forest stood at the edge of the cemetery. It would offer cover to stop, to think, to grieve.

Throat burning, I'd almost reached the shelter of the woods when Oghul stepped out from behind a dead palm tree. "You!" He held a torch and wore his trademark frown.

Dread seized me. He was either going to be my savior or —if he knew what I'd done—my executor. I didn't know what I was going to tell him.

Oghul doused his torch in the sandy soil.

I glanced behind me and saw troops swarming the guard station.

At least they'd call the medics.

If Marc is still alive.

A cold wind whipped through the cemetery, rattling the dead trees. The berserker loomed, menacing in the dark, the beads in his hair clacking together, the whites of his eyes glowing red. "Where is Dr. Belanger?"

A new kind of fear lanced through me, and I felt my throat go dry. I wasn't up for any big misunderstandings with a brute who could rip me in half. My finger danced on the trigger of the gun.

"Marc stayed behind to help me escape," I said, voice shaking only slightly. It was the truth. As much as I was willing to give.

I could tell Oghul didn't believe me, not fully at least. He shifted from side to side like an angry bear.

"He's with them," I said, looking for any sign of Marc. They'd positioned troops outside and were sliding the heavy doors closed. "They don't know he helped me."

Oghul growled low in his throat. "Then we will leave now."

"I need my—"

He handed me my pack.

"Right." I slung it over my shoulder and stuffed the gun back into my pants as Oghul set off through the tangled underbrush.

I followed, wading through knee-high debris. There were dried palm fronds, twigs, even a few petrified coconuts.

"The woods" felt more like a giant dried-out hedge. You'd have to be desperate to even think of getting frisky out here. The branches dug into my pants and scratched my arms.

"You could not shoot me with your gun," Oghul said, the full moon shining bright on his back.

"I wasn't going to shoot you." I wasn't that crazy.

He grunted. "Not with an energy disruptor." He shoved a neck-high branch out of the way and let it rocket straight back at me.

I caught it, but not before it stung my hand pretty good. "What does a disruptor do?"

"It makes me angry."

I fought the urge to kick him in the back of the leg.

"To mortals. What does it do?" I needed to know. Desperately. "It won't kill them," I asked, digging at the strap on my shoulder, "will it?"

Oghul didn't even bother to turn around. "I do not know."

My stomach churned with guilt and regret and a dozen other emotions I hadn't even had time to process yet. I had to talk to Marius. He'd given me this stupid thing. Surely he knew what it did.

If we ever made it out of this place. The underbrush had grown thicker, taller too. Trees weaved over us in a skeletal canopy. "Where are we, anyway?"

Oghul continued shoving his way through the dead forest.

This was too bizarre. There were no trees in Limbo. No bushes.

Not unless you counted hell vents.

I came to a dead stop, heart pounding in my throat. "Where. Are. We?"

Oghul kept going. "Almost there. Another twenty paces."

Panic seized me. “This is a hell vent.” This was worse than getting shot.

Hell vents were direct lines to the underworld. Sure, demons dressed them up as tempting oases, but they were there to steal your body and soul.

The berserker turned. “This *was* a hell vent.” He shrugged. “As you can see, it is dried up.”

Yeah. Sure. “How do you know?”

He reached down and snapped a twig.

I took one step back, then another. The entire structure might be unstable. Was the ground vibrating? I thought it might be. I’d heard of vents opening up in the ground, sucking people straight down. Only I couldn’t see anything on the ground but dried-out plant debris.

“No, you do not go the other way,” Oghul said, as if I were some petulant child. “This vent. It has been dormant for centuries. Otherwise, we would have lost our souls a long time ago.”

Was I going to hyperventilate? I thought I was. “I can’t believe we’re having this conversation,” I gasped.

A branch caught me and I shrieked. Any second I could be cast down into Hades.

“Come,” he said, reaching out a hand to me, “we are closer to my horse than we are to the edge of this vent.”

No way was I holding hands with a berserker.

If I was smart, I would have broken away and never looked back. I would have, if I’d had any clue where to run. My luck, I’d get lost in this macabre jungle. We were surrounded by dead, dry, twisted debris. And skeletons. That was definitely a skull in a nearby pile of leaves and rot.

“I’m damned if I do, and damned if I don’t,” I said, my voice hitching.

Oghul didn’t get it. “The cracks, they are not so bad up ahead.”

"Goody." He saw cracks.

I swallowed, hard, and glanced behind us. I could try to trace my way back, but I had no illusions of what I'd find in the enemy camp. Marc was injured—or dead. The guards were looking for me. And I had absolutely nowhere to hide unless I wanted to lead them straight back to Marc.

After he'd sacrificed everything for me.

I scrubbed a hand over my eyes. Marc had entrusted my escape to Oghul. That had to mean something.

The Mongolian sneered. "I do not know why the doctor loves you. You are a pain."

My heart twisted. "He told you he loves me?" It shouldn't matter, but it did.

"Let's go," I said to the berserker.

We pushed forward. This time I moved slower, even though it was impossible to see the ground in front of us.

Dormant or not, hell vents were designed to tempt people before sucking them straight into the underworld. I didn't know what kind of traps were set in here, or what creatures might have survived even without the lush, tempting jungle that usually came with eternal damnation.

My heart stuttered as Oghul and I reached a break in the trees. "That's not—"

"No. The vent is forty paces farther. This is where we stop."

Moonlight shone down on a small clearing of cracked dirt, littered with tumbleweeds. In the center stood the largest, sleekest horse I'd ever seen. It was pure white, with furs draped over its back.

"*Áni.*" The berserker smiled for the first time I'd ever seen.

The horse stomped, the muscles in her legs and shoulders flexing.

When we drew closer, I realized the dangling bits on the saddle were finger bones.

All of the sudden, *Áni* didn't seem like the best idea anymore. "We're just going to ride on out of here?"

"My *Áni* is the fastest horse in Norway," Oghul said, cupping his hand to help me up.

"All right," I said, taking him up on it. I hated to break it to him, but we weren't in Norway. Besides... "You look Mongolian."

"I was adopted."

"No kidding?" Far be it from me to know how berserker society worked. I just hoped they rode fast horses.

This one was a killer to mount. I grunted, clinging to the side of the beast. I tried to avoid the clacking finger bones as I struggled to get a leg over. My thigh muscles ached as I finally managed to straddle the horse's wide back.

The saddle shifted as Oghul took his seat behind me. The fur on the saddle was coarse and thick, like that of a wolf. I secured my duffel in front of us and gripped *Áni*'s pommel with both hands.

He seized the reins and we took off. *Áni* dashed straight for the tree line. I cringed, ducking low. As far as I'd seen, this horse had no wings.

We were ready to crash headlong into the trees when we wisped through them instead.

What? I choked. I had no voice.

Below me, I could see the outline of my legs straddling the horse's back. It was as if they were made of smoke. My arms and my hands as well had taken on the same vaporous hue. I realized with a start that we were passing through the trees.

The world had gone silent, as if we were wrapped in a cloud.

We dashed out into the desert wastelands, through the

old army lines. I didn't even feel the pull of the Great Divide. We streamed through it like specters in the night.

The first streaks of dawn broke over the horizon as we raced through the lava fields, through the desert that divided them from the MASH 3063rd.

Home.

We saw Father McArio's hut on the edge of the minefield. He stood near the wrought-iron fence he'd fashioned for his sculpture garden. It was alive with metal birds and flowers. Father was forever taking trash and discards and turning them into art. He stood eyes closed, lips moving, at the start of a new day.

We whisked past, through the maze of discarded junk and vehicle parts that crowded the minefield, until we reached the edge. *Áni* cantered and then trotted to a stop.

The smoky sensation lifted.

I'd actually made it back. Part of me had wondered if it was possible. The air smelled familiar, clean—with a hint of desert dust and antiseptic. I could hear the comforting sounds of camp beyond the minefield. It was like coming home from a long, long trip.

I cleared my throat. "Thanks," I said as Oghul dismounted. I tossed my duffel onto the ground, and he held me steady as I swung a leg back over the horse. "I like the way you ride." We should have done that the first time.

He looked at me evenly. "I take one passenger." He handed me my pack. "Dr. Belanger leaves you with me out of last resort." He remounted his horse.

Okay. So we weren't going to kumbaya. "I'm glad you were there," I told him.

Oghul grunted. Ah, well. The corners of my mouth tugged up as I began walking toward camp. *Home.*

Two steps later I stumbled over a trip wire and a cold, fishy waterfall landed on my head. I shrieked, covering my head too late as the slimy, wet bodies tangled in my hair. Dancing sideways, the rancid water soaking me to the bone, I flicked the mess onto the ground.

Sardines.

The stench was unbearable. I rubbed my face with the one semi-dry spot left on the end of my sleeve. Disgusting.

The Mongolian giggled like a schoolboy. "You did not see that coming." He clutched his stomach, bending atop his horse. "I did not see that coming, either! I like this place."

I should have tossed a fish at him.

"*Skal*," he said, raising a hand in goodbye before he and his horse disappeared into a plume of smoke.

Right. Sure. Leave me alone in the minefield with a bucket of dead fish on my head.

The sun had broken fully over the horizon. I'd have to hurry if I wanted answers from Marius. He was usually late to go to bed, but when he did, it would take the entire old army to rouse him.

First, I had to change out of the enemy uniform.

I glanced at the empty, fish-littered path behind me. It appeared deserted.

Just to be safe, I ducked into a dilapidated ambulance to change. It smelled like hot metal and dirt. And now, sardines. I shimmied out of the old army uniform pants.

Checking the pockets, I saw I still had the rock I'd picked up from the old army lines. I transferred it to my new army surgical scrubs, then rubbed some of the fish water out of my hair with the pants. It didn't really work.

Quickly, I completed the rest of the change. I buried the uniform and headed down to camp.

I passed two nurses as I dashed down the hill.

They chuckled at me. "Rodger was right," the younger one called.

"I don't want to know," I grumbled as I headed toward

the tiny vampire lair we'd cobbled together for Marius at the edge of the swamp.

Whatever they were talking about was probably my private business—a concept nobody around here seemed to understand.

Stars, I hoped Marc understood what he was doing when he asked me to shoot him.

The problem was, I knew Marc too well. He was noble to a fault. Part of the reason I'd agreed to sneak into an enemy unit in the first place was that I knew he'd do anything to keep me safe.

I just wished he hadn't had to prove it.

Merde. I kicked up a small cloud of dust as I skirted around the tar swamps. I'd lost all objectivity as soon as I'd gotten alone with him. It was so easy to fall into our old rhythm, probably because I'd wanted that in my life for so long. It was a familiar place, one I'd treasured even as I mourned him.

But it wasn't my reality anymore. This was.

The peacekeeper will find love as a hideous new weapon is born.

Didn't mean I'd get to keep the love. Or halt the weapon.

I pounded on the rough wood door of Marius's lair.

"Go away," he said, sleepy. "I'm brooding."

"Stay awake," I hollered through the wood. "I need to talk to you."

"Petra?" Marius shifted on the other side of the door. "You stink."

"At least I got your attention." Focus. "That gun you gave me," I said, lowering my voice. "Marc got shot."

I heard shuffling inside. "Your human?" he asked, more awake.

"Yes." I waited, my gut filling with dread. What was he not telling me? "Marius?" I yelled.

"I never thought you'd shoot your ex-lover."

I leaned my forehead against the door. I didn't either.

I wished I could take back the last thirty-six hours. Call a do-over.

His voice sounded hollow. "The disruptor gun was to protect you from the ghost."

Yes, well, the ghost hadn't required deadly force. He couldn't blow up the other MASH camp or he would have already. So I'd shot my friend instead.

"Where did you hit him?"

"Square in the chest," I said.

"Good. A head shot would kill him. Anywhere else, he might have a chance."

Dread washed over me. "Give me odds." I didn't want any gray around this one.

Marius's hesitation was palpable. "Twenty percent. Maybe. I'm sorry."

I squeezed my eyes shut. I'd screwed up. Big time. Marc had come back to me whole and alive and I'd blasted him with a supernatural weapon. All so that I could escape back here and know he was dead or dying and that I'd never see him again.

Tears stung my eyes.

I pushed off the door. "Thanks, Marius."

Marc had left me—possibly forever—so I could live on, fight another day, figure out what in Hades we were going to do about Dr. Keller's superweapon.

Alone.

I had no idea if he was alive or dead.

Being with him had felt so comforting, so familiar; well, this feeling did, too. I had lived with this heaviness in my heart before.

I reached down deep in my pant pocket for the rock I'd taken from that dig we'd stumbled on.

There'd been an accident there—one that the old army

wanted hidden or they wouldn't have brought their casualties to that classified area. I had to think that the excavation had to be connected somehow with Dr. Keller's formula gone wrong.

The shard felt cool against my fingers.

I owed it to Marc to push on. It was the only thing I could do for him.

My roommate Rodger had been a geology minor in college. He also collected rocks—somewhere among the *Star Trek* action figures. He might know what this was, or at least where to look. I glanced over at our hutch on the edge of the swamp. I just hoped he was home.

CHAPTER FOURTEEN

I BANGED into our hutch and tossed my duffel bag onto the floor.

Rodger was still organizing the action figures he'd brought back from his leave. At least that was what I hoped they were doing spread out all over my cot.

My roommate stretched out on his neat and clean bed with an Avengers comic book. "You're back." He started to sit up. "Whoa!" He gave a gross-out look. "What happened to you?"

"The minefield," I said, looking for a place to sit.

Rodger leapt up and began clearing action figures, for their sake more than mine. Heaven forbid the vinyl-caped Jawa from 1978 get fish goo on his original, factory-sealed packaging.

"Oysters or chicken guts?" he asked, making sure the twelve-inch masterpiece edition of Captain Kirk was safe from my stench.

"Sardines," I said, sitting, not caring about my blanket and sheets. They were washable.

Now that his children were out of the way, Rodger was impressed. "Nice one." He whistled under his breath.

"I don't have time to worry about it," I said, resting my head in my hands.

"Actually, I think you should."

That's right. Rodger had an uber-sensitive werewolf nose. He'd just have to suffer.

"I shot Marc."

"Damn." Rodger slumped down next to me.

That didn't begin to cover it.

He sat with his elbows on his knees, trying to get me to look at him. "Marc was the enemy?"

I cringed. Yes, Marc was technically the enemy, but, "No, I didn't shoot him because he was on the other side." I explained the horrible mistake I'd made.

Rodger's eyes were going bloodshot. "Marc might be okay," he said, rubbing his face with his sleeve. He dropped his hands. "We've both seen patients with twenty percent odds pull through just fine."

But we usually saw them die. "The worst part is, I have no idea." I stood, unable to sit for one more second. "Before, I knew Marc was dead. I could at least try to deal with it," I said, pacing the hutch. "Now he could be clinging to life, in pain and alone. He could have gotten caught anyway. He could be getting court-martialed or shot. They could be shoveling dirt over him at this very minute, and I don't know." I'd failed him. "I'm not there."

"I understand," he said quietly. I stood looking out at the bubbling tar swamp, and we just *were*. Rodger knew I was right and that he couldn't make it better. So he just chose to be with me. It helped. Maybe.

I didn't know anymore.

"Before, there was at least someone to blame," I said, chest heaving. I felt hollow. "It was the old army's fault. They took him. They put him on the front lines. It was their fault when the enemy slashed his throat and left him to bleed out on the ground. He left me because they took him from me." I dropped my head, not wanting to say it. But I had to. I owed it to Marc to at least face what I did. "Now it's all me. I pulled that trigger. I ran, not knowing if he'd make it. I left him."

My throat felt raw. I'd been prepared to never see him again, but I wasn't prepared for him to cease to exist. Not again.

Rodger pulled me into a bear hug. I sank into him, taking the warmth and the comfort, needing it like I needed my next breath. "I just wish I knew somebody on the other side," he said, almost to himself.

I swallowed hard. "Me too."

Marc would contact me if he could. He had to. In the meantime, I just had to hope and pray. And help him any way I could.

Rodger pulled back, his face grave. "He could be okay. You have to remember that."

"I know." I meant it. I tried to smile as I patted him on the arm. "I have a question for you," I said, wiping my nose on my sleeve.

"Yes, you may borrow my soap."

I laughed despite myself. *Merde*, I was a mess.

"I found something on the other side," I said, digging in my pocket for the crystal. "I don't know what it is, but I thought you might."

He took it and held it up to the light. "Titurate?" He inspected it closer, rolling it over in his hands, exploring every nook and cranny like a kid with a new toy. "It is! Where did you get this?"

I explained while my roommate continued to ooh and ahh over the piece of rock. At least I'd asked the right person.

"So why is this rock so special?" I asked, worried for a moment he was going to want to sleep with it like a teddy bear.

Rodger shook his mop of auburn hair out of his eyes. "It's the hardest crystal ever," he said, holding it up as if I was supposed to be able to see that. "Eeeee!" he screeched at it.

Now I'd seen everything. "Please tell me you're not singing to a piece of rock." I sniffled.

"Eeeee..." he continued, his voice warbling, sounding like a dying seal. "I'm working it."

"Try not to work so hard."

"No, see." He turned the crystal sideways, as if that would help. "You hit the right sound frequency and poof! The entire crystalline structure collapses. You're basically left holding nothing. Well, a fine dust. But you really can't see it and it's basically nothing. Or so I've heard."

"Okay," I said, trying to sort through the rock geek code. "So basically, you're trying to break my crystal."

"A friend of mine had a video. It's gorgeous. The whole thing goes up like a mini-fireworks display and then—poof! It's the only use for something like this. Other than to put in a collection. Which would be so amazingly cool." He inhaled like I'd been holding him underwater. "Can I have this for my collection?"

"Not if you break it."

He grinned like a groupie. "My rock club is going to freak out."

I knew he was into this, but... "You have a rock club?"

Rodger couldn't stop playing with the crystal. "Where do you think I go every Tuesday afternoon?"

I had no idea. I was usually on shift.

"Just kidding." Rodger grinned. "Rock club is every other Saturday. I do LARP on Tuesdays."

I didn't care. "Do you think somebody in your rock club will know more about this?"

"Maybe." He shrugged. "One thing's for sure. They are going to have puppies."

"Seriously?"

"Actually, no. Only I can have puppies." Rodger grinned. Luckily for him, he got back on track before I slapped him. He held the rock up to the light. "I've only seen one other titurate crystal, and that was at a show in Brighton. It wasn't even for sale. The guy was just rubbing our faces in it." He laughed. "Everybody kept trying to make it break."

"You think you stood a chance?" I asked.

"You never know."

I doubted this guy would have left his rock out where just any *eee* could smush it. I reached for the stone, but Rodger dodged me. "It must be a hard frequency to hit," I said.

"It is," he said, fondling it some more. "Look." He dug under his bed for a massive box of books. Shoveling through the pile, he found one on crystals and flipped through it.

"You want to hand me the rock while you do that?"

"No." He found his page. "See here? That's a picture of it."

Lo and behold, it was. I did have a genuine titurate on my hands. Although I didn't know why we were still looking at a picture when Rodger had the real thing in his tight fist.

"They don't call it the Crystal of the Gods for nothing."

Okay, well, "Can you find what else it does? Other than turn to dust?"

"How about I go do it while you shower?"

Ha, ha. "I'd actually like to go with you." It was my rock. My responsibility. "I want to hear firsthand what your friends have to say."

Rodger cringed. "Um. Yeah. I don't think you'd be welcome with some of these guys."

He had to be kidding. "I'm not hip enough for rock club?"

My roommate gritted his teeth. "I had to make up a few stories while you were away."

I had a bad feeling about that. "What kind of stories?" I asked slowly.

He clutched the crystal to his chest, but his eyes were on me. "You were gone for two days."

"A day and a half." And he was stalling. "Rodger?"

His eyes grew wider. "Nobody could figure out why I'd come back from vacation and volunteer to work two double shifts."

"Rodger!"

"I told everyone that you were in the minefield, setting pranks," he said quickly. "That worked...for a while. But then a bunch of people saw Marius come out of there smiling, so they thought you two were out hooking up."

Glory be. "And you told them what?"

"I told them maybe you were," he said, voice rising, shoulders up around his ears. "It seemed like a good cover." His teeth clenched in a nervous smile. "But then Marius said no way he was with you and he thought he saw you with Shirley."

"At least I have good taste." Shirley was an awesome person.

"You *did*," Rodger said, gaining confidence when he realized I hadn't tossed him through the hutch wall. Yet. "But then Kosta asked Shirley if that was true, and you know she was thrilled because she's been wanting him to get into her for months, so she said that you were out there hiding things."

"What?" I gaped.

"You know, like pranks. Maybe storage."

"Why didn't she just tell him I was in my lab, working on the anesthetic for immortals?"

Rodger sucked his lips into his mouth. "That would have been a great idea."

"Okay," I said, pacing again, "so now I'm hiding gods-knew-what in the minefield." I could live with that.

Rodger took a deep breath.

I stopped. "What?"

"It would have been fine except that things are disappearing all over camp."

Unbelievable. "I've only been gone for two days!"

"A day and a half. And there's no reason to yell," he said, getting his hackles up. "*I* know you're not a thief."

"But everybody else?"

Rodger cringed.

He'd been lying for me, along with Marius and Shirley, and all of their stories stunk worse than I did with fish on my head.

"I'm going to kill you," I said, going after him.

He zigzagged out of my reach. "Not if you want to find out about your rock."

"I'm going to toss all of your action figures out into the swamp."

"There's no need to get nasty."

"Everyone is talking behind my back."

"Now, that part is true."

There was nothing sacred in this MASH camp, nothing private. And that was when we were dealing with boring little details like who switched shifts with whom and who had one too many shots of Hell's Rain at the officers' club.

"The gossips are going to have a field day with Petra the vampire lover/friend-crushing/klepto who spends all of her time in the junkyard."

"At least you have a sense of humor about it," Rodger offered.

"I'm going to get a shower," I grumbled.

* * *

I got more looks than I'd ever gotten walking the fifty feet to the shower tent.

"How's your boyfriend?" A clerk in a yellow robe winked at me as she ducked out of the shower tent.

I gritted my teeth. "Marius is not my boyfriend. Shirley is not my girlfriend, and I didn't steal anything."

Her nervous laugh made my stomach pinch.

I braced myself and ducked into shower stall number two. I had absolutely nothing to be ashamed of. Except for shooting Marc.

See? No matter how bad things were, I could always make them worse.

I stood under the lukewarm spray for a long time before soaping up my hair.

"I believe you," said a Southern voice on the other side.

"Who's that?" I asked as the stinging soap ran down in my eyes. I hadn't even known someone was there.

"Fogarty. Cafeteria service."

I blasted my face and head with water. "You're from Georgia, right?" She liked to talk about Cajun cooking. I just wished they'd let her make some real food.

"Um-hum. The trouble started when the four-star general and his mama rolled into camp two days ago."

"Really?" I asked, soaping up. A four-star mama's boy.

"He's just a demigod general, but she's a goddess, so Kosta's doing it all up. They're in for a general inspection." Fogarty's water shut off. "He's okay. But I've heard she has sticky fingers."

I placed a hand on the damp wall between us. "Have you told anybody?"

Her towel slipped off the hook. "Now, I think you know that's treason."

Right. To accuse a goddess. Damn.

"You're just going to have to suck it up. But like I said, I know you didn't do half the stuff I hear."

"Thanks," I said, wondering just which half she did believe. "How did you find out about this goddess?"

"Her name is Eris."

I tapped a finger against the wood shower wall. "I should know who that is." I needed to borrow one of Rodger's books again.

"Greek goddess of chaos."

That sounded about right. "I'll bet the next prophecy says something about her," I muttered, grabbing the soap once again.

"No. The second prophecy already came in."

My soap clattered to the floor.

"We were all watching this morning. I'd still be there if I didn't have a shift at eleven."

I braced a hand on the stall door, willing myself to breathe. I said a quick prayer that the next prophecy would give me a glimmer of good news. Some indication that we'd be able to stall the weapon or free Dr. Keller or that—please God—Marc would be okay. I needed it so bad right now. I needed to at least hope. I let out a shaky breath. "What did it say?"

"Oh, yeah. Sorry," she said, gathering up her shower caddy. "Death comes with a gift."

CHAPTER FIFTEEN

MY HEART BEAT WILDLY. "*Death comes with a gift*? What does that mean?"

But she'd left the shower hut.

Marius's gun wasn't a gift. He'd take it back as soon as the sun set.

I had to see this.

Hands shaking, I rinsed most of the soap off—hopefully—and grabbed my robe. No doubt the television in the mess tent would be tuned to the Paranormal News Network. PNN was the only channel it got.

With my shower caddy in one hand and the other clutching my robe closed, I made it all the way to the south side of camp in three minutes flat.

"Is it still on?" I asked one of the motor-pool guys as he held the door open for me. I didn't think he'd planned on it. It was more like I barged past him.

"Nice outfit," he said, giving me the once-over. "I like the new you."

"Can it, Lazio."

"You'd better watch out," he called after me. "Kosta is

wanting us to be a little more buttoned down. Inspection and all."

Yeah, sure. I had more important things on my mind than polished boots. The mess tent was only half full, which was still pretty good for midmorning. Coffee stirrers, confetti, and half-eaten bowls of popcorn cluttered the long tables. No doubt there had been a fierce Oracle Watch party going on earlier.

Gods, I was so out of touch. I hadn't even been gone that long. Worse, I was disconnected from the MASH-19X as well, unable to contact anyone and even ask if Marc was alive. Not that I wanted to cavort with enemy units, but come on, I needed to know.

One way or the other.

The TV blared an ad for the Dyson Werewolf Heavy Duty. With twelve times more suction to capture the thicker, denser hair most vacuums missed.

I never understood why those women in the commercials looked so happy to be vacuuming. As far as I was concerned, a lack of housework was one of the main advantages of living in a hutch in the middle of the desert.

Craning my neck past a giggling bunch of corporals, I spotted Shirley sitting on a table near the front, her red hair stuffed into a loose knot.

"Hey, lover," I said, depositing my shower kit onto the table.

"Smirk all you want," she said airily. "It got Kosta's attention."

"Is that all you think about?" I asked as she cleared off a space for the rest of me.

"Yes."

Far be it from me to judge. I scooted up next to her. "I hear death comes with a gift."

"They've been analyzing it all morning."

"And?"

"See for yourself."

My nerves tangled as I sat and waited through the endless commercials. "You're not at work?" I asked her.

"I'm getting Kosta a cup of coffee."

"And doing a mighty fine job of it."

She snorted. "He's yelling at a bunch of supply clerks for playing washers with tank parts. General Argus caught them. It'll be a while." She reached behind me for the popcorn bowl. "So I'm actually doing a good job. The colonel's coffee will be hot when I get back in twenty minutes."

"Way to work it."

"I'm learning."

The news came back to the overly tan, large-toothed grin of Stone McKay, lead anchor and the only werewolf to make *Non-People* magazine's Sexiest Supe Alive list five years running.

He folded his hands on the desk in front of him. "We're now going to Mount Lemuria, where the Oracle of the Gods has delivered the second prophecy in what many are hoping is a three-part drive to curb the violence in this centuries-old immortal war. Prama Nandi is there."

The camera cut to an attractive young Indian reporter with camera-perfect skin, glossy lips, and hair so shiny that it sent up glints of light. She wore a curve-hugging purple trench coat.

This was serious journalism.

"I'm on the scene where the oracles have just delivered the second prophecy." She lowered her chin. "Death comes with a gift."

I ran my hands through my wet hair. Yes. *But what did it mean?*

The words *Second Prophecy: Death Comes With a Gift* ran on a ticker at the bottom of the screen.

Prama flipped her hair back. "While speculation is running rampant about what sort of gift death would come with, as of yet we have not heard personal commentary from any of the three oracles."

The camera cut to head shots of the soothsayers. Only these weren't studio shots. I supposed it was hard to get a twenty-six-hundred-year-old diviner to dress nice and pose. So they had photo stills.

There was Radhiki, in a bloodstained sack and staring in horror at the camera.

There was Li-Hua, her stick-straight black hair tangled around her face as she held up a large femur bone.

There was Ama, with blood-red streaks painted across her ebony cheeks. She'd lost her sack and was instead made decent on top by a black censor's rectangle.

Shirley nudged me. "Makes you feel better about every bad class picture you ever took, am I right?"

No. I couldn't believe these were the people directing my life. I'd worked hard in school. Studied when I could have been going to parties. I'd worked hard to try to become a decent, productive member of society, and instead, I was sitting here in Limbo, waiting for instructions from a woman who couldn't even remember to wear her sack.

The camera cut back to Prama Nandi staggering over large rocks as she tried to get close to a mountain cave. "I'm going to see if I can get any of the oracles to come out and give me their personal take on this latest prophecy. This will be a PNN exclusive."

A large boulder crashed down the mountainside. She ducked as it landed outside the cave, partially blocking the entrance. "Rocks have been falling like this every time I try to get close," she said, with a conspiratorial note, all the while moving closer.

Another boulder crashed down, and she made a startled

jog forward a foot or so. "There's a definite growling going on inside as well. Can you hear that?" She held out her microphone toward the dark entrance to the cave, then brought it back, smiling. "My sources haven't confirmed this, but I'd say these oracles don't want to be disturbed."

She held a hand over her head as a shower of smaller rocks began pelting her and anything else within ten feet of the cave entrance. The camera shot shook.

They flashed back to Stone McKay in the newsroom. He held on to something in his ear. "Prama, we're going to get back with you when you have one of the oracles ready to talk." He flashed a smile to his viewing audience. "In the meantime, let's hear what everyone is saying on Twitter."

A logo zoomed up onto the screen: *Oracle Watch 2021* it read, in stylized Greek script with a mountain in the background. It landed on the screen with a boom.

Then another smaller logo flashed up next to it and landed with a lighter sound. *Death comes with a gift.*

And wouldn't you know, there was a little present next to it.

I wanted to strangle somebody.

Stone McKay grinned. "BloodSucker1497 says: *death can't possibly come with any kind of a gift because once you are dead, you can't enjoy presents.*"

The comment appeared in a blue box next to Stone's head. "I suppose that's one way of looking at it," the anchor ad-libbed as the next Twitter comment popped up.

"PrincessPeanut says: *this oracle fails to consider the greatness of immortals. It completely excludes them and is just one more example of mortals trying to take gifts that aren't theirs.*"

Stone raised his eyebrows. "Interesting theory."

I groaned. "Why do I care what PrincessPeanut has to say about the fate of the world?"

Shirley shrugged.

Stone McKay waited as another comment flashed up on the screen. "EXfangirl22 says: *Typical for three immortals to look at death as a gift. They don't have to die.*" Stone winced. "Ouch."

Shirley handed me the popcorn. "You have to admit EXfangirl has a point."

More like they were all giving me a headache. Didn't anyone get it? "It doesn't matter what she thinks or what Stone says or what any of us make up," I said. "The oracles have spoken. Death comes with a gift. Now we just have to wait and see what happens." And pray it wasn't about Marc.

I knew from experience that it was next to impossible to predict how the oracles would come to pass. I just hoped this one hadn't already come true.

A burly-looking MP clomped up to us. He was a cyclops, like the rest of them. And he didn't look happy. "Kosta is looking for you," he grumbled.

Shirley slid off the table. "Whoops."

"What? Are you trying to get in trouble?" Sometimes I think she riled Kosta just to get his attention.

The guard stepped between us. "Not you. Her," he said, pointing to me.

My pulse quickened. "Me?" I asked. "What did I do?"

He shrugged.

Please don't let him find out about my little field trip.

Stomach churning, I let the MP lead me back to Kosta's office.

Shirley walked next to me, occasionally blowing on the thick mug of coffee she'd poured on the way out of the mess tent. "He likes it hot, but not too hot."

"Can you please freak out with me?" I asked, pointing to the huge MP in front of us. "What could Kosta possibly want with me?"

"It sure won't be a fashion consultation." She grinned, tugging at the sleeve of my robe.

"Yeah, thanks." Way to get my mind off things. I wasn't only being summoned to the commander's office. I happened to be naked except for a thin pink robe. I clutched the top of it with one hand, closing it tighter.

"Let me know if you see General Argus." I'd duck around a corner.

And I'd forgotten my shower caddy in the mess hall. Great.

The PA system crackled.

Attention all personnel. Incoming wounded. We need every available surgeon. Step to it. At least four full choppers are on the way.

"Good luck," Shirley called as I made an about-face and began jogging toward surgery.

Rodger was pushing the door open when I got there. "You hear?" he asked, his auburn hair sticking every which way. "They're unloading a special forces unit up there."

It took everything I had to keep from charging the hill to the helipad. Mind swimming, I pushed into the prep room. It couldn't be Galen. There were a lot of units out there, doing Lord knew what.

The only way I could help them was by keeping calm and putting them back together.

I stood at the long sink by the change room and scrubbed my hands until they hurt. Rodger stood on one side and the cranky Dr. Thaïs on the other. Thaïs had been arrested for about five minutes after he'd nearly gotten me killed on my last adventure. It hadn't stuck. The immortals had way too much pull around here, and he'd used every bit of his.

At the moment, I didn't even care.

Hands up, I banged into the OR, still in my pink robe. Like I'd had time to change. Nurse Hume stood ready with my gown. He barely lifted an eyebrow as he tied me into it and slipped on my gloves.

"I've got one!" an EMT yelled, bursting in through the back.

"Over here," I ordered, pointing to my table as I rushed to get a look at the soldier's condition. It was one of ours. Cobra Special Forces unit. Not Green Hawk, like Galen. I felt guilty for being relieved.

He had burns to his chest and left arm. "Wait." It wasn't an artillery burn. "This is some kind of napalm."

"I don't know what it is," the EMT said as he and his partner hoisted my patient up on the table. "But don't touch this stuff. It's burning every one of them alive."

I glared at him over my mask. Our patient could hear him. They all could.

"Don't listen to him," I said to the man on my table. A sheen of sweat coated his face, and blood gurgled from his lips. "I've got you."

"Get his uniform off now," I ordered Hume. I readjusted the large silver light over my table, aiming it at his chest. I tried to keep the emotion out of my eyes as my nurse peeled the cloth away.

Kosta stood next to me. "Basilisk venom." He cursed under his breath.

I'd studied it, but I never thought I'd see it. The hellish creatures were supposed to be extinct. The black goo had eaten into the soldier's chest cavity, through it.

"Make him comfortable and move on," Kosta said into my ear.

Goose bumps skittered up my arms. "I'm going to need blood and saline," I ordered. He was going to be losing fluids. In a few minutes, there wasn't going to be any skin left to contain them.

My gaze flicked across the crowded ER. I didn't want to look down at my patient. I didn't have time to bond with him. There were more coming in.

But I did it anyway. His eyes were unfocused, his skin cold. He was in shock, which was almost a blessing. I took his shaking hand and squeezed. "I'm sorry. There's nothing I can do."

He deserved to know.

The soldier squeezed my hand back.

I caught Father McArio's eye and he hurried over.

I dragged off my gloves as Father leaned close and murmured something in the man's ear.

"Robichaud," Kosta hollered. "Over here."

I jogged down two rows of tables, hands bare. Kosta stepped back as they lifted one onto the table in front of him. "It's just an arm," he said, leaving to meet another case coming in the door.

Only an arm.

He was a Japanese demigod, built huge, with piercing gold eyes. His left hand wrapped around his right bicep. Underneath, the entire right arm lay black and oozing. "It's coming off," he said, through gritted teeth.

My heart pounded in my ears. "It has to," I said, accepting gloves from Holly.

His face reddened. We didn't have much time. As it consumed his lower arm, the venom was moving up, looking for more.

"We're going to need to tie you down," I said. Anesthetic didn't work on immortals. He'd be awake as I sawed his arm off.

"No. Don't tie me." He came as close to pleading as a demigod could. He swallowed. His head came off the table. "I have a fear."

"Okay," I said quickly, accepting the bone saw from Holly. We didn't have time. "I won't do it. But you're going to have to lie still for me." I placed a hand on his shoulder. "You can do this."

There were tears in his eyes. "I deserve it. I'm a killer."

"You're a soldier." We all were. "We do the best we can." Sometimes, it wasn't enough.

He screamed as I cut.

When the arm was severed, I tied off his wound, careful to make sure none of the venom touched his skin. He was clean. In fact, he was healing as I stitched.

It was a good sign, a textbook case.

He lay heaving, staring at the ceiling.

I pulled off my gloves. "You're going to be okay."

The tidal wave of patients had ebbed. And as I took in the bodies on the tables, I realized most of them were dead or dying.

"Doc," my patient said, his voice dry, his eyes pleading, "does it even matter, what we did out there today?"

I had to think it did, but I wasn't sure. "We matter," I told him.

An orderly wheeled him away, and I stood for a moment, eyes closed. This was awful. Inhuman. The official line was always the same. Immortals had to stay awake during surgery. It was impossible to put them under.

I refused to believe it.

I was on the verge of discovering how. I knew I was close. I had to figure this out. I *would* do it.

I opened my eyes to find Holly watching me. "Do you really believe that?"

"What?" I asked, wiping my wet cheeks.

"That we matter." She watched me as if the answer meant a great deal.

It wasn't only the soldiers. It was all of us. We needed to know that we suffered for a reason. That death had a purpose.

But did we make a difference? I didn't know.

"Of course we matter," I said, dragging off my cap, plopping it onto her hand. "Now leave me alone. I have to go see Kosta."

Whatever heinous crime he wanted me for, I was almost glad. I'd pay whatever price he wanted, and then I'd argue my case for anesthetic research. I needed more time to focus, more resources, at least a decent lab.

I charged into Kosta's outer office. Shirley sat on the floor with a stack of files. "How'd it go?"

"It was surgery," I said, walking up to her.

Shirley's desk and filing cabinets occupied the back wall, broken by a thick wood door. The rest of the room lay bare, well, unless you counted the banker's boxes stacked everywhere.

I gave her a hand and she stood. "Kosta in?" I asked.

"He was just about to send our friend after you," she said, glancing at the MP by the door. I hadn't even seen him when I came in. Shirley dug through the top drawer of her desk and came out with lipstick and a small compact. The MP and I exchanged a look while she did her face.

"You look gorgeous," I said, wishing we could hurry it up. I wanted to find out exactly what Kosta had on me: going AWOL or theft.

Then I'd ask him for a favor. This was going to go just dandy, I could tell.

Shirley rapped on Kosta's door.

He gave a grunt and she entered, with me behind her and the MP taking the rear.

The colonel's office was straightforward, just like the man. He sat behind a standard military-issue desk, his shaved head bent over a stack of documents waiting for his signature.

Ancient battle shields lined the wall behind him, trophies from battles won. He'd been granted immortality after the campaign against Athens, but he sure hadn't let it go to his head.

"Thank you, Shirley," he said, without looking at her. "Stay outside, Kryon. Sit your butt down, Dr. Robichaud."

I took the hard wooden seat opposite him.

Just what kind of trouble was I in? I wished he would just come out with it.

The door clicked closed behind me, and Kosta kept writing.

No doubt this was an ancient Spartan war tactic. Freak them out until they spill.

I sat straight, shoulders back, and realized I'd forgotten to change after surgery. I was still wearing my pink robe.

Merde. I gave in to the urge to retie the belt.

At last, Kosta raised his head. A raised scar sliced down his right cheek and over his lip. The word in camp was that he'd gotten it in the Battle of Thermopylae.

He looked me up and down, scowling. "This is out of uniform, even for you."

I gave up on proper military form and crossed my legs. "If I'd known the wounded were coming, I would have dressed up."

He tossed his pen down onto the desk. "Where have you been, and what have you stolen?"

"Nothing," I said quickly. "You know me." He hadn't exactly been a mentor, but we'd worked together for seven years now. He'd seen me with patients. He knew my character.

"I was doing research," I said, "working on the sphinx venom anesthetic." It was almost true. I would have been doing that if Marc hadn't convinced me to wander over to the dark side.

Kosta grunted. "For thirty-six hours?"

"I got caught up in the work," I said, beginning to warm to my role. "It's important. You saw what just happened in that operating room."

He looked at me for a long moment. "So your colleagues simply made up stories."

"We're talking about Rodger, here. He didn't know where I was, so he improvised."

Kosta chewed on that one. Rodger could have earned a PhD in bedlam, and we both knew it.

He leaned back in his chair, still watching me. "Then who is the thief?" he asked, hands folded over his chest.

Like I was going to accuse the goddess of chaos. "I think you know," I said slowly.

He watched me for a moment. Kosta had a solid-gold BS detector. No question I'd set it off and it was pinging like crazy. Only my explanation made a lot more sense than anything else he'd probably heard.

He gave a sharp nod. "We won't speak of it again."

I tried not to look too happy. "Gladly." Treason wasn't at the top of my to-do list.

He scratched his chin. "It's good you've been keeping up with your research." His gaze wandered to the shields lining the wall. "Terrible scene back there. I'd give anything if we could find another way."

Kosta glanced at me, his fingers drumming on the desk. "The visiting general was in the OR just now."

"Good." I'd been trying to get HQ interested in what I was doing.

It turned out, before I'd sicced Jeffe on an immortal, none of the sphinxes had dared to ever raise a hand—or I suppose in this case a paw—against a warrior.

Good thing Jeffe and I never realized that.

And that the immortal he'd attacked was the forgiving type.

We'd learned, quite by accident, that sphinx venom could knock out an immortal.

I thought the discovery would get some attention, or at

least some research money. I'd applied for an office, supplies, for any kind of help the New God Army could give me. So far, my requests had been met with stone-cold silence.

"General Argus of Rhodes wants to talk to you," he said.

I stood. "Perfect. My paperwork is in the lab. I'll meet with him anytime. Anywhere."

"Stick around. He'll be here any minute."

I blew out a breath. Okay. Fine. I could do this. From the stories I'd heard, Argus seemed to be a fairly logical guy. Hopefully, I'd be able to talk him into a trip to the lab.

Kosta crossed his arms over his chest.

I fought the urge to rearrange my robe again as the silence stretched between us.

"*The* Argus, huh?" I asked, just to make conversation. I'd studied him back in mythology class in undergrad. Argus had one hundred eyes. And he was here, in camp. "I thought he was supposed to be off guarding Zeus's lover."

Kosta looked put out. "Zeus's wife turned her into a cow. That Argus is dead. This is his great-grandnephew. He only has four eyes." From the look on his face, Kosta wasn't a fan. "He brought his mother."

Ah, yes, Eris, goddess of the sticky-fingered.

Kosta eyed me and I heard his office door open.

We both stood as General Argus strolled in wearing battle fatigues with four stars at the shoulders. He was bald, soft, and reminded me of a fatted calf. Yet his gaze was calculating, wary.

He inspected me like I came with the camp. "This is your doctor?"

He had a heavy Greek accent. Obviously, he didn't get out much.

Kosta grunted. "She's a model soldier," he said, lying through his teeth. "This latest round of surgery pulled her out of the showers."

A sneer curled the general's lip. "I'll get to the point. The army has no interest in changing the way things are done. However..." He stared at me, as if he could see into me by force of will alone. "What happened in that OR was disgusting. You sure this drug of yours can work?"

"Yes," I said, adjusting my robe. I hoped. "But I need time, resources"—something besides a homemade lab on the edge of the minefield. "I've got a list of things that can make the research go a lot more smoothly."

"I can give you three days."

"Excuse me?"

Shirley broke in. "General, you have a call from Apollo."

"I'll take it in the VIP tent," he told her.

Argus turned back to me. "I have a meeting in three days. If you can give me solid proof that this drug of yours can work, I'll back your bid for funding."

Impossible. "I need more time than that." He saw the value. He'd said it himself.

"Either you can do it, or you can't," the general spat. "Which is it, Doctor?"

He didn't give me time to answer before he strode out of the room to take his call. Kosta saluted him. I was too shocked.

I needed this chance. Soldiers like the ones I'd seen today deserved it. But my work was preliminary at best. I didn't know how I was going to pull proof together so fast.

"He's nuts," I hissed.

Kosta gave me a hard look. "He's willing to stick his neck out, at least temporarily. I'm glad you were at it hard these last couple of days."

"Me too," I said, wondering just how I was going to get the rest of my work done in three days.

I'd just have to do my very best. Live in the lab. Force

Rodger to keep up my schedule at the hospital. He certainly owed me.

I took a deep breath, making sure my robe stayed closed. "If you don't mind, I'd like to get back to work."

Or right to work, as the case may be.

"Fine," Kosta said, getting back to the papers on his desk. "And, Robichaud—"

I paused at the door.

"Put on some pants."

CHAPTER SIXTEEN

I HEADED STRAIGHT to the lab. Well, I stopped to put on some pants first. Rodger had left the hutch, hopefully to consult with his rock-club buddies. I didn't even bother to move the new stash of geek-tastic action figures from my bed. Or from the top of my locker. Or the front of my bookcase.

My mind raced with everything I had to get done. I needed something beyond *sphinx venom will knock out an immortal.* I needed to show how we could use that knowledge to develop a controlled anesthetic.

Quickly, I changed into surgical scrubs and a pair of tennis shoes. The Limbo suns beat down hard, making the inside of the hutch steamy and the outside even worse. Sweating, I scraped my hair back into a ponytail as I made my way out of camp and up through the cemetery.

There was no way to predict how fast research would go. The idea of doing several weeks, months, maybe even years of work in three days was staggering.

I shouldn't even attempt it.

It wasn't like I could just phone this one in. Surgery was pressure enough, and that was the part of the job I enjoyed. I was never meant to be a researcher. I would never have taken this on except that it was important.

Sphinx venom could knock out an immortal. It was an amazing discovery as far as I was concerned. Frankly, I was shocked HQ hadn't given it more weight.

No, they wanted proof that I could use it.

It seemed I wasn't going to get any investment until we had a sure thing, which negated the need for a lot of investment.

I wanted to punch something.

We were talking about a potential breakthrough here. I understood the gods didn't necessarily rush to embrace change, but come on.

I kicked a rock and reached into my pocket for a stick of Fruit Stripe gum as the leaning heaps and jutting peaks of the junkyard greeted me. It was hard to make a difference in this war. This was my shot.

My responsibility.

My current lab stood just inside the minefield, past a large char mark on the ground where my last lab had been. I preferred keeping flammable experiments away from camp. Plus, the minefield offered a degree of privacy. People had to go out of their way to bug me.

It still didn't stop them—not completely.

I shoved open the door marked *critical care*. I'd commandeered it from the pile of junk that had been the old intensive care unit. After a patient escaped, HQ had approved steel doors and double-thick walls. I'd taken the leftovers.

In fact, most of my new lab was our old unit. It had been designed to break down quickly and easily, in case our unit needed to redeploy in a hurry. So Marius had relocated it here. As a vampire, he was superstrong. Plus, he understood the value of a good lair.

The pinewood walls were smooth and clean. I had a basic floor and a roof. This was junkyard luxury.

As usual, the place smelled like desert dirt and the sweet, fig scent of sphinx venom.

It was dark inside. Marius had sawed two windows that let in some light, but mostly dirt and dry air.

I lit the lanterns that hung throughout the long, narrow room. Electricity would have been nice, if only to hook up the steel refrigeration unit I'd acquired, and even some of the plug-in burners.

It was dangerous to have fire around some of the fluids I was testing.

But I'd applied for an electric hookup along with everything else I'd asked acquisitions to provide. HQ had denied it lock, stock, and barrel. Said it was unnecessary. Extravagant. As if the generals in charge knew what that meant.

Father McArio had built me a small desk in the center of the lab to hold all of my papers and reports. I'd positioned old cafeteria tables on the walls to the right and left. The only other furniture was a small cot Father had set up in the old storage hold in the back.

When you got right down to it, a separate room was a needless luxury. I could sleep in the lab.

I rubbed my eyes as I opened my notebook and prepared to get started. The key was to find a solvent to mix with the sphinx venom that would allow us to control the amount of time an immortal was knocked out.

As soon as the venom got into a person's system—mortal or immortal—it completely took over. I'd never seen a toxic agent run so rampant.

The venom on its own could put an immortal under for up to seven days, which was dangerous. Any anesthesia carried a risk. I wasn't about to submit critical patients to a week of it.

Plus, it was impractical. Recovery would be overwhelmed. And if the Old God Army knew our soldiers were asleep and defenseless, they could slaughter them in their beds.

I pulled up a stool and studied my notes.

We had to be able to manage the delivery and effects of the venom. Incendiary chemicals that were deadly to mortals, but like candy to demigod warriors, seemed to work best. The challenge was finding the right amount and then stabilizing it.

In three days.

Still, work felt good. It was better than focusing on what I'd done to Marc, or on everything I'd lost.

Death had been certain the last time. Marc was gone. I had no choice but to move on. Now I wasn't sure of anything. I didn't know if Marc was alive or dead. I didn't know if the world would end or not. I didn't know what part I had to play to stop it all.

I ran a hand through my hair and tried to focus.

One step at a time. First, I worked on a combination of eighty-seven-octane unleaded gasoline and the venom. It was the mildest combination I had so far that would (in theory) work, with the least amount of risk.

Sure, it would torch the lab if it came in contact with any sparks from my Bunsen burner or the lanterns hanging from the ceiling above me. But such was the nature of the beast.

I heated the solution carefully. I'd always liked the smell of gas, in theory. This much so close was making me a little dizzy. I edged nearer to the window and wished I had a fume hood.

Still, it was better than the peracetic acid. That solution had smelled like liquid fire. It worked beautifully in tests, and I was almost ready to try it on an immortal volunteer. But it explodes violently at 100 degrees Celsius, which is 212 degrees Fahrenheit. I figured that could be safe. Turned out my metal storage shelf did get that hot under the baking Limbo sun.

Thankfully, I'd had to leave for a shift in the clinic.

I measured out five milliliters of venom into a graduated cylinder and then added twenty ml of gasoline. I worked on various combinations throughout the afternoon. Mixing and testing them for effectiveness and stability.

And—Father McArio would be proud of me—I even remembered to step outside every hour or so. For the first few batches at least.

I'd learned that after mixing and a stabilization period, I could gauge each anesthetic's impact on the immortal metabolism with reasonable certainty by testing it on patient blood samples and measuring breakdown rates.

I rubbed my eyes as I sat on a stool in front of my desk, recording breakdown rates. The gasoline wasn't performing as well as I'd hoped. At this rate, patients would be waking up mid-surgery.

There was a gentle knock at the door. "Petra?"

Father McArio.

I winced. If it was anyone else, I would have told them to scram.

My eyes felt like sandpaper. I rubbed them as the door opened behind me, letting in shards of blinding light.

"Rodger said you might be in here," the raven-haired priest said, holding a tray that smelled like warm bread and meat.

Leave it to him to bring a bribe. My stomach growled.

"How hungry am I when mess hall food starts smelling good?"

"That's the spirit," he said, easing the door closed behind him. He wore a black shirt and clerical collar, along with fatigue pants. His nose wrinkled as he took a whiff of my latest concoction.

I smoothed the hair out of my face. "I'd love to, but I can't stop for dinner. I'm way behind."

"This is breakfast." He set the tray on the only clear spot on my desk.

Oh. No wonder I was ready to pass out. I picked up the tray and set it on top of my notes. It wouldn't hurt them. Besides, the gasoline was a bust. General Argus wouldn't be seeing these files.

It was rehydrated scrambled eggs and bacon. There was nothing else like it. Literally.

I scooped up a big bite that managed to taste both runny and sticky at the same time.

Father watched me. "You should rest."

I appreciated his concern, but... "I'm way behind." What I'd needed was food. I hadn't even realized how starving I was until I'd started eating. I bit into a crumbly mess. Mmm...biscuit.

Father walked casually through the lab, clucking over spreadsheets and test tube holders, but I knew what he was going for.

Sure enough, he peeked behind the curtain to my little sleeping room in the back. It hadn't been used. He didn't show any reaction. "I think all of us appreciate the dedication you're showing with this anesthetic research," he began.

"But," I began.

Let's just have out with it.

"Well," he said, in that overly patient tone of his, "I was just wondering. Is there something else driving this? Something you'd like to talk about?"

Hmm...like the fact that my research, important as it was, might not even make a difference if the old gods wiped us out with their new weapon? Or maybe the fact that I'd shot and quite possibly killed the one man who could put a stop to it?

Perhaps it was the fact that I'd spent all day and all night beating my head against the wall over formulas that didn't work. Meanwhile, time was running out. And although I appreciated Thomas Edison's little ditty about how he was so much closer to discovering electricity because he knew nine-hundred-and-something things that *didn't* work, I frankly didn't have that kind of time.

"Petra?" Father pulled up a stool.

"I've got nothing," I said, scraping the last bits of egg from the metal tray.

"You're frightened," he said, as if he were just figuring it out himself.

I closed my eyes. Put a lock on it. "I don't have the time or the emotion for this."

He folded his hands in his lap. "You don't have to deal with it right now. But maybe telling me will help ease the burden. You know you can talk to me."

Sure, I'd told him all kinds of things over the course of this stupid war, but I'd never had to tell Father I'd shot a person. And so I did. I told him what had happened at MASH-19X. How I'd leveled a disruptor at Marc, how I'd run. "He trusted me to help him," I said, hoping Father would understand, needing it. "Instead, I might have killed him."

"I'd like to help," he said. Father was still looking at me like I was a good person. I didn't deserve it. "I know you care for him."

I shook my head. I couldn't *not* care for him. And while it had been beautiful before, all it did was hurt me now. I sighed. "For a large part of my life, I was sure he was the one."

Before this war. Now all I knew was bloodshed, suffering, and death.

I couldn't do anything about Marc, but maybe I could do something to ease the pain for these soldiers.

Father placed his hand over mine. I hadn't even realized how hard I'd been clutching the leg of my scrubs. "I'll check with some of the chaplains on the other side. He's at the MASH-19X, right?"

I nodded, loosening my grip.

"They may be able to see how he's doing."

All I could feel was a hollow ache. "I really think I killed him."

We sat in silence for a long moment. Finally, Father spoke. "Tell me. Would Marc punish you for what you did?"

What? It was crazy. "Of course not."

"Then be kind to yourself. For him."

I didn't know what to do. I planted my elbows on my knees and ran my hands through my hair. "I don't want to talk about this anymore."

"Would you like to pray?"

"No."

Father lowered his eyes, understanding. "Then I'll pray for you." He paused. "At least promise me you'll get a few hours of sleep."

I gave a one-shouldered shrug. "I'll try."

"That's not the same."

I slumped, fighting the urge to roll my eyes. "I don't want to lie to a priest."

He smiled at that.

"I'll rest when I can," I said. When I'd reached a stopping point.

That seemed to satisfy him, or at least make him realize he could bring the cot to the doctor, but he couldn't make her sleep.

He took the empty tray. "Can you tell me why there are several metal cans of lighter fluid outside your lab?"

"Oh, goodie." They'd arrived.

We walked outside, and he helped me gather them up and set them up along the right wall.

"I'll rest after I work on these." I did a quick calculation in my head. Six gallons. Excellent.

Father gave me a long look.

"I promise."

We both knew I was lying.

* * *

Hours later—don't ask me how many—I'd worked my way through a sleeve of saltine crackers, a pack of water bottles, and a half-eaten sandwich, courtesy of Jeffe. He'd come in for an extraction and stayed for a catnap—or more like a pass-out-on-my-notes-and-drool nap—before I kicked him out.

At least I'd learned that the only solvents to have any kind of an effect on the venom were the flammable liquids with low autoignition temperatures. Luckily, we had plenty of those around: gasoline, ethanol, liquid hydrogen. I was going to try to work my way through the top ten.

Three failed formulas later, my head felt like it was ready to explode. If that weren't bad enough, Rodger pounded on the door. "Hello! Land of the living here. How are you doing?"

I was spilling ethanol down the side of my graduated cylinder, thanks to startling noises made by overeager werewolves. "Go away."

My eyes and throat stung from the constant chemicals, and I could barely think straight unless I was focused and working.

He clomped up behind me. "This isn't a race."

"It actually is." General Argus had told me himself he wouldn't be able to argue my case without solid results. If I didn't have anything to impress the higher-ups, there was no telling what they'd do.

They could decide my time was better spent in surgery. They could take my work and give it to another scientist.

They could shut the project down altogether—force me to ingest my own experiments, like they'd done to the doctor who'd experimented with hormonal birth control for goddesses. Of course, they wouldn't see any difference between estrogen and ethanol until it was too late.

I remeasured sample number four. "I have until three o'clock on Thursday."

Rodger glanced at his watch. "Which means you have ten minutes."

"What?" I spilled the sample again. I thought I'd kept track of the days better than that. I was reduced to counting on my fingers while Rodger tossed a rag on my ethanol sample. "Monday I came out here," I said. "Tuesday I saw Father..."

My roommate thumped a clean set of military fatigues onto my lap. "Time to get dressed, Cinderella. Come on," he said, easing me off the chair. "Less counting. More moving."

I ran a hand through my raving-crazy-woman hair. I hadn't left the lab in three days. "I need a shower."

Rodger sniffed. "Er, yes, I would have thought you'd have taken a shower in the last three days. Obviously, I was wrong." He rechecked his watch. "Nine minutes."

"Stop pressuring me," I said, fingers unsteady as I dragged off my scrub top. There was a moist towelette packet with my breakfast utensils. I ripped it open and gave myself the most pathetic sponge bath of all time.

"I talked to my rock-club buddies," he said. "Guess where titurate comes from?"

"Now is not the time for twenty questions," I ground out, trying to locate the towelette under my arm.

"Transylvania, but it's all mined out. You want to know the only other place you can find it?"

"I'm breathless," I said, realizing my moist towelette wasn't all that moist anymore.

"Limbo. It's formed when layers of rock are compressed by the heat of Hades."

So what was up with the hush-hush mining operation? "Why keep it a secret?"

Rodger had his back to me. "Are you almost ready? Six minutes."

I struggled into the clean shirt. "You know I hate the uniform."

"Sorry to break it to you, but first impressions count," Rodger said as I tried to fit my feet into my pant legs.

I really did need to sleep.

A bang at the door made both Rodger and me jump. "Robichaud!"

I yanked my pants up and struggled with the button as Kosta burst into the lab, followed by General Argus looking even pastier than before.

"Excuse me, sir," I said, saluting, hoping my pants would stay up. "I was under the impression I was meeting you."

Kosta strolled up to me, his nose wrinkling. "The general here decided he'd like to inspect the lab for himself."

I could tell neither one of them was impressed.

Rodger made a quick escape while I focused on General Argus. He wore an impeccably pressed uniform and a chest full of shiny medals. His hard eyes dissected me from head to toe. Then he turned, and I saw that he literally had eyes on the back of his head—two of them. They canvassed my tables like something on the bottom of his boot. "I thought you were hard at work."

"I am, sir. Here," I said, heart racing as I gathered the notes on my desk, "let me walk you through what I've been doing."

He wasn't listening. He picked up a used test tube. "This isn't impressive at all."

He held the test tube up to the light, which was a really

bad idea since we were talking about lanterns and lighter fluid.

I shot a look to Kosta, who moved in on the side.

"Can I see that, General?" Kosta asked.

Argus handed off the explosive tube. "I take it you don't have my anesthetic."

For Pete's sake. "Not yet."

He raised a brow. "Can you provide me with inarguable proof that you're close to an anesthetic?"

My stomach clenched. I desperately wanted to lie. "No. Not exactly."

"You're working too slowly." He fingered through my notes. "You need help."

He wasn't walking out. At least not yet. "Let me show you what I have so far. I think when you see it, you and your superiors will agree that this project is worthy of funding."

"You will have a partner."

No. "With all due respect, sir. I don't work well on a team." I'd hated group projects in school, and I despised the thought of one now. Having to work with someone else, having to explain things, would only slow me down.

He continued as if I hadn't spoken. "You will relieve her of all her other duties," he said to Colonel Kosta.

"We can put her on emergency backup only," the colonel said, guarded. "If the fighting starts up again, I'd like to have as many docs as I can on the roster."

"I've been tasked with a peacetime responsibility," the general said with a barely disguised sneer. "The New God Army is to work with the Old God Army on...special projects. This will be one of them."

"Okay." I wasn't against sharing research. In theory. Anything that helped alleviate suffering on both sides was ideal. Still, "I don't see how I can work *with* the enemy on this."

I glanced at Kosta, who gave me the *shut-up-and-do-it* narrow eyes.

"Perhaps if you'll allow me a week to come up with a workable plan," I added.

One week to try to get out of this.

"I already have a solution," the general said, in the way of out-of-touch big bosses. "The Old God Army has volunteered a top researcher to work with you, in this lab."

"Perhaps we can talk about some better equipment," I said, digging for the report I'd already given the army. It detailed what I'd need.

"You will discover an anesthetic within the month."

Sure. Why not? "Listen, sir. I can't guarantee—"

"You will discover the anesthetic," the general said, daring me to contest him again. I didn't.

The general stared me down. "Do not disappoint me. Or make me look foolish for trusting you."

I took a deep breath, the rush of fumes making me a little dizzy. "Of course not, sir."

Kosta crossed his hands over his chest. This was over his head and we both knew it.

Argus grunted, satisfied. "Now you will meet her."

My mouth slacked open. She was here now? So much for even pretending I had a choice.

I might have been better off before the army had taken an interest in my work. At least then I had autonomy, the freedom to come to my own conclusions at a reasonable, human pace.

Kosta opened the door to admit my new team member. So he was in on it, too.

I stood still, as if ready to face the firing squad. This doctor had better be good. She'd better not slow me down or screw me up or make this impossible task even worse.

She'd better not be an I've-got-all-the-time-in-the-world immortal.

But nothing I could have imagined prepared me for what I saw.

Marc walked through the door.

CHAPTER SEVENTEEN

I STARED.

It was Marc. In the flesh. A walking, talking Marc. At least I thought he was saying something. His lips were moving. But it wasn't registering. I thought I'd killed him.

Deep down, I'd known. I'd been ready for the fact that I'd shot him to death.

My pulse beat wildly against my throat. I wanted to run up and hug him, kiss him, tell him I was so relieved to see him. But he was the enemy. It would be dangerous to admit I knew him.

I exhaled as the tight fist around my heart loosened. It was enough to know he was whole and alive...and standing next to some strange woman.

She had to be a goddess.

She was supermodel-gorgeous with long brunette hair that belonged in a Pantene commercial. Her floor-length, filmy gown was made of dew or spiderwebs or something equally see-through. The thing clung to her to the point where it left little to the imagination. She preened, fully expecting Marc's undivided attention. She got it.

I couldn't have been more shocked if she'd leaned over and kissed him. Which would get me instantly smited because I'd have to at least try to haul her off him.

Get a grip.

My mouth slacked open. I had to do something, say something.

"Oh my god."

General Argus bristled. "What did you say, Captain?"

Kosta waved him off. "A mortal term of endearment," he said, glaring at me. "Dr. Robichaud, you have the great honor of meeting Nerthus of the sacred grove. She's a four-star general in the Old God Army."

Sure. I could tell by the uniform. "It's an honor to meet you," I said, going for a bow rather than a salute.

She licked her lips. "This is my special associate," she said, leaving off his name.

You couldn't even tell I'd shot him.

Marc looked amazing, as usual—lean and powerful in old army tan. The cocky goddess might be enjoying the view, but she had no idea how I'd once had every hard-muscled, drop-dead-sexy inch of him memorized.

She drew a polished fingernail down Marc's arm. He stood there and took it, almost acted like he enjoyed it. What the hey?

It sliced me to the core to be this close, yet have to act like I didn't even know him. Then watch her touch him on top of it.

I had no idea what was going on with her—or why he wasn't breaking her immortal arm. Okay, maybe it would be a bad idea for him to resist like that, but he could have at least managed an eye roll, if only for my sake.

Sure, I'd shot him, but he was the one who'd thrown himself so willingly at death. He'd stood in front of that gun, knowing it was coming. Now after he'd just put me through the ringer thinking he was dead—again—he had the gall to take part in this little show?

I crossed my arms over my chest. If this was his way of getting back at me because he'd found out I'd dated when he hadn't, he could bite me.

Nerthus turned sour when she looked at me. "This is your lab?"

"Yes." It was a dump, but it was the best I could do on my own.

Nose wrinkled, she strode down the aisle between my cafeteria-style lab table and the desk.

Meanwhile Argus started pawing through the research notes on my desk. I stifled the urge to snatch them back. It wasn't like he knew what he was looking at. Worse, he was getting them all out of order.

Nerthus peered at my ethanol test like it was a dead rat. Holy heck. It was about to boil over. I hurried over to my workstation and flipped the burner off.

The goddess held up a hand. "Let me handle the rest."

And with a nod from her, Marc donned my thick rubberized gloves and moved my caustic sample over to my cooling rack like he owned the place.

Yeah, she was really helping.

"It's a little overcooked," Marc said, my safety glasses over his eyes as he double-checked the sample. "But it's stable."

Fan-fricking-tastic. Another lab spared.

While my personal life got even weirder.

"What's this?" the goddess asked as she touched the cool white pad stretched out underneath my sample rack.

"Icy Hot patch," I answered quickly. "It was the only thing I could find." Unless you counted the two-ice-cube allotment I was given at the mess tent.

She inspected the bread ties holding it in place. "How can you expect to do real research in this...hovel?"

Marc moved to stand next to her. "It's a disgrace, my lady."

Of all the—I didn't mind Miss Gauzy trash-talking my place, but Marc?

At least my lab wasn't haunted.

I held my temper in check. "I've been doing this on my own. My funding application was denied."

"That's not true," General Argus bristled. "I approved it myself."

That sneaky, lying...

I shot Kosta a look.

He ignored me.

Fine. It took everything I had to keep my face pleasantly blank. "I appreciate your foresight, General Argus. Funding this project would serve both armies," I reminded them. "I've already established that sphinx venom is safe to use on immortals. If I can determine a delivery vehicle to administer the proper dosage, we can begin volunteer testing." It wasn't like this was going to kill anybody. "I have a report—"

"I saw it," she said, flicking her gaze up at the lanterns overhead like they were hairy, fang-toothed bats. "That's why we're here." She leveled a look at me designed to make me feel both inferior and grateful. "You've been chosen to take part in a peace initiative between our side and yours. Our sides will work on the anesthetic together. I have already been in contact with Old God Army acquisitions." She sneered at Argus, as if she knew he was full of it. "They will provide you with everything you need."

Wow. Okay. In that case, "I'd really prefer direct funding." I could order things myself through Shirley.

The goddess turned a scathing look on me.

Argus dropped my notes all over the floor. "Do not curse her," he ordered, his beady eyes on the goddess. "We need both the mortals to work."

My stomach curled.

Kosta approached Nerthus, placing himself in between me and the goddess. "She knows your will is divine." He glanced back at me. "And that the report lists her needs."

I didn't dare speak.

A curse from a goddess could mean anything from blindness to being turned into a pigeon for all eternity.

Wisps of smoke curled from Nerthus's ears.

Marc leaned close to her. "One tragedy is enough, my lady."

She puzzled at that. "One?"

He drew a hand down her arm. "The greatest tragedy is that I will miss you."

She softened. I couldn't believe Marc had actually spouted that inane horse puckey. Or that she bought it.

I bristled. In the Old God Army, the women had to play slave to the men. But what about the goddesses? Did they have the right to demand services of the mortal men?

She looked ready to take him into my back room and christen the lab.

A new thought curdled in my stomach. What kind of price had Marc paid to come back to me?

I cringed inside as she ran her fingers through the hair above his ear. "I'm sorry to leave you in a place like this."

He inclined his head toward her. "If it's what you wish me to do, I'll manage."

Oh, barf.

She turned her attention to me. "You will greet your new partner."

Nice of her to get around to the rest of the introductions.

"This is Captain Belanger," she continued.

"Good to meet you, Captain." I kept my voice even.

He gave a swift, impersonal nod. He was so close, I could have touched him.

Nerthus eased a gleaming lock of hair over her shoulder. "General Argus will be your contact on the ground," she said to both of us. It seemed she had better things to do.

Argus studied Marc, then me, with the appraising kind of look a gambler would give a racehorse at the track.

I kept my chin high and my eyes forward.

"We expect results," he said.

Impossible ones.

Argus folded his hands behind his back, making a show of it. "You'll send me a daily report."

That he wouldn't understand.

His eyes narrowed, as if he could read my thoughts. "You will make this joint venture a success."

The *or else* was implied.

CHAPTER EIGHTEEN

I KEPT my back straight and my voice even. "I'll begin updating Captain Belanger immediately."

It was the only thing I could do. Marc and I stood facing each other. The air lay heavy, soaked with everything we couldn't say.

Marc cocked his head, watching me. "I look forward to working with you."

"It'll be interesting," I told him.

The goddess paused, as if she could sense the energy between us. "I'll be watching you." She gave Marc one last glance before following Kosta to the door.

"Understood," Marc said as the door slammed closed behind them.

He grinned at me.

"What the?—" I began before he silenced me with a kiss.

"I thought I was never going to see you again," he said, kissing me again.

I pulled away. "I thought I killed you."

"Evidently, I'm hard to kill." He grinned. And when I didn't smile, he added, "I went into asystolic arrest due to an immediate and simultaneous depolarization of my myocardial cells." He held up a finger at my horror. "But the good news was no intracranial hemorrhage. My burns were superficial. And they got me into emergency treatment before I got worse."

My heart sank. "I really did almost kill you." He'd gotten so lucky.

"It was basically like getting struck by lightning," he admitted.

"Can I see your burns?" Had I hurt him by hugging him?

"They're mostly healed, or at least they don't hurt anymore," he said, releasing the top three buttons on his uniform and displaying part of a shiny, red scar. "In a month, you won't even be able to tell. We have a burn serum that is out of this world."

"Our side doesn't." But I supposed he knew that already.

"They put me in a ward usually reserved for the gods," he added quickly, as if trying to get it out of the way,

Ah. "Is that where you met your goddess?"

He had the good grace to blush. "She took an interest in me," he said stiffly. "But come on, you know it's nothing."

"She didn't seem to think so." Marc tended to act first and think of the consequences later. "What did you promise her?" I drew my fingers down his arm in the exact same place she had. I wanted to erase her.

"Nothing," he gritted out.

"You're playing a dangerous game," I warned.

"She'll lose interest soon," he insisted. His gaze locked with mine. "In the meantime, I'm here for you."

The peacekeeper will find love as a hideous new weapon is born.

A horrible thought crossed my mind. "What if you were supposed to stay back on your side and prevent Dr. Keller's research from being weaponized?"

He caught my hand. "I searched the lab again before I

came here. There's no trace of the formula we were working on. Whoever killed Dr. Keller took it and is long gone from MASH-19X."

It was bad news, but not exactly a surprise. Plus, the second prophecy had already been announced. That meant, for better or worse, the first had come true. "What do we do now?"

He drew me close. "We make your anesthetic work. We do what we can to make a real difference in this war. I thought a lot about that while I was laid up." His fingers caressed the nape of my neck. "I thought a lot about you."

The man should have come with a warning label.

He looked down at me, so tender. His lips brushed mine. And then I didn't want to talk anymore, or think. "I'm a mess," I murmured as his teeth grazed my earlobe.

"You used to kiss me after I went frog hunting with my dad."

He'd come back smelling like the bayou. "You never gave me a choice." He was so darned happy and cute when he came back.

"Not giving you one now." He caressed the small, sensitive hollow of my back that only he knew about.

"Well, in that case..."

I could barely put a thought together as he drew me to him for a mind-numbingly perfect kiss. It was sweet and heady and sensual all at the same time. I savored it. Him.

This was my moment, my time with Marc. Everything else might have been decided for us—where we lived, whom we fought for, whom we were allowed to love—but we could decide this: to be together in this moment.

And so I drew him back to my little room, to my narrow cot to talk, to laugh, to kiss. And when we finally wore each other out, I fell asleep in his arms.

I slept well, knowing I had someone to watch out for me,

someone who cared. Marc had come back to me at last, for as long as I could hold him.

* * *

I woke several hours later to find myself alone on the narrow cot. Liquid bubbled in the lab on the other side of the curtain, and I heard the thud of a book opening along with the scratch of a pencil on paper.

Rubbing the grit from my eyes, I fought my way past the flimsy curtain to find Marc crouched next to a bubbling sample, scribbling notes.

I ran a hand through my sleep-tangled hair. "I should have briefed you before tackling you and then taking a siesta."

He smiled. "It's okay," he said, going back to writing. "I understand your notes. I know how you work."

"You'd better watch that ethanol." It was at a rolling boil. At that rate, he was going to lose his sample.

"Oh, the ethanol mixture blew up," he said, glancing back at me. "I'm surprised it didn't wake you."

Ha. I'd slept harder that I'd thought. "Seems you could have set a bomb off."

"Let's hope it doesn't come to that," he teased, tossing his pencil down. "I'm trying the liquid hydrogen mixture now. Let's hope it doesn't burn the lab down."

"I missed this," I confessed, drawing close. "I missed us."

He shot me an easy grin. "Me too." He reached out and laced his fingers with mine, gently tugging me the rest of the way into his arms. "I mean, what are the odds that we'd come together like this in the middle of a war?"

"Well, you were the one who hunted me down," I said.

After ten years.

I had to try to let that go if we had any shot of making this work. And speaking of that, what were we doing anyway?

A buzzer went off, and he glanced back at the sample. "It's at temperature," he said, turning back to the table.

"Great." I found a pair of lab glasses, double-checked the temperature gauge, and then shut off the heat while he prepared the sphinx venom.

He gave me an uneasy smile, so full of...what? Hope? "Here goes nothing."

We both braced ourselves as he added the venom. I watched it swirl down into the liquid hydrogen. So far, so good.

"If we can develop an anesthetic that works," I said, eyeing the sample. "If we can please Argus and your Nerthus," I added, because with the gods, that was always the trick..."maybe we can use that success to learn more about what other projects the gods have going, specifically that new weapon."

Marc drew his gloves off. "It could work. I mean, I was already on the weapons project once. And we obviously work well together."

Maybe it all came down to that. Maybe this anesthetic would do twice the good—it would help the soldiers, and it would show the gods they had a winning team in Marc and me. "If we could stop that weapon, if we could fulfill the prophecies and end this war, think of what that could mean."

Marc winced. "Petra, I—"

"The imprisoned dragons would be free," I said, my excitement growing. "Our friends and colleagues could go home. Us, too. Instead of being on opposite sides, we could actually *be* together."

"I want that, too. I'd love it." He tossed his gloves in the trash bin under the table behind him. "But don't get your hopes up."

"Have a little faith," I prodded. "You don't think we have it in us?"

He planted his hands on his hips, at a loss for words for a brief moment. "I think we have a lot going for us," he said guardedly. "I think we can make this anesthetic work. I think we have a good shot at worming our way into weapons research."

"And destruction," I added, with relish. We'd rob the gods of their awful weapon. "*Death comes with a gift.* Our gift will be making that deadly weapon fizzle out."

"But realize this"—Marc went on, as if he wasn't even listening—"whatever good we do will be because of you and me. Us. Not because of some ancient prophecy."

Fair enough. "You don't have to believe for the prophecies to work." I sure hadn't in the beginning.

And Marc was...Marc. He always had to be in control. I should have known he'd never accept the idea that something larger—something he couldn't control—was at work.

"Petra." He closed the distance between us. "This war isn't going to end," he said, as if it were fact. As if we could make no difference at all. "The gods have been fighting for thousands of years, and they'll be fighting for thousands more. Humanity doesn't have a chance." He shook his head sadly. "We don't have a chance, at least not like we did in New Orleans."

I didn't understand. "So why did you start things up again with me, physically, if you have no intention of sticking around?"

"Because it's you. It's us," he said, as if we had no other choice. "We can be together. For now," he clarified. "Until we find the anesthetic. Or until Nerthus and Argus tire of us. And if we get lucky, maybe we can do more research together and eliminate the weapon. But we're still on opposite sides. We still have the same problem we did ten years ago."

When he'd let me go.

I felt myself grow cold. "What exactly are you saying?"

"Petra..." His voice was rough. "I love you, you know that."

"And?" I demanded.

He flinched. "I never wanted to be with anyone else."

"And?" I pressed.

I needed to know where we stood, what he truly thought about this. Us.

He winced and said it straight. "This is great for now, but when we're separated again, and we will be, I can't do the distance thing again."

And there it was.

I leaned back against the table. "I don't believe it." After all this, he was still more than ready to let it all go.

"What did you expect?" he asked, half demanding, half pleading.

I don't know. "Peace."

He drew both hands through his hair. "We're on opposite sides of an immortal war."

"Oh, thanks for the news flash," I said, stalking away. I hadn't thought of that one.

"I'm only being honest," he said, following me, as I tossed my lab glasses onto the table. "I'd never lie to you, Petra."

He could at least sugarcoat it.

I turned to him. "Then are we torturing ourselves if we can't be together?"

He stood, helpless. "I don't know. Maybe I shouldn't have come."

"Nice of you to think of that now." After he'd barged into my life again, after he'd kissed me and held me and made me want him all over again.

He pulled off his lab glasses. "This is important work," he said. "But that's not all. After seeing you again and spending time with you on my side, I just wasn't ready to let you go."

Lovely. "I'm so glad you got what *you* need."

He took a step toward me, reaching out a hand. "Don't be that way. You were certainly glad to see me earlier."

I held my ground, my cheeks heating when I thought of exactly how glad I'd been.

"You also needed to know I was alive. I saw your face when you shot me. I knew it destroyed you to do it."

This might destroy me worse—having him and losing him again.

Well, unless I could fulfill a bunch of ancient prophecies channeled by soothsayers on a lost island. It wasn't like they had a schedule. Who knew how many prophecies there would be, how many years they could stretch out?

And how this latest one might even come true—*death comes with a gift*.

Right then, I felt like strangling Marc myself.

He drew a lock of hair back from my face. "Can't we just be together for now, enjoy now?"

That was what Galen had said before he left me.

Merde. Why was I setting myself up for this again? It was like I had a masochistic need to get my heart stomped on and splattered against the wall.

But it didn't have to be that way. I could choose. I couldn't control this, but I didn't have to be destroyed by it, either.

I looked up at the man who had stolen my heart all those years ago, the one who had stolen it again in the time we'd been together this week. And I drew a line. "We can be together," I told him, seeing his relief. "We can work together." I'd even ogle his backside. Because, let's face it, what red-blooded female wouldn't? "But I'm not signing up for love and kisses and a future you can't promise."

He'd gone stiff. "What does that mean exactly?"

"We can be friends."

"We are friends," he said warily.

"Just friends. Nothing more."

"You've got to be kidding me," he said, as if I'd told him I was going to become a nun. "You don't know what I had to pull in order to get this assignment. It was one in a million, I finally have you back—and you want to be friends?"

That was our mistake—in a nutshell. "You don't have me back," I said, ignoring the hurt in his eyes. I didn't have him back, either.

I didn't know what he'd had to do to make it here, but I knew it was temporary. And that he was giving only what he could on this particular day, this week, this month.

The Marc I'd fallen for, the one I'd known in New Orleans, had never held his emotions in check. He never held back his love. He was all or nothing—just like me.

This war had changed a lot of things.

A bead of sweat slicked down the side of his face. "So you're expecting me to be here with you every day and not touch you?"

"Bingo."

"I can't live like this."

"I say that every day."

But he was right. This was going to be our own particular brand of hell.

To be here, alone. Constantly tempted with what we'd given up at the whim of the gods.

I wanted to hold him more than I'd ever wanted anything in my life. I was raw with it.

But I couldn't have him, so I might as well save myself the grief and the pain. Last time I'd fallen, it had taken me ten years to get over him. If I tripped again, I might never recover.

He stared down at the rough wood floor. "So what are we really?"

"Lab partners, partners in crime," I said as he cursed

under his breath. "But I'm not letting you break my heart again." No more than he already had. "Just friends," I said, holding out a hand for him to shake.

He didn't take it.

"If you truly care about me, you'll do this," I warned.

I could see the emotions warring inside him. Good. He might as well feel it too. I didn't want this. I didn't choose this. But I'd do this for us and make the best of it.

"Friends," he said, reaching out to take my hand. He drew it up and kissed the top of it. "Until you change your mind."

"Let's just stick to work," I said, trying to figure out where I'd tossed my lab glasses. I had to check the sample.

His lips formed a thin line, but he didn't offer any comment as he joined me at the table.

The sample had evaporated completely.

Great.

"So that one's a bust," he said, reaching for my lab notes without even looking at them.

"So we'll try another solvent." And another one. We'd try until we found one that would allow us to control the effect of the sphinx venom. "When do you think your side will start sending equipment?"

"Knowing the goddess? It's already on the way."

"About that—" I stiffened. "How well do you know the goddess?"

"Jealous?" he challenged.

For a second, I didn't know what to say. I was too tired, too raw.

Regret flashed across his features. "I'm sorry. That was a jerk thing to say." He shook his head. "Nerthus means nothing. I know I sound like an idiot when I talk to her, but courtly words make her feel good. And it got me on this project."

"Why?" I asked.

He softened. "I wanted to see you again."

Damn the consequences.

"It's too dangerous." He had to understand that. "What if she turns you into her slave boy?"

"I don't care," he said simply.

I sighed. The man was impossible. "Yes, well, our last group project didn't turn out so well," I pointed out, trying for a little levity.

The burn mark marred his chest. I was still amazed by his bravery.

He caught me checking him out and gave me a tight-lipped grin. "Reconsidering?"

He wished.

I planted my hands on my hips. At least this time, he'd sought me out despite the consequences. He didn't just let me go on with my life, thinking he was gone.

He paged through my notebook. "I heard about this project when I was in the hospital. They needed someone fast. I made a personal appeal to Nerthus."

"Must have been a good one," I said dryly.

Still, forces were at work. That much was clear. I just didn't know what it meant. "The prophecy said death comes with a gift."

"I'm not dead yet," he said, quoting a Monty Python movie we used to watch. He went back to the notes.

Yes, well, he might not believe, but I did. Marc was here with me for a reason. And it wasn't so he could rip my world apart again.

If I just kept my wits about me, we could use the time together for good, for healing. And maybe, just maybe, we'd find what we needed to survive.

CHAPTER NINETEEN

MARC INSISTED I take care of myself while he prepared a new sample and organized my notes. That was the one good thing about having Marc here; I trusted him—well, with everything but my heart.

It was so easy to fall into old patterns with him. To just live and enjoy being with him, but I had to take it for what it was—a reminder of what I couldn't have.

So I vowed to keep it light. Enjoy it for what it was.

Take a shower, for heaven's sake.

He bent over my notes, engrossed, as he scribbled his own ideas in another journal. "You'd better not be a spy or something," I said, brushing past him as I headed out for the showers.

"I think that was you," he called as I left him in the sad, stifling little lab.

Good point.

I made my way out of the minefield, careful of the pranks. Although I wasn't sure a pot of fish over my head would make much of a difference anymore.

I needed a thorough scrubbing and maybe a few more

hours rest. I tried not to feel guilty about that. Marc was as good as me, maybe better with his research background. But we had an anesthetic to discover, a weapon to stop, and three oracles who thought death came with a gift.

Still, it felt good to let go for five minutes.

I kicked up a small cloud of dust as I zigzagged through the cemetery. I'd left my shower kit back in the mess tent, but it was probably long gone by now. Besides, there was no way I was going to show up there looking like a minefield disaster. I headed for my hutch instead.

"Hey, roomie," I said, charging in the door.

Rodger wasn't there. His stuff sure was. My bed was lined with three dozen boxes of various Jawas, Ewoks, and bounty hunters. Marius's bunk was spread with busts of Spock and Kirk, along with plastic-wrapped T-shirts that said things like *The Death Star was an inside job* and *Party like a Vulcan*. Then there were a stack of *Star Trek* logoed plain red shirts on the shelf between their bunks that just said, *Expendable*.

Rodger's bed was laden with every action figure known to man. Then he had *Doctor Who* bobbleheads on my bookcase and comics on the stove (a real wise move there). I touched my fingers to the cast-iron surface. Okay, it was cold. But still...

The floor crunched under my feet. I looked down to see that Rodger had laid out his entire rock collection. What? Did he still think he was in his three-bedroom house in Earlsfield?

Cursing under my breath, I avoided most of the rocks and managed to reach under my cot, where I found a new bar of soap, a fresh bottle of shampoo, another towel, and about seventy-five baby Yoda pencil sharpeners.

It was official; I was going to kill my roommate.

In the meantime, I crawled into my bed for five minutes.

It was too close and too soft and I didn't care that this was my last clean set of sheets.

I'd slept like the dead last night—maybe it was that argument with Marc—but I still felt wiped.

Action figures tumbled to the floor as I curled up and closed my eyes.

Five minutes.

It was pure bliss. And as soon as my eyes fluttered open, I knew I'd rested way too long. Sunlight streamed through the open windows of the hutch. I'd blown the evening, all of the night, and if my guess was correct, a good portion of the morning. I lay on my side, blanket clutched to my chest, and felt—good.

The grit had left my eyes. My head had cleared. My body felt rested and awake. I reached down for my soap and shower goodies, noticing that Rodger had carefully laid out his figurines on his bed for once.

Served him right.

Maybe that was what the men in my life needed—a swift kick in the pants. Maybe Rodger wouldn't take over my space if I didn't let him. Maybe Marc would think twice about playing fun-for-now with my heart if I kept it friendly but professional between us.

Too bad I'd be driving myself crazy at the same time.

Soap and towel in hand, I banged out the door.

There weren't many people out this morning, which meant it was late. Everyone was probably at work already or holed up until lunch.

Good. No distractions. I'd get clean and go straight back to the lab.

I'd almost made it to the showers when a goddess stepped into the path in front of me.

She held a silver flame in her open palm, her arm bent, like a waitress holds a tray. An emerald barely there dress clung to her every curve. An array of tiny diamonds on invisible strings ornamented her neck and chest like a carpet of stars. They sparkled in the light of the silver flame.

I glanced behind me, hoping, praying she was here for someone else, but we were alone.

Silky blond curls cascaded down her back and curled over her shoulders. Her skin itself seemed to glow.

"Finally," she huffed. "I was beginning to think I couldn't detect your presence in camp."

That wasn't creepy or anything.

"My apologies," I said, trying to recall the formal language the goddesses preferred, wondering what in Hades she wanted with me, and frankly—wishing I'd been five minutes faster to the shower.

She flipped her hair back. "So what was the little bitch wearing?"

Er... "Who?" My mind raced. "Your goddess...ness?"

"Nerthus," she said, as if I'd hit my head on a rock. "My son said you met her."

So this was Eris, goddess of chaos.

Lucky me.

I wished with everything I had I could start walking again. Or that someone, *anyone,* would interrupt us. I didn't want to get involved in a supernatural episode of *Real Housewives*. I was so close to a good dousing and a shampoo. But there was no way I was going to risk the goddess smiting me.

She rolled her eyes. "Argus has four eyes and he can't even tell me what Nerthus was wearing."

"Well..." Maybe we could make this quick. "It was this whitish, almost see-through dress, with these little webby things..."

"Um-hum," she said, waving her hand to hurry me along. "What was it made of, mortal?"

Come on. Really?

"Er..." My fashion statement most days consisted of scrubs.

"Did it sparkle?" she demanded.

"Maybe." When you got right down to it, all goddesses tended to glow, and I'd honestly had my mind on other things. "It looked almost wet." And painted on.

"Evening dew," she said as if it were obvious. "How unoriginal. She's just got to play off the whole desert motif with a water theme."

"Right. Well, if you'll excuse me," I said, bowing, praying this freak would let me go.

"No!"

My heart leapt as she thrust out a hand.

She glared daggers at something behind me. "Those peasants tried to get too close."

I looked back and saw a group of nurses giving her a wide berth. I wished I could do the same.

Eris leaned in close enough for me to smell the sweet honeysuckle of her breath. "So who's the secret transfer?"

My temples began to pound and I fought the urge to take a step back. *Marc?* "I'm not sure it's a secret, necessarily."

"Cut the crap. Who's Nerthus after?"

I'd make a horrible diplomat. "I'm not sure she's after him exactly," I said, trying to walk the line.

Eris brushed me off. "That whore would do anything." She frowned, then brightened in about one second flat. "So what does he look like?"

This woman was going to get emotional whiplash.

And had she looked in the mirror lately? She was a goddess. She didn't need to be hot after some mortal captain just because some other goddess might think he was cute. "Aren't you involved with someone?"

She waved me off. "I'm always involved with someone."

She drew a few fingers along her collarbone. "So what's he like?"

Mine.

I shifted my towel and shower supplies to the other arm. "I just met him. I don't really know."

"I'm not even allowed up there," she said, pouting in the general direction of the lab. She sneered, her voice going startlingly cold. "Argus forbid it."

The air between us iced over. I could see my breath. I clutched my soap and towel between us, as if that would help.

Just like that, the chill vanished. She tilted her head. "Can you get me into the lab for a peek?"

What, was she flirting? I could see her dress getting shorter, tighter; it hugged her breasts so that the thin, supple fabric left little to the imagination.

Yeah, that wasn't going to work on me.

"I'll have to ask my superiors," I said, wishing I could buy her a clue.

She didn't need to be acting this way. She didn't need to dress like a floozy for attention. It was ridiculous. She was the kind of girl who could be with the cutest guy at a party and still feel the need to flirt with every man in the room.

She lowered her chin. "Get me a picture of the hot doc."

"Who?" I asked, just to be difficult.

Eris was a goddess. Her skin glowed. She could probably go three years without a shower and still look perfect. She had the god of thunder and fertility for a boyfriend.

"The mortal," she said, twirling a finger around a golden curl. "What does he like?"

I couldn't resist the urge. "Fruit Stripe gum." I was running low. "And Reese's Peanut Butter Cups." That one just came out. "Ooh...and Oreos," I said, trying not to get too excited. "The kind with the double stuff."

Be careful.

I'd said I didn't know him well.

What the hey. "He told me he'd kill for a Mo's Pizza, extra-large with pepperoni and onion," I said quickly before I lost my nerve.

The goddess tilted her head. "Mo's?"

I adopted my clinical persona. "I think it's some place in New Orleans. Topside. Nerthus doesn't know anything about it," I added, almost as an afterthought. But I knew.

I knew.

Her lips curled into a smile. "Go, mortal. Learn all you can about this captain."

"Anything you wish," I said. But the goddess had already stalked away.

Okeydokey. I wasn't quite sure what to think about that. I couldn't believe I'd just used Marc to get a pizza.

My stomach growled at the thought of piping hot cheese, crispy crust.

I was still thinking about it when I ducked into the shower tent.

"It's Petra," a young nurse called, securing her pink towel under her arms. "What were you doing talking to a goddess?" she asked as she ducked out of the stall at the end.

"Well, you know goddesses..." I said, praying it would drop.

It did.

"You look like you've been busy," a supply clerk said, making it sound like I'd been out at the rocks for three days.

I twisted the shower nozzle. Crisp, refreshing water cascaded over my head, my shoulders. "I've been working," I said.

"On that new doc in camp?" Her voice echoed against the water.

"I heard he was a dragon," the nurse said.

"Um...I didn't ask." I hadn't.

Technically.

"Did you see him walking through camp? He's such a hunk."

I closed my eyes. Could I just have a minute of peace?

"I know. I love the broody type," the woman next to me said. "I shot him eyes and he didn't even react."

Another one giggled. "You know he saw you."

I was sure he did. Marc didn't miss anything. It was what made him such a good doctor, among other things.

"So what's he like, Petra? You looked kind of smug when you walked in here."

I'd been thinking about pizza.

"Did you flirt with him?"

"He's my lab partner."

What was I supposed to tell her? He was my first love? That I was trying to convert him back into a friend?

If anyone found out we'd ever been an item, he could be yanked from my project, smited, chained to a rock. The goddesses did not share very well.

All I wanted was a long hot shower. Heck, I'd take a lukewarm one. I wanted to wash my hair five times and wallow under the water.

And then maybe hope for that pizza.

As for Marc, he was off the table.

CHAPTER TWENTY

It was high noon by the time I dropped my shower stuff off at the hutch. Rodger was there, and if I wasn't mistaken, he was unpacking more *Star Wars* figures.

"You've got to be kidding me," I said, dropping my shower kit on a pile of Jawas.

"Petra!" Rodger leapt over the *Millennium Falcon*, as well as a good portion of the Rebel fleet, in order to rescue all the stuff he'd stashed—yet again—on my bed. At least he'd changed the sheets.

I sat on a pile of T-shirts. "In case you haven't noticed, this is my bed. My pillow." I resisted the urge to toss it at his head. I might have spoiled Rodger with all those nights I'd spent in the lab, but... "If you think you're going to make me sleep out there with Marc, you're nuts."

"Marc is back?" Rodger's bushy eyebrows shot up. He plopped down on the T-shirts next to me, Jawas forgotten. "I thought he was dead."

I gave him a sideways glance. "Marc is in my lab."

"I love this," he said, gold-rimmed eyes twinkling.

"No, there will be no loving in the lab. He's leaving soon,

and even if he wasn't, he's the worst possible man for me to get involved with."

Rodger shrugged. "Sounds like you're already involved."

"You're not being logical," I told him.

"Sure. That's the problem," he said, too amused for my taste.

He didn't get it. Marc wasn't the same person I'd known in New Orleans. "He's changed." It wasn't just the scar on his neck, or the burns on his chest; he was harder, not as trusting. He couldn't open up. "He wants all of the fun and none of the feelings."

Rodger rested his elbows on his knees, considering it. "Are you saying this war hasn't made you a little more guarded too?"

I stood, grabbing for my jacket. "Can it, Rodger."

"I'm just saying you should give the guy a chance."

"I did." Before he'd told me it was temporary. I dragged a comb through my hair before I left. "What do you know about relationships anyway?"

"I'm in one."

"But it's not a futile one," I said, pointing the comb at him.

Rodger sat, silent.

Oh, darn. I tossed the comb onto my nightstand.

I wanted to say something to make it better, but I didn't know how. *Sorry* wouldn't cut it.

"I've got to get back." I left the hutch and headed for the lab. I hadn't done the best job combing, so I just ran my fingers through my hair as I walked.

I felt awful for Rodger and his wife. They'd had a strong marriage, a true partnership. He was a homebody who loved his kids. Now he was reduced to writing letters. He'd never see them grow up, never get to kiss his wife goodnight or hear about her day...not until the mail arrived a month later.

They were casualties of war, just like Marc and I had been.

My stomach did a few flip-flops as I made my way up the hill through the cemetery. It was over between us. It wasn't like I was going to fall for him. I'd told him we were just friends. If he pushed me, I'd stand my ground. I could do this.

I just didn't relish the idea of working so close to him.

When I got to the lab, I was relieved to find Jeffe there. He and Marc sat outside in the sunshine, doing extractions.

Of course Jeffe was there. It was Friday. I gave myself a mental shake. It hadn't been on my radar with everything else going on.

The sphinx held out one large paw as the venom from his claws dripped into the test tubes in Marc's hands.

Jeffe was in full question mode. "Yes, but if you *had* to choose a goddess, who would you choose?"

Marc shrugged. He sat on a crate as he held the sphinx in position. "I told you. I'm not worthy of a goddess."

"Very clever." The sphinx nodded. "Okay. Here's one. Where were you transferred from?"

He didn't give an inch. "That's classified."

"Hmm...very good."

Marc released him and the sphinx stood. "What is the average life span of a lobster?"

He paused. "In the ocean or in a tank?"

"The ocean," Jeffe said, waiting for Marc's response. The sphinx danced in place. "Did I get you?"

"They can live more than a hundred years," I said, thunking the sphinx on the head.

Jeffe planted his butt back on the ground. "I was asking Captain Belanger."

"Yes," I said, "but if he gets it wrong, we don't want you honor-bound to eat him."

The sphinx scratched his chin with his free paw. "That is

true." He shook out his mane. "My apologies. It is just that I do not have my notes."

"Yeah, that explains it," Marc said.

Obviously, he hadn't spent much time around sphinxes.

"Those in the camp trust me to ask their questions," Jeffe said. "I make detailed notes. I leave nothing to chance."

Marc held a sterile cloth over Jeffe's paw while he deposited the test tubes in a holder. He caught my eye. "Father McArio came by. He brought us sandwiches."

"No, thank you," Jeffe said, "it is taco salad night in the mess tent."

We let the sphinx go while I helped Marc clean up outside. I was almost tempted to follow Jeffe. I didn't want to be alone with Marc, even if he was just my friend and this was purely a research project.

Rodger said I'd changed. Maybe I had. But if so, it meant I was wiser, stronger. I knew better than to let Marc get to me.

Merde. I was so tired of being on guard. I wanted just one day, one hour where I could take some comfort, bury myself in the crook of his arm, kiss him like I had when he'd arrived at my lab.

"You'd better watch yourself," I told Marc, retrieving a few of the Band-Aid wrappers that had fluttered out of the trash. "I ran into Eris down there, and she is all into you."

"I don't even know an Eris," he said, accepting them, wrapping the whole thing up for biowaste.

"Nerthus does."

"This is worse than high school," he muttered.

Welcome to my world.

He held the lab door open for me, and I hesitated.

For heaven's sake. I could do this. I could be alone with him. I was a doctor, not some randy teenager.

I caught his eyes; he was watching me with a sort of

puppy-dog look. He cleared his throat. "I think you were really close with the peracetic acid," he said.

"Interesting," I said, watching him. This was bad. I was going to have to be the strong one, or we wouldn't last the night.

"Peracetic acid isn't our answer," he went on, "but milder seems to be better."

"I wouldn't have thought it."

Sphinx venom was designed to quickly overtake an entire nervous system. It obliterated anything I'd tried to use to dilute it. Which was why I'd assumed stronger was better.

"Are you going to go inside?" he asked, still holding the door.

Right.

When I entered, I saw he'd rearranged the two lab tables. Anger flashed through me before I realized why he'd done it. We had a new lab oven to sterilize our equipment, and a washing station.

"Believe me, I thought twice about touching your things," he said as he watched me survey his changes. He'd moved both worktables to the back, which was technically more efficient.

"Where'd you get all this?"

"Nerthus."

Of course. He'd gotten us new battery-operated burners, real cooling racks. His new layout was also more practical. There was more room to move too, which didn't explain why Marc and I stood so close.

He cleared his throat. "I know it's not mine."

"It's okay," I said, finding my voice. "I like it."

He was too close.

I wanted to be mad, not because I felt it, but because it would put some distance between us. I was used to owning my anger. Now I was afraid of it. I didn't have a tight enough hold. Letting loose around this man could open me up to, well, his tongue in my ear in my newly redesigned lab.

I stepped back, almost stumbling in my haste to get away. "So have you found anything interesting?" I asked, heading for his notes on my desk.

He'd worked through the rest of my top ten list of solvents. All of them had been too harsh. Ugh.

I took a seat on my stool. Leaning back against the rough wood, I braced the papers on my knee and paged through the progress he'd made overnight. He was good. His work was thorough, precise.

He'd finished the ethanol testing and managed to rule out diesel fuel and liquid hydrogen. He'd worked fast. Of course, the new equipment hadn't hurt. "I could kiss you," I said under my breath. "Ouch." I lifted my head. "Sorry." It was a dumb thing to say.

At least he looked as miserable as me. "I've worked with highly volatile neurotoxins before. But nothing like this."

"Yes," I said, examining the notes, forcing myself to focus. "We're going to have to switch directions on this." It was frustrating. "We're losing time."

"It's not good news. I know." He stood his ground. "I have to admit, it's nice to be working on something good for a change."

True. His old project terrified me. As much as I didn't want him so close, with me, we were doing good. And it was better than having him at work on that killer weapon. I turned to face him. "How close do you think they are to finishing?"

He shook his head. "It's impossible to say. Dr. Keller talked about needing a pathway." The lantern light played off his features, making him look even more stark, mesmerizing. "The toxin acts like a virus. The good thing is that once it's inside the body, it's not replicating fast enough to overtake someone's system."

He touched my hand and I felt it everywhere. His closeness was almost overwhelming. He ran his fingers along the edges of a cut I didn't even know I had. "In its current state, the virus will make people sick, but it won't kill them. We have time."

Gently, I pulled my hand back. "Until they develop a pathway." This was all so screwed up. "Hopefully we can get through the prophecies before that," I said, daring him to doubt me.

He didn't.

"Don't worry. I'll be a good friend," he said, putting an emphasis on the last word.

It vibrated through me. "Will you?"

I needed to know. We were working together. I had to feel like I could focus, and right now all I could think about was what it would be like to touch him back.

Maybe I should just drag him over to the cot and get it over with. Then it could be just physical and not this terrible, aching emptiness.

He knew his limits. He held his true self back. I couldn't even try. It wasn't me.

I tilted my head, studying the raised scar that cut across his neck.

This cool detachment, this separation, it never would have been possible for Marc, either. Until this war.

He hitched his breath as I ran my fingers along his raised flesh. His skin colored as I touched the smooth skin below.

Could I break through to him?

Did I even want to?

My thumb lingered at the base of his throat. "What have you suffered that you decided it was better to be alone?" What had he seen? Had it been worse for him?

He lowered his head. "I've operated until I could hardly walk out of the OR at the end of my shift. I've watched soldiers scream on my table as their organs went liquid from poison because we had nothing left to neutralize it. I've watched my patients left for dead."

And been left for dead himself.

"And it was better to do it alone," I said.

He swallowed. "Yes."

Maybe he was right. I didn't know. But one thing was certain. I wouldn't try to make him feel. I wouldn't dredge up the pain and the longing and the suffering he'd buried just to find that part of him he'd lost, that part of him I'd loved.

It was too hard. He'd suffered too much. And I refused to leave him broken when it was time to say goodbye.

CHAPTER TWENTY-ONE

When night fell, we heard a knock at the door. Marius poked his head in. "Sorry to interrupt, but Medusa needs you."

Marc and I were at my desk, working on a list of milder solvents. I stood. "Is she okay?"

His face was drawn. "She thinks she might be feeling some contractions. She's in the clinic. Nobody wanted to treat her. And she has a prejudice against vampires."

"I'll take care of her," I said, heading out. Medusa knew me. Besides, I didn't want anyone treating her if they weren't comfortable. She'd sense that. Every patient had a right to feel like their doctor was 100 percent focused on their care.

"You've been spending a lot of time in your lab," Marius remarked as we headed through the minefield.

I didn't want to talk about it. But I did owe him one. "Thanks again for talking to me about Marc." I knew he'd been ready to sleep when I went pounding on his lair.

He nodded. "I'm just sorry I didn't have better news."

"He's fine." I leaned close so no one would hear. "That was him back there."

Marius's eyes widened. "You mean the dragon?" He shook his head, as if I'd said something crazy. "Why didn't you introduce me?"

I shook my head. "I'm a little off when it comes to that man." Understatement of the year. "And how did you know he was a dragon?"

Marius shrugged. "I smelled him." He walked next to me, hands in the pockets of his white doctor's coat. "Shifters recover much better from a disruptor blast. You gave me the impression he was human."

"Oh," I said, startled. "He lives like one," I added lamely, as if that made a difference.

"No wonder Rodger is busting a gut," Marius said as we crossed the street toward the clinic. "I can always tell when he has a secret."

"He'd better not say anything about Marc and me. I can't let it get out that Marc and I used to be together."

"You're not now?" he asked.

"No," I said, wishing it didn't hurt so much to say.

"Don't worry," Marius said quickly. "I'll do what I can to keep things quiet." He opened the door to the clinic for me. "Besides, the more they talk, the less they believe what they say."

I sure hoped he was right.

* * *

The waiting room was crowded, which I took as a good sign. Word was getting out about the care we offered here.

I took Medusa's chart and headed for a room in the back. "Did you get a urine sample?" I asked one of the nurses on duty.

She shook her head *no*, her thin nose wrinkling slightly at the thought.

Come on. I knew Medusa could turn a person to stone, but she was also a creature in need of care. She didn't need us tiptoeing around her.

"Give it to me," I said as the nurse went to retrieve a small plastic cup. I'd handle it myself.

Medusa had just done her thing, a common occurrence with pregnant women, so I had another nurse fetch me a bottle of water.

"Drink," I told her while I took her vitals.

We did a full examination, and it turned out the Gorgon just had some indigestion.

She ran her hands over the slight roundness of her green scaled stomach. "My apologies. I feel foolish."

"Don't." No need for that. "I'm glad you came in."

Her stomach rumbled. "It must be the jelly beans. I cannot get enough."

"Your weight gain is fine," I said, double-checking her chart. "Just make sure you balance the sugar with plenty of veggies and good-for-you foods." I took her mostly full water bottle and watched as she shifted on the crinkly paper that covered the examination table. "Are you taking your prenatal vitamins?"

She hissed. "They are like horse pills."

The water in the bottle began to boil. Yikes.

She didn't notice as I capped it and practically threw it onto the counter behind me.

Her eyes darted. "It is like the time Athena made me swallow the three-pointed trident of Neptune."

I glanced back at the bottle. It was still bubbling. Incredible. I knew some of my patients had powers, but I didn't usually see it firsthand.

"Are you taking your prenatals?" I asked again.

"Yes," she grumbled.

"Good." That was all I'd needed to know.

As eager as I was to get back to the lab, this was one of the parts of being a doctor that I enjoyed the most. Medusa might like to thrash her tail, but I knew she was taking good care of herself and her baby.

I sent her up front to schedule her eighteen-week ultrasound. Then I stayed behind to change the paper on her exam table and grab the leftover water bottle. It wasn't my job to clean up the room, but in a way I felt like I owed it to the poor Gorgon not to have that nurse in here with her wrinkled nose and her prejudices.

Afterward, I checked out of the clinic and headed to the minefield.

Cool and collected.

If I could do it with an ancient Gorgon, I could at least attempt it with Marc.

I arrived just in time to see an immense wooden cart pull up to the lab. It was hitched to two white cows with leafy garlands around their necks. We both cringed as the oversized wheels of the cart ground against a wrecked wheelchair. It screeched against an old metal storage locker as the cows dragged it for several yards.

I walked up to him. "That's something you don't see every day."

He wore a slightly pained expression. "Nerthus likes cows."

"So do I. Medium rare with a baked potato."

There was no driver, at least none that we could see.

We walked around to the back. "So I'm assuming the last delivery didn't come by cow."

His jaw tightened. "Try Nerthus in a string bikini."

For a goddess, that was playing hard to get.

Marc lifted the cover on the rear of the cart and my heart stuttered. "It's a generator!" The other boxes held metal lab tables, more uniforms for Marc, and—I held up a red man-thong. "What is this?"

He pulled a box of electric lights off the cart and groaned.

"Is this the goddess's version of underwear?" I asked, stretching it between my fingers. This was too precious. It even sparkled. "I'd love to see you in this."

"I thought we were just friends," he said, reaching for another box.

"We are," I said before he got any ideas.

"Maybe I'll go commando," Marc said, heading into the lab.

Like I needed to be thinking of that all day.

We soon realized we also had a full set of worship books dedicated to Nerthus, as well as a framed lock of her hair. Ew. I was half tempted to burn it for testing.

No extension cords for the generator, but Marc put in a request.

"Tell her you miss her," I said, checking out the generator as he filled out the paperwork.

"What?" he choked out. "You don't think I'm already the mortal flavor of the week?"

Well, he wouldn't be mine.

He lowered his pen. "Why are you so determined to push me away?"

He had to be kidding. "Do you want an alphabetic list or maybe just Top Ten style?"

There was a sharp rap at the door. "Pizza."

No way.

I opened it up to find a rather annoyed Horace hovering outside the door. "Ahem, I come in the name of Eris the most high and beautiful goddess." He rolled his eyes. "The supreme deity with the most beautific gifts, the perkiest bosom, and the best sense of style."

"Really?" Marc asked.

Horace shrugged. "It was on the note card. She isn't allowed to come up here, so I'm supposed to send her regards and check you out." The minor god craned his neck in the door to get a handle on Marc. "Um-hum. Okay." He handed me the pizza. "Bye."

"This is ridiculous," Marc said, holding the pie.

I shrugged. "You know the goddesses."

He frowned. "I'm not talking about that."

"Sorry, Marc. I'm not going to get into it." I sat on a stool, as far as I could get from him, willing him to respect the distance, honor what we'd said would never happen between us. "Let's just have some pizza."

* * *

The next day, Father McArio dropped by with Fitz the hellhound and helped us put everything together. We paid him back with my favorite item in that day's cart—a two-by-four-foot ornately framed picture of the goddess.

"This is certainly a nice frame," Father said as he hoisted it up. "You really don't mind?"

Marc walked him to the door. "We'll say it got lost in transit."

Frankly, all of the gifts were making me nervous.

Eris had sent presents as well—massage oils and silk sheets. And muffuletta sandwiches from Central Grocery in the French Quarter.

"What is this?" I drew an ornate glass jar out of a box. "It's filled with bubbles."

Marc winced. "Don't open it or she'll know we saw it. Just"—he motioned to a stack of boxes near the door—"put it in the bottom of one of those."

Fat chance. I rested it on my hip. "What is it?"

He ran a hand through his hair. "It's a divine telephone. You break the bubble and call someone."

"I like it," I said, wondering whom I could possibly call.

"No. Nerthus will know if you use one."

Figured. And she'd know we didn't call her. "Fine," I said, shoving it under a box of slave-boy costumes. I hoped Nerthus wasn't going to pop by and ask Marc to dress up for a surprise inspection.

Subsequent deliveries from Nerthus brought us a state-of-the-art fume hood, a lab-grade refrigerator, and two crates of pinecones blessed by the goddess.

But no extension cords.

We couldn't hook up the lights without them. We'd ask, only to receive a binding cord. Or a cord of wood. Or once, even a board. Finally, we had Jeffe draw a picture while he was in for a venom extraction.

As we worked through our options, we struggled with exactly what kind of solvent to use that would act as a neutralizing agent for the venom. I was beginning to think a natural substance just wouldn't cut it. As mere mortals, that was frustrating because natural solvents and chemicals were all we had.

I was careful not to touch Marc as he pored over a medical text. "What about poison?"

He kept reading, absorbed. "Be reasonable. Nerthus isn't that annoying."

I leaned up against the lab table, trying to work it out in my mind. "The harshest solvents we have aren't strong enough. We haven't even had one substance show real promise." The sphinx venom was just too strong. I adjusted my stance. "Hear me out. How is it any different from what they're doing at the University of Buffalo?" Last I'd heard, they'd found a way to use tarantula venom to combat heart attack deaths.

He was listening now. "Venom as a neutralizer. That could work."

"It could," I said, getting excited. "You think you could score us some?" Both sides had been using poison as a weapon for some time now. I handed him the forms. "Ask for the spittle of the Cerberus first," I said. Cerberus was the three-headed dog of the underworld. "You know—dogs and cats..."

"I'm going to get Britney Spears perfume as well," he said, writing down the second most common poison to the gods.

"Yes. Perfect." We could use some good-smelling solvents in this lab. And it wouldn't kill us if we spilled it.

Marc glanced up at me as he wrote. "There's the blood of Medusa."

Right. "I'm seeing her the day after tomorrow."

Or sooner. It seemed like Medusa was in the clinic every day. She'd reported coming down with the divine plague, blood humors, and flesh-eating bacteria, all of which turned out to be simple morning sickness.

I prescribed saltine crackers.

And confiscated the water she boiled. She really needed to watch her temper.

The next morning, we received our poisons and our extension cords. We got to work on the poisons first. Then, after we'd turned our eight o'clock report in, I sat back to watch Marc work, shirtless. I'd miss the view once the air-conditioning started up.

"The lights look nice," I told him. He'd installed standard lab fluorescents over our work area, and a tabletop lamp in the back. "You always were good with your hands," I murmured as he climbed down from the chair he'd been standing on.

The muscles in his arms worked as he rubbed his hands clean on a white towel. "Are you coming on to me?"

Of course not. "I'm just observant."

He caught my wrist. His eyes glittered as he drew my hand toward him and kissed each fingertip.

A windup timer on the lab counter dinged.

"I'll take a look," I said. And when I slid our latest test formula under the microscope, I froze.

Our solvent had not only neutralized the sphinx venom, it had eaten our healthy cells, too.

We were going in the wrong direction. At least with the spittle of Cerberus.

Marc examined the results on the other lab table. "The Britney Spears perfume ate our sample."

I rested my head on the top of the microscope. If our most potent earthly and limbo-based solvents were too weak, and our immortal poisons were too strong—what then?

My eyes fixed on the water Medusa had boiled on her last visit to the clinic. It wasn't a poison, like her blood. It wasn't a natural substance, like gasoline or ethanol.

Marc followed my gaze and took the bottle. "What?"

"I'm thinking," I said slowly. I picked up the nearly full bottle, turning it over in my hands.

"It's just water," I said, handing it to him. "But it might possibly be enhanced."

Medusa boiled it when she got mad. I hadn't asked her about her household, other than to talk about crib safety. Still, according to myth, Medusa lived on an island surrounded by a toxic lake. So if she was doing something to the water...

"Let's try it," Marc said, taking a dropperful. I capped it and returned the bottle to the table next to me.

It could work.

Just then there was a rap on the door. "Hello!"

Father McArio.

"Come on in," I said as he opened the door.

He backed in, holding two large bags in his hands. "A troop of dancing girls delivered this to me by mistake."

He had Krystal's hamburgers. I could smell the burgers and the onions as I took the bags from him.

"Stay for dinner," I said, taking out burgers and onion rings. Eris had sent a ton.

"You talked me into it," Father said, pulling up a lab chair next to me. "How is your work going?" he asked us.

"We think we might be onto something," Marc said, preparing the samples.

"I'm glad to hear it," Father said, unwrapping a burger. "Wondrous how the goddess kept these so hot."

He uncapped the bottle on the table and brought it to his lips.

Oh no. "Wait!"

But it was too late. He'd taken a drink.

"Is there something—?" His question ended on a gurgle.

He tried to swallow and couldn't.

"Father." I grabbed for him as he started to collapse sideways. *No, no, no*. "Father, stay with me."

I eased him down off the chair and onto the floor.

Marc joined me. "What happened?"

"He drank our Medusa water."

Father's skin heated. His breath came in pants. "Ohmygod." I rushed for my stethoscope.

His heart was beating at 120. One thirty. It was too fast. His pulse was rapid.

"Can you tell me your name?" Marc asked, taking his blood pressure.

Father's voice slurred. "Can't feel. My hands."

"Hold on," I said, fighting to keep my voice steady. Nothing in my medical research books ever said anything about Medusa water. Heck, I hadn't even thought about it until a minute ago.

I tore through the boxes in the corner, looking for Nerthus's gift. Where were goddess bubbles when you needed them? Finally, I found them under about a thousand rose petals. I uncapped the jar and squeezed a hard globe, but it refused to pop. Fricking thing was made for superstrength. I dropped it on the floor and stomped on it.

It burst open, filling the tent with spicy incense.

A cloud formed and a dove fluttered in the middle of it. "You would like to speak with the goddess?"

Oh, sure. Talking doves.

Think.

"No, I don't want to talk to the goddess," I told the bird. "Put me in touch with Medusa." Could it even do that? "Please."

The bird fluttered. "Medusa the damned, the serpent goddess, the executioner of men—"

"Yes, yes. Scourge of Kisthene's plain." We didn't have time for this.

"One moment, please."

"Hurry up," I ordered.

Father had maintained consciousness, but had begun to pant. "His heart rate's one thirty-five," Marc said.

Not good.

"Doctor?" Medusa hissed.

I looked back to see her slithering up to the vaporous cloud, which was starting to resemble a wall of smoke. She held a basket of skulls in one hand and a trident in the other. "The morning sickness has eased. I was decorating the baby's room."

"Good. Look. I need your help. This man"—I glanced at Father behind me—"he drank some water you boiled back at the clinic."

The rattle on her tail shook. "That was very foolish."

"Yes, well, he assumed a water bottle was a water bottle,

and this isn't helping me," I said, getting a rein on my emotions. "What can I do to treat this?" I refused to think that I couldn't fix it.

Her eyes widened and the snakes in her hair hissed. "It is deadly. I told you."

Just like she told me she'd laid off the chocolate. I knew that look.

"Medusa," I said slowly, "this man is my mentor. And my friend."

"You do not understand." She slithered uncomfortably, dropping skulls out of her basket. "My lake must be deadly. My touch is poison. I am the scourge!"

"You can be the scourge," I said, voice rising, "I get you are damned. That's fine. But you can trust me. I'm your doctor. And this time, I need your help."

Her expression clouded. "I don't owe you—"

"No, you don't," I said quickly. "I want to treat you. I care about you and your baby." Damn the ancient Greeks and their tit-for-tat way of doing things. "I'm not asking because I have some favor stashed away. I'm asking because you can tell me your health issues and I need your help."

She snarled, showing off a double row of razor-sharp teeth. The water in our test tubes bubbled behind me. "Fine, but he cannot hear."

"Who?" I demanded.

"The mortal doctor."

"Marc?"

"You've got to be kidding me," he growled as he stood and exited the room. Thank heaven he didn't argue.

Medusa watched the door close. "Give him the fruit of the finut tree. It grows thirty miles due south from here. One taste and he will be cured." Her eyes hardened. "Do not tell anyone."

Thank you. "I won't tell," I said, wishing I could hug her, glad I couldn't.

One taloned hand found her rounded belly. "Motherhood is making me soft."

Yeah, well, I wasn't leaving anything to chance. "I need specific directions on the finut tree."

She gave me a hard stare. "You will find it growing in hell vents."

I choked.

Medusa rolled her eyes. "It has a long brown trunk and purple fruit. Truly, must I draw an *X* over my heart where you could stab me and kill me?"

Okay. "Got it." I looked to Father on the floor. "How much time does he have?"

Her lip curled up in a sneer. "I don't know. I like my poison to work somewhat slowly so that the so-called heroes who invade my island will wallow in their regret." She shrugged. "But they usually drown pretty quickly in the lake."

"Thank you," I said, knowing she'd made a sacrifice, willing to make another one as I grabbed for my field jacket and a lantern.

"Goodbye," she said as the plume of smoke dissolved.

No telling how long it would take me to find the hell vent and start climbing a tree.

Don't think about it.

There was no choice here. I rushed to the bedroom and found a pillow for Father's head. "I'm going to save you," I promised. He reached for my hand, tried to speak, but couldn't. I resisted the urge to check his vitals again. It wouldn't matter, not if I couldn't come back with the antidote. "Marc is going to be here with you," I said, standing.

I found Marc outside, next to Father's Jeep. "Get in there. He needs you."

"Why? Where are you going?" he asked as I slid into the driver's seat.

"Special mission for Medusa." I fished the keys out from under the floor mat.

He grabbed my arm. "Over my dead body. I'm not going to let you get yourself killed."

When he put it that way, it didn't sound all that appealing to me, either. "Stay here," I said, firing up the Jeep.

"What the hell?" I heard Marc holler as I sped south, on my way out of camp.

Pretty much.

Thirty miles. Due south. Hell vent.

God help me when I got there.

CHAPTER TWENTY-TWO

Palms sweating, I gunned the engine out of the minefield and onto the Limbo plains. The night was black and ominous. Of course I had no way to navigate. It wasn't like I had a road or a compass or...anything.

Real smart, Petra. The constellation Hito was in the south tonight. I'd use it as a guide.

While a lot of the constellations on Earth were named after heroes and gods, the ones down here were for those who strove valiantly and failed.

My stomach twisted. It had better not be an omen.

I clutched the steering wheel as the Jeep bounced over the uneven ground. I could barely see in front of me in the darkness. Forget headlights. Someone might see. We might not have standing guards or Shrouds like the Old God Army, but I sure as heck wasn't going to advertise the fact that I was going AWOL.

Again.

Focus on Hito. I steered straight for the hero who was beheaded by none other than Medusa. Either the fates were having a field day, or I was getting paranoid.

I hit a big hole, rattling the Jeep and my teeth.

I'd never been this far out of camp by myself, on the ground, unprotected. There were packs of wild imps in the desert that would tear you apart in seconds. If they didn't get me, I could just as easily drive into a sinkhole, Limbo's version of bottomless quicksand.

It wasn't like I'd brought emergency flares or the disruptor or even a fricking bubble to call a goddess.

What was I thinking?

Father. I was thinking about Father and how he was in pain, dying at this very moment. I didn't have time to pack a bag or plan a trip. My main focus had to be the antidote. There was no choice, no wavering. So I pressed on.

Death comes with a gift.

Well, I didn't want one. Not if it meant losing my friend.

My pulse raced. I could feel my heart in my chest. I was hyper-aware of the vast desert cloaked in night. Every rattle of the Jeep. Every pounding over rock meant I was one breath closer to the hell vent.

Please, Lord, let us get out of this and I'll be a better person. I'll find the anesthetic. I'll stop lying to Eris.

I'll let Marc know how much I love him. I'll kiss him silly.

My eyes and throat grew dry, my hands stiff from gripping the steering wheel as it vibrated and jolted with the Jeep.

I was going in the right direction. I'd find my way back to him. I had to believe that or I wouldn't be able to take the next second, much less what would happen afterward.

And then I saw it—a large shadow looming out of the desert, dead ahead.

I took a deep, shuddering breath. I never thought I'd be so glad to see a hell vent. This had to be it.

My arms shook.

This was it.

It was on me before I knew it. I hit the brakes so fast I skidded sideways.

"That was...disturbing."

I shoved the Jeep into park, glad to survive my own driving.

Arf!

I whipped around, ready for imps or flesh-eating locusts or whatever else was out here.

Fitz sat in the back seat, his tongue lolling out. *Arf!*

Of all the creatures I didn't need out in the middle of the Limbo desert... I reached out and petted his furry puppy head. "Stay in the car."

I needed to see if I could find a weapon.

Hand braced on cool metal, I scrambled down the side of the Jeep facing away from the hell vent and circled around the rear. Father had to have something in the back. He'd be crazy to go ministering to lost souls unarmed. I yanked open the hatch next to the spare tire, and my hands closed around a large black strongbox.

"Ha!" I bit down a shout.

Fitz jumped into the back, sniffing at my hands as I flipped the clasp. I felt around. This thing was custom. The soft foam lining was cut to hold whatever Father would need on the road. My fingers closed on a flashlight—*thank you*. I clicked it on.

The soft, round beam fell on a large metal cross nestled in the gray foam. There were vials of oil and water, and one of those long purple stoles priests wore around their necks. This one was bloody and torn at the bottom.

But where were the weapons?

I didn't see any. I searched under the stole.

There was a brown book with gold lettering underneath. *Rules for the Roman Ritual of Exorcism.*

Hell.

"You gotta throw me a bone, Father." I tore out the foam lining, scattering pictures of saints. I'd known he was an exorcist. He'd helped me with an enchanted dagger a month or two back, but to think that he was out here in the wilds of Limbo, practicing without any real weapons? It was insanity.

I examined the stole, half tempted to put it on. There was a medal near an embroidered cross at the top. Fingers shaking, I took the medal and pinned it onto my hip. Saint Isaac Jogues. The martyr. Way to go, Father.

A final scan of the back of the Jeep showed no weapons, not unless I wanted to hit something over the head with the wooden cross. I took the cross and stuffed the holy water in my pocket.

I was a good Catholic.

Mostly.

I braced myself. I raised the cross in one hand and the flashlight in the other as I headed for the hell vent. A dark form glinted on the desert floor dead ahead. I about fell over sideways when my light landed on it.

A bronze dagger thrust blade-down into the desert floor.

I knew that knife.

It was as long as my hand, with a compact handle and a triangular blade. This was no army-issue weapon. It was old and ornate. The grip was wide, wrapped in leather. The top curved to form the head of a serpent.

I'd seen this knife before. It had been mine. I'd lost it in the desert while fighting for my life. And if I drew it out of the soil, I might never get rid of it again.

"What is this place?" I muttered, gripping the cross tighter as I left the knife to the desert.

To my right, I heard a moan. Yikes. I'd left a few soul-sucking Shrouds back here once upon a time.

I smelled gasoline and death.

Heart in my throat, I shone my light on the source of the

noise. Bodies littered the ground. There had to have been at least a dozen old army soldiers slaughtered. The carnage was sickening.

Among the dead lay the coiled, smoking bodies of imps.

Fitz whimpered, sniffing the ground.

A sweet breeze blew in the palm trees, not ten feet away. With it, I could feel the electric undercurrent of evil slide over my skin.

"Help..." a woman's voice called from the mess, weakly.

I winced, and for one guilty moment, I wished I hadn't heard.

I was already in the middle of an emergency medical case, one that involved my friend and my mentor. I was here to save Father McArio, not get involved with whatever the Old God Army was doing right on top of a hell vent.

Stopping could cost Father his life. Judging from the carnage I'd seen, the injured soldier could easily be too critical to move, or to treat here. She probably wouldn't survive.

Merde.

My light glanced over a smoking, wrecked Humvee. The bulletproof windows were shattered. The tires had been slashed, one completely torn off. There were gouges in the metal sides.

Then I saw something move. I trained my light down on the crumpled form of a woman. She clutched a bloody towel to her neck. Light brown hair fell from a messy bun into her eyes. They widened when she saw me.

At that moment, I felt a piece of me crumble. I steeled myself and went to help.

"Are you a priest?" she asked, her words thick as I knelt down beside her.

She wasn't Catholic or she'd know.

"I'm a doctor," I said, propping my light up on an ammo case.

Blood pooled under the injured woman, and I felt my adrenaline surge. Her neck wasn't our main problem, not if she could still talk. She was pale. Her pulse was thready. I inspected her legs. Her pants were torn and bloody. I probably wasn't going to be able to move her without opening something up. I had to see more.

"Do you have a knife?" I said, taking a quick peek at her neck. I was right. It was bad, but it could wait. Her legs, on the other hand... "We need to cut these pants off."

"No knife," she said, every word an effort.

"None?" Unbelievable. I didn't know who was equipping these old army soldiers or what they were doing here or how I was going to find a... My stomach plummeted as the truth slammed into me. "Mother Mary on a biscuit."

I stood, anger pulsing through me as I grabbed the flashlight. "Just a second," I said to my patient, horrified, amazed, and resigned. "I don't believe this," I muttered, stalking back to the ancient knife right where I'd left it months ago, half buried in the sand.

A wise man I knew said once that the universe always had a plan.

Sometimes I really hated the universe.

I reached down, grasped the leather handle, and yanked the dagger from the soil. Yep. I knew this one. Intricate, time-worn carvings wound down the blade, and there was a sliver missing from the tip.

Heaven almighty.

I hurried back to the soldier. "You still with me?"

She nodded and watched as I used the knife to slice away her pants. It was as if she'd been attacked by wild animals. "Let me see your canteen." I shrugged out of my scrub top, leaving only my white tank as I dumped water on my shirt and began cleaning the blood away. All of the cuts were deep, jagged. These things had mauled her.

My patient was edgy, fearful. She could see how bad it was. "You just hold on. I'm going to help you."

She gave a weak nod. "I wish you were a priest."

"Yeah, well, don't give up yet." I found the source of the worst bleeding. The imps had nicked an artery. I reached down for my boot, tugging the laces off.

She lolled her head to the side. "Why do you have a cross on the side of your Jeep?"

She was talking too much. She shouldn't be feeling up to talking. It was a bad sign. "I borrowed it from a friend," I said, hoping she'd let it go. Patients sometimes got a surge of strength at the end. I didn't want to think I hadn't reached her in time.

I tied off the makeshift tourniquet and began treating her other wounds as best I could. She'd lost too much blood.

"I'm Dr. Robichaud, MASH 3063rd. Our camp is about an hour back. As soon as I get you stable, I'm going to put you in my Jeep and take you there."

I glanced back at the hell vent. Maybe I could get Father's antidote first. No. Guilt swamped me. The delay could kill her.

Or him.

Hades.

But I'd already made my choice, hadn't I?

I'd chosen duty over my friend.

My patient began to shake. She'd lost too much blood. "This is going to hurt, but I need you to try to stand."

It was a struggle, but we managed to get her into the passenger side of the Jeep.

I'd left the dagger behind on the ground, but I wasn't fool enough to think it would stay there. One problem at a time. I reached in the back for the foam lining of Father's exorcism kit, letting the soldier use it as a pillow.

"Thank you," she said, bracing herself against the pain. "You saved me."

I appreciated her confidence, but we weren't out of the woods yet. "You relax," I said, starting up the Jeep. Every vibration had to be like razor blades to her sliced-up legs. She was still bleeding.

We sped away from the hell vent and headed due north to camp. I hoped I was going straight. I'd forgotten to look at the stars.

Please, God, guide me. Let me find a way to save her and Father, too.

But even as I drove, I knew I'd chosen. This girl would bleed out if I didn't get her back. Father would die if I didn't get the fruit.

Tears stung my eyes. He was my mentor, my friend, one of the greatest men I'd ever known. He was also here to save people like this young soldier.

He was Saint Jogues, the martyr.

Arf! Fitz leapt from the back and into my lap. Dang, I'd forgotten all about the dog.

"Stop it," I said, depositing him in the back.

Meanwhile my patient was trying to open the Jeep door. "Hold up." I ground to a halt. "You can't do that," I said, dashing around the front so I could open and close her door. Then lock it.

"Please." She grabbed at my arm. "I'm dying. I want to see the stars. I want to go home."

She was delirious. I helped her sit up straighter. "You have to stay put so I can get you back," I said, checking her bandages.

She smiled and leaned against me. I knew that kind of look.

"No," I told her, ordered her. "This is not over." I checked her pulse. It was weakening. It was inevitable. She'd lost too much blood. It tore at me.

I knew it. I'd known when I chose her. She was dying.

Jaw clenched, I watched her rise. Her spirit hovered over the body I held, beautiful and free from pain. She looked even younger, happy.

"You can see me," she said, delighted in her discovery. Her voice was strong and melodious. She glanced behind us, then back, smiling. "It can't touch me now."

I wet my lips. "I don't understand." Had something out of the hell vent followed us?

She touched a hand to her mouth as sadness crossed her features. "Souls who pass too close to a hell vent are sucked into Hades."

Her revelation stunned me. I'd had no idea.

She stood taller, hands clasped. "You saved me."

Tears pricked at the corners of my eyes. "I'm glad." It was all I'd ever asked for in this war.

She nodded and turned her face to the heavens. And then I watched her rise until she was just a whisper of a cloud in the night sky.

I stood for a moment, recovering, trying to make sense of it. I knew I'd done all I could. She'd been as good as dead when I'd picked her up. It was senseless. It was wrong.

Sighing, I raised my head and just about choked when I saw the dagger resting on the dashboard.

CHAPTER TWENTY-THREE

I TOOK A SEAT. "OKAY, FITZ," I said, grabbing the dagger, wrapping it in my bloodied scrub top.

The soldier's expression was oddly peaceful. I reached down and closed her eyes.

Then I eased the knife into my pocket and shifted into gear. We made a sharp 180, sending Fitz scrabbling against the vinyl back seat of the Jeep. "Let's go back."

We lurched over scattered stones. The hellhound rode directly behind me, his head out the side and his tongue lolling. I was glad one of us didn't know what we were in for.

I just hoped we weren't too late.

The shadow of the hell vent loomed across the desert ahead. It was both heartening and terrifying. Every primitive instinct in me screamed to turn back. I braced myself. I could do this. I had to.

My stomach churned. Just a few more minutes and we'd be there. I just hoped the fruit wasn't high up in a tree. I wasn't sure I'd be that great at climbing, especially if it was built like a palm tree. Why didn't Father have a rope in his exorcist kit? Or as long as I was wishing, a ladder?

I pulled the Jeep close to the wrecked Humvee and returned the soldier's body to where she had almost died. The Old God Army would be searching, and I didn't want her family to wonder.

Then I drove south a bit and killed the engine.

Fitz jumped out, wagging his tail. *Merde*. "You don't know what we're getting into, buddy."

My nerves jangled. I double-checked my cross and the holy water in my pocket. As for the dagger? I didn't think it was going anywhere.

A sweet-smelling breeze blew from the vent. Palm trees swayed, inviting me to enter.

"Okay, doggie. We need the fruit from a finut tree. It's round. It's purple. On a long brown trunk." That was all we knew.

I'd just have to gather anything and everything that looked close. The dog whined as we drew closer.

"Believe me, this isn't how I'd plan it," I said, focused on the tree line as Fitz trotted next to me. "Father is real sick. This is an emergency."

Bracing the cross under my arm, I unscrewed the holy water and dipped my fingers. I touched them to my forehead, my chest, and both shoulders, ready to take all the divine intervention I could get.

"Here, buddy." I reached down and touched some to Fitz's collar. If we were overdoing it, well, I had a feeling the Lord would understand. I just hoped He was watching.

I returned the bottle to my pocket as we skirted the edge of the jungle. I could hear rustling in the trees and then a child's laugh. My hair stood on end. "Maybe I should get the exorcism book."

Then again, I had to wonder if my soul was pure enough for that.

An ugly knotted tree rose among the dripping foliage. It was maybe ten feet in.

Fitz barked and dashed straight into the hell vent. "God almighty," I said, pushing my way into the dense foliage, refusing to look down, trying not to touch anything more than the branches blocking my way.

Please let me get out of this alive.

Wet leaves smacked against my arms and legs. I held up the cross, keeping them away from my face as my flashlight bounced off Fitz's dark form. The air smelled fresh. Flowers bloomed all around us. I could hear the chatter of the birds and the rush of water nearby.

Then the darkness lifted and it was beautiful. It was like the sun had risen over the most perfect day I could imagine. I felt warm and alive and glorious.

I knew it was an illusion. It couldn't be real. But I wanted to run and play. My hips wiggled despite myself. I felt *free.*

I clutched the cross tighter, the wood digging into my skin.

Heart pounding, I began my search, trying not to get distracted by the exotic flowers or the chattering monkeys swinging in the high trees. Father didn't have much time. And I worried I'd get so turned around I'd never make it out of here.

Fitz stopped in front of an ugly tree.

"That's disgusting." It was twisted and knotted. The trunk was too thick and leaned to one side. It had dense, scraggly leaves on the top, along with wilted brownish purple fruit. "It's rotted and—yuck." Those weren't leaves on the higher branches. They were locusts.

Fitz dug his paws against the thick trunk, spewing rotten bark. The trunk oozed thick pus.

That couldn't be it.

There was beautiful fruit in the trees all around me. If I

just wandered more, searched harder, I could find the pretty purple ones.

I blinked hard, remembering my Catholic school. The devil delighted in temptation. He specialized in making evil irresistible. So if I was supposed to keep my hands *off* something... I took another look at the tree Fitz was pawing and tried not to wrinkle my nose at the small purple fruit on the high branches.

Do it.

Before I could think about it too much, I scrambled up the curved trunk. Rotting bark came off under my hands and legs as I climbed, but I didn't care. I kept going. I made a beeline for the fruit and grabbed hold of a piece. It wouldn't come off the tree. Blast it. I tucked the cross under my arm again, unwrapped the knife, and sliced it free.

The tree shook, and a scream shattered the night. I dropped the cross. Hell and damnation.

I leapt to the ground. *Run.*

A red, potbellied demon landed on the path directly in front of me. It spewed black venom as it cackled.

I waved the dagger at it. Fat lot of good that would do me. The thing would have to be on me before I could use it.

Panic seized me. I was going to die in a hell vent, eaten by a demon.

A thunderous growl split the night. I was afraid to look, unable to move. The demon's eyes grew wide as a giant black beast stalked out from behind me.

It was half dog, half wolf, and growing larger by the second. Fire licked at its fur. Red eyes tore through the darkness. It snarled and snapped up the demon, devouring it whole.

Clutching the knife and the fruit, I ran. I ran like I've never run before. I zigzagged past trees. I leapt over a stream. Holy hell. I was turned around. But I couldn't stop.

Run.

Monkeys chattered in the branches on both sides, making chase, playing as I made a mad dash for my life and my soul.

The jungle grew darker, denser.

I pushed forward, through the blackness. Through the biting cold. Branches smacked me in the face, tree limbs ripped at the fruit in my hand and the dagger in the other. The chattering monkeys morphed into fanged monsters. They leapt on my back, tearing at my skin and my hair.

The beast snarled behind me, snapping up monsters and biting them in half, their bones crunching.

I burst out of the hell vent. I stumbled over the rocks of the desert, afraid to look back.

The raging beast rocketed past me, leaping onto the Jeep. It tore off the back gate as it climbed into the rear. It was Fitz! He was shrinking, but not fast enough.

I shoved the fruit in my pant pocket, threw the knife out the window, and fired up the Jeep. I gripped the steering wheel and gunned it due north.

Pain seared my neck. I touched it, and my hand came back covered in blood.

I clutched for the purple fruit. It was still in my pocket. Hallelujah.

Please don't let me be too late.

We bounced over the desert in a blur of fear and panic.

Fitz jumped into the passenger seat, looking normal—for a possessed hellhound. He jammed his head out the window as we sped for home.

We made it across the desert, through the minefield, past the mangled helicopter. I cornered around the hickey horns van and towers of scrap metal.

The air was sour; the dirt was up my nose. I was back home.

I had the antidote. I didn't succumb to the hell vent. Or to Father's pet.

Now I just had to pray it wasn't too late.

I brought the Jeep to a screeching halt outside the lab and rushed inside.

"He's in the back," Marc said, wide-eyed. "What happened to you? You're bleeding!"

I pushed my way through the curtain. Father lay pale and unmoving.

"He's bottoming out. His pulse is at fifty," Marc said, coming up on the side of me. "Let me see your neck. Something *bit* you."

"I'll live," I said. Father McArio might not. He was weak, but alive. *Thank heaven.* I braced the fruit against my chest, tearing into it like a ripe tomato.

He wasn't conscious. He couldn't eat, so I dripped the juices into his mouth. They ran over his cheeks. I touched the soft flesh to his tongue. "Father? Are you there? Can you hear me?"

His eyes flew open and he coughed.

Hallelujah.

"Drink the juice," I said, ripping off a fresh piece.

"Damn it, Petra," Marc said, checking Father's vitals, then going back for surgical gauze and antiseptic for my neck.

He treated me while I treated Father. "I had no idea whether you were alive or dead. Do you have any idea what that's like?"

"Yes." I did. "It sucks, doesn't it?"

I returned to Father. Some of the color was coming back to his cheeks.

He'd passed out again, which was actually good. His body would heal better that way.

Father coughed. Marc checked his pulse, glaring at me the entire time. "He's at seventy."

"He's stable." Thank heaven.

"Then come on," Marc said, not taking his eyes off me. "We need to talk."

This should be fun.

"Outside," I said, standing.

"Now," Marc said, hot on my heels as I pushed through the curtain and strolled through the lab. "Do you have any idea what it's been like trying to save him while the whole time I'm thinking I should be saving you? You were out there. Alone. You could be getting stabbed, blasted to hell, sliced up by imps. Did you even think before you took off?"

We charged out of the lab, and he got a good look at the half-trashed Jeep.

"My God," he said, turning me around. "What the hell are you doing taking these kinds of chances?"

"Right. But it's okay for you to make me shoot you and wonder if I killed you."

He balked at that. "I survived."

"I didn't know that!" My voice broke as I shouted.

It felt good to finally let it out.

I took a step closer to him. "And what about what you did when we were breaking into the lab? You just jumped into that vent without a gas mask."

"I'm a dragon. I can handle it."

"I didn't know that! You're always running off. Thinking you can sacrifice yourself. Expecting me to suffer and you don't even think about what it's doing to me."

His eyes narrowed. "This isn't about me. I sacrifice. I gave up everything so you didn't have to sit back there in New Orleans and wait around for me for the rest of your life."

That was rich. "You think you're so noble, but you're not. You're taking the high road. It may sound moral and superior, but what you're really doing is running away from the people you love. You're not sacrificing. We are."

He looked at me like I was nuts. "That's bullshit."

It was the truth. "You're asking me to be there for you, and then you keep putting me through this."

He stood for a moment, silent. "You just ran off on me."

"It feels pretty lousy, doesn't it?" It was twisted. It was messed up. "I may have shot you, Marc, but you stepped in front of the loaded gun."

He always had to be the noble one, and it sounded great on paper, but what it really meant was that he left people like me holding the bag. "You want it all. You want me. You want things to be the way they were. You think you can have it for a few days or a week or however long we happen to be together until I never see you again."

He shook his head. "I didn't choose that," he said, his voice hoarse.

"No, you didn't. But you're asking me to do something that you're not willing to do yourself. You're asking me to love you. You're asking me to be with you. But you're blocking yourself. You're playing it safe. I can feel you holding back. I know it, Marc, because I've had the real you. I had you when you were sweating it out with me on the roof of your walk-up. I had you when we couldn't think of anything but what it would be like to finally graduate and be together. I had you when I found that ring."

It was like I'd slapped him. "I was going to ask you on your last day of residency."

All the fire drained out of me. They'd come and gotten him the Sunday before. "I know."

"How?" The pain in his eyes stole my breath away.

"Because I know you, Marc."

He squeezed his eyes shut. When he opened them, they held a sorrow so deep it tore me in half. "I can't do it," he said.

I nodded. The kicker was, I understood.

It was just too hard.

He stilled. "So where does this leave us?"

"Alone."

"Petra?" Father's voice called from the lab, weak and questioning.

We rushed to the back room, where our patient was trying to sit up. He had his hand to his throat.

"Are you thirsty?" I asked, supporting his back as he leaned forward and coughed.

"I'll get him something," Marc said, brushing past me.

He brought back a bottle of water and helped Father tip it to his lips.

I wiped the sweat from the priest's forehead. "How are you feeling?"

"Okay, I think," he said, looking around, as if wondering how he'd gotten into my back bedroom. "My head could be better."

Marc checked his blood pressure as Fitz jumped up on the bed and lay next to his owner.

"What happened to me?" Father asked.

I removed his boots and pulled the covers up over him. "It's called medusa water. She gets mad and it boils."

"She's a patient of yours," he said, reaching down to stroke Fitz. "Be careful. Medusa has been banished. She's not of the immortal world and she's not of ours."

"What are you saying?" Marc asked.

The priest considered the question. "Medusa is an entity unto herself."

Marc didn't look too happy about that.

"So is Fitz," I said as the puppy rolled over so Padre could scratch his belly.

Father glanced past me. "Is there supposed to be smoke in there?"

We headed into the lab, and sure enough, red vapor

billowed from the medusa water-sphinx venom vials. I shared a glance with Marc.

"I'll take a look," he said. "Why don't you take care of Father?"

Father was trying to roll to his side. "If it's all the same to you, this padre would rather rest up at home."

"Actually," I said, taking a closer look at his dilated pupils, "I'd rather have you in the recovery ward." Better safe than sorry.

He made a face. "Is that truly necessary?"

"Medically speaking? Yes." He'd be under strict observation, unlike here. "Besides, Jeffe is on shift tonight." Father had been teaching the sphinx how to play poker. It would give them both something to do.

Father nodded. "Very well."

I brought a wheelchair up, and we got him moved and settled in. After Marius examined Father again and practically tossed me out of recovery, I made my way back to the lab.

And as I passed the burned-out helicopter, I felt an unmistakable heavy weight in my pocket.

I stopped, felt the outline of it through my scrubs. "Oh, no." I closed my eyes briefly.

Not again.

But I had to see. I had to know. And so I drew the bronze dagger from my pocket.

I studied the curved handle, the blade with the tip missing. It was the same knife I'd pulled out of the sand in the desert, the same one I'd tossed out of a moving Jeep on the way back to camp, the same bronze dagger that had stalked me on my last adventure.

"I should have chucked it into a sinkhole," I muttered, returning it to my pocket.

Still, it had to mean something.

The oracles had been clear: *Death comes with a gift.*

"Not my fault death's a lousy gift giver," I muttered, leaving the burned-out helicopter behind me.

When I made it back to the lab, Marc was busy at the microscope. "Anything?"

"Yes," he said, angling the microscope toward me.

I looked through the eyepieces and adjusted the microscope until I could see fat, round cells. The medusa water had neutralized our sphinx venom.

We did it.

Numb, I pushed away from the sample. "Well, that's it, then."

"It is," Marc said. "Good news. You don't have to deal with me anymore." He moved past me toward the door, careful not to touch. "I'm going to take a walk. Why don't you announce it to the general?"

I should have stopped him, but I didn't as he banged out the door and out of my life.

CHAPTER TWENTY-FOUR

We set up the official test in a private room near the recovery ward. Marius waited in the OR, scrubbed up and ready for surgery, in case anything went wrong.

And it very well could. Drugs like this usually went through a litany of tests before they were allowed to be used on real people, or immortals in this case. But the order had come straight from General Argus: Test now.

I just hoped that if there were complications, they'd pull it and let us refine the active dose. You never knew with the gods. I finished taking our patient's vitals as Marc wiped his arm with an antiseptic swab, preparing for the injection.

"How are you doing?" I asked the burly special ops soldier.

He nodded in recognition. "I'm doing." It was the immense Japanese demigod I'd had on my table. I'd cut off his arm, and still, he'd volunteered to help test this drug.

He was brave, giving; he was one of the good ones. I just hoped we wouldn't let him down.

"We're going to put you out for only about fifteen minutes." I wanted to give a small dose the first time.

He nodded, a thin sheen of sweat betraying his fear. Immortals as a rule didn't like giving up control. This one hadn't even wanted to be tied when I severed his arm.

I squeezed his hand. "No worries."

Kosta gave us space. Argus did not. I flexed my shoulders, angling for a little breathing room as I inserted the needle into our patient's arm.

We'd know in ten seconds if this worked or not. I squeezed the plunger and began the countdown.

"Ten, nine, eight..."

The soldier's eyes fluttered closed.

"Pulse is steady," Marc announced.

I nodded. "Seven, six, five..."

"Breathing is normal."

"Four, three, two. One." I pulled the needle out and glanced up at the monitors.

Our patient was out.

"Can he feel anything?" the general asked over my shoulder.

Marc checked his pupils, then the monitor. "He's functioning, but under."

The general beamed under his mask.

We did it. We found a way to help. I touched my patient's scarred shoulder, feeling a hundred things at once. Relief, pride, joy, sadness that it had taken this long.

Argus edged me out of the way. I did a double take as he unsheathed a wide-blade hunting knife. "What are you—?"

I watched, shocked, as the general buried the knife in my patient's chest.

The monitors screamed. Kosta seized Argus's arm as the general twisted the knife and yanked it out.

He was sweating, triumphant as he held the bloody blade. "You're right! He didn't feel it." Kosta shoved him. Argus stumbled back, a bloodthirsty leer in his eyes. "We did it!"

Marius rushed in.

"Help me get him out of here," Kosta thundered, his scar white, expression murderous as he and Marius half shoved, half dragged the general away. But the damage was done.

"I need suction!" Marc said as blood poured from the wound. "Crushed rib, collapsed lung," he continued, examining our patient. "I don't know if it got the heart."

I hurried for our instruments. Sweat gathered at my surgical cap as I suctioned the blood. The blade had torn a hole through his left lung, above the heart.

Damned gods.

I'd looked this man in the eye. I'd told him he'd be okay.

He did this for me.

Marc's brow knit as he worked.

"We only have fifteen minutes," I reminded him.

Less, actually.

"Give him more," he barked.

"We don't have any more," I ground out.

Marc's fingers slipped in the blood, and he cursed under his breath.

The anesthetic would keep our soldier out for a quarter of an hour if it worked right. Please let it work right.

We had to have him stitched up and healed in less time than that or he'd wake up in the middle of surgery.

Sweat slicked his brow as Marc reinflated the lung. "I don't think it went any deeper," he murmured, focused.

I suctioned the blood. "Five minutes."

His forehead crinkled. "I can't make him heal any faster, Petra."

"Try."

I suctioned as Marc stitched. We guided the muscle as it grew back together. We guided the ribs, leading the broken bones as they re-formed.

"How are we doing?" he asked as we both pulled back,

bloodstained gloves poised over our patient as his skin knit together.

"Less than a minute."

Marc closed his eyes and exhaled.

I wiped a damp, sterile cloth over his chest, cleaning away the blood. His vitals looked good. Chances were, we'd done it. I wanted X-rays just in case.

Our patient stirred. He was early. His skin was still red and raw.

"Holly," I called, "can you get in here?"

The soldier blinked, staring at the ceiling. I slipped off my bloody gloves and reached for a new pair. "How are you feeling?"

Confusion trickled across his features. "I don't know." His eyes flickered over me. No doubt I was pale. I hid behind the clinical calm I'd perfected from years on the job.

His gaze darted to Marc, then back to me. "What happened?" he asked.

"You were out for almost fifteen minutes," I answered. "You didn't feel anything, did you?"

He shook his head.

We'd tell our patient later what had happened. As for now...

Marc had pulled on a new pair of gloves as well. "If you don't mind, I'd like to order a few tests, just for documentation."

He nodded.

It had worked.

We did it. We'd developed the first humane solution I'd seen come out of this vicious combat.

And tested it brutally.

I gave my patient a reassuring squeeze. Just when I'd thought there could be hope in this war, I was reminded that it could never be that simple.

Holly joined us, scrubbed in and ready to take over. "Kosta wants to see you at the officers' club."

"Lovely," I said, giving my patient one last look. "I'll come see you tomorrow."

Marc and I headed back toward the surgical locker room.

He pulled off his cap and I did, too. I yanked out my ponytail. "Why can't we just go to Kosta's office?" The commander knew I wasn't a big drinker. Besides, after the stunt Argus pulled, we had a lot to discuss.

"Come on," Marc said, his hand sliding across my shoulder. "Commander's orders."

Yeah, well, I wasn't a big drinker. Even less when I was rattled. What I needed right now was control.

We entered a square room just behind the surgical prep area. Lockers lined up on opposite walls with a few benches in the middle.

"He stabbed him," I said low, wadding my gown and shoving it in biowaste. "He yanked out a knife and buried it to the hilt."

"How much do you know about Argus?" Marc asked, tossing his gown on top of mine.

"Not enough," I admitted as we headed out of the physicians' locker room and into the night. I'd been so eager to pursue the anesthetic, so focused on getting it right, on helping patients like my amputation case. I didn't stop to think whom I might be trusting.

"Maybe your commander knows something," Marc said as we made tracks for the officers' club.

I didn't doubt it. Kosta was a barracuda. And if he didn't want to use his office, I had to wonder if the conversation we were about to have was going to be off the books, so to speak.

The run-down shack that served as the officers' club stood on the edge of camp, close to Kosta's quarters and the VIP tent.

The tin roof was loud as heck during the monthly rainstorm, but it gave the bar its bite. Large gutters funneled down into tanks that captured Hell's Rain. Rodger had measured it at 180 proof.

Marc and I attracted more than a few stares as we wandered past the wooden bar toward a table in the back.

"It's the dry doc!" a mechanic at one of the front tables yelled out.

"Hold on to your glasses. She's got sticky fingers!"

"Rodger finally drive you to drink, Robichaud?" another yelled before they saw me walk up to Kosta. Just that quick, the peanut gallery quickly turned back to their drinks.

Marc and I pulled up a chair at a wooden table in the back. Kosta sat, red-faced, in front of a drink he hadn't touched.

"Argus is giving his report to HQ," Kosta said, the scar on his lip white.

Marc sank into a chair. "What do you want to bet he leaves out the part about stabbing our patient?"

"How is he?" Kosta asked, eyes on the door.

"He'll live," I said. It wasn't the point.

The bartender brought us each a clear glass of Hell's Rain. It smelled like lighter fluid and lemon Pledge.

My fingers curled around the glass. I wanted to rant. I wanted to yell. I wanted to list everything I hated about this war and this place and the injustice of fighting for an army that didn't care whether we lived or died, whether we suffered, if we had lives, or if we loved.

But Kosta was my commanding officer.

Besides, he knew.

"Congratulations," he said, raising his glass to us before downing it.

Some party.

I dipped my pinkie into my glass and tasted it. It scalded

my tongue and made my eyes run. This was worse than the time I tried tequila.

Lazio leaned back from the table next to us. "You have to drink it fast." He held his up and downed it like a shot.

Ew. What was the point?

Marc sat scowling. His hair was tousled, his mouth wide and firm. His complexion was ruddy, as if he'd just gotten back from a bike ride instead of a mad rush to put a man back together.

My silent appraisal seemed to annoy him. He threw back his drink and punched it down so hard the table rattled.

"I'll be sure to write up something for your file," Kosta said to Marc. "Can't guarantee it'll do any good, coming from our side."

That's right. Marc was leaving.

I'd known all along it would come to that. I'd accepted it. And still I felt like a part of me would never heal.

Maybe I did need that drink.

I raised my glass before I could think about it too much.

"That's it," Lazio called from the next table, reaching for another one. "Let's toast. To tonight's prophecy!" He held up his drink as everyone at his table clanked their glasses, Hell's Rain sloshing out onto the table.

I grabbed Lazio's arm as he moved to drink, spilling half his glass.

"Oh, hey, awwww..." He shook his wet arm.

"What prophecy?" I demanded.

He looked at me like I'd gone off the deep end. "They will fire the weapon and bring an end to suffering."

"Fire the weapon?" I asked, fighting for my voice. "They actually said 'Fire the weapon.'" I hoped he was drunk.

He chuckled. "PNN's been repeating it all day. They're going crazy trying to figure out how the last one came true."

Death came with a gift. Like the dagger in my pocket.

I rushed to the bar. "Turn on PNN." The bartender shrugged, reaching under the counter for an old transistor radio. It whined as he turned the dials, trying to find the station.

"Hurry up, hurry up," I said, turning the thing around, doing it myself.

"He will fire the weapon and bring an end to suffering," said a woman on the radio. "But what weapon?"

One that could destroy us all.

"Well, it's obvious the gods have something planned, and they will tell us in their own good time."

"Yes, but which side?"

I felt Marc behind me. We had a pretty good idea which side.

"What is it?" Kosta sat down next to me. It was more of a demand than a question.

I had to trust him. It could be all over soon. "We think the Old God Army is developing some kind of weapon," I said, keeping my voice low, watching Marc. "They have a virus, deadly to humans, but no pathway."

Kosta sized up Marc. "Do you have information on this?"

He was silent for a moment, his shoulders drawn tight. "I could be tried for treason if I told you."

The colonel thought for a moment, nodding slowly as he came to his decision. "I can make arrangements."

Marc studied him as the radio pundits went on about this new superweapon and what it could mean. "My side has a superbug. As of now, they don't have an efficient way to get it into the population."

To Kosta's credit, he didn't grill us on how we knew. That would come later.

If we survived.

He watched Marc carefully. "How long have they been working on it?"

Marc looked peeved. "Don't know."

"They've had all the time in the world," I stated.

Kosta held up a finger. "Not necessarily." His eyes narrowed. "If you want to get anything done in this army or the other one, you've got to do it fast. You can never count on the moods of the gods. At least not for long."

"What if it's a pet project of a god?" Marc asked. "One with a particular hatred for humans?"

"It kills anyone who's not immortal," I added.

"I'll be damned," Kosta said under his breath.

I glanced around the bar. We were huddled near one end, ignored by the booze swillers all around. It was amazing to think that this could be the last night for many of them. For Marc. For me.

"Think about it," Kosta said slowly. "They'd need something that can take over a system, kill humans while at the same time, knock out any immortals that would try to help. It couldn't be liquid. There would be no way to inject everyone. It would have to be airborne. Like a powder."

I gasped. "Our anesthetic could easily be converted into powder."

The sphinx venom could act as the ideal pathway for the virus.

Kosta stared at me dead-on. "All they'd need is some type of delivery mechanism."

Some way to disperse it.

Marc drew up, rigid. "The crystal powder. They have titurate."

My body went numb as it sank in. We'd made their weapon work. We'd given the gods the ultimate killing machine.

Kosta slammed his hands onto the bar. "I'll go get Argus."

"We'll get our samples from the lab," I said, pulse pounding in my ears.

Bar patrons scattered as Marc and I ran for the lab. I was almost afraid to know what we'd do when we got there.

We could destroy it. Torch it. Burn our research. I'd even go AWOL for real this time, run away with Marc so they could never find us. Our research would be lost. The gods would never know how we'd discovered the pathway or what they could do to fire their weapon.

We reached the lab and threw open the door.

It was trashed. Tables overturned, glass shattered across the floor, papers strewn everywhere. My boots crunched over broken vials as I grabbed for my notes. They were old. "These are no good." I dropped them, plowed through the papers, trying to find anything that mattered.

Marc dug through the mess on the tables. "Our samples are gone." He shoved past the boxes of unused equipment, digging for something, anything, but we knew.

I heaved a stack of papers at the wall, kicked the overturned desk. It was over. They'd stolen it.

We were finished.

Out of breath, I stood helpless in the ruins of our research.

We'd lost.

We thought we were instruments of good in a horrible war. In truth, we were putting together the final piece in a giant killing machine.

"Come here." Marc found me, pulled me into the warmth of his chest.

I clung to him. I'd been naive, cocky. I thought I could trust the powers that be to keep us alive, or at least not try to kill us.

I was wrong.

And now every human was going to pay the price.

Marc was stiff, unyielding. "Think," he said, his chest

rumbling under my cheek. "We can do this. What do we have to neutralize the anesthetic?"

"Nothing." We hadn't made it there yet. And even if we had, I didn't see how we'd deliver it to every man, woman, and child in the known world.

There was nothing that would combat the pathway, only time. And that was something humans didn't have.

They will fire the weapon to bring an end to suffering.

I'd thought I could stand up, change things. Bring it on, I'd said. Well, we had. We'd brought about Armageddon.

CHAPTER TWENTY-FIVE

"HEY," Marc said, holding me by the shoulders, "we're going to figure this out."

I didn't see how.

He released me. "We've got to go see Argus."

Yeah, I'd like to have a few words with the brutal SOB.

Our quick walking turned into running, and soon we were sprinting through the minefield. I'd have to keep my temper with the general. This was about damage control, finding a way to retrieve our notes and our pathway before it was too late.

We dashed past the burned-out ambulance, leapt over the trip wires.

The Old God Army had to have someone in camp, an agent close enough to know when we'd broken through, one who could act before we even knew we were a target.

Argus might be sick in the head, but he was one of our generals. He had a very real stake in this. He'd been the one to encourage us to research together. He'd set us up with equipment and funding from the Old God Army. He'd given us space to work, time. A deadline.

He'd trusted Nerthus.

We zigzagged through the graves in the cemetery, scrambled down the low rise and into camp.

I had to see the general. I had to know. If it was Nerthus and he could stop her, maybe we had a chance.

And if it was Argus who had betrayed us...

If he was the one poised to end all humankind, maybe we could end this.

A bone-deep chill shuddered through me. The bronze knife slapped against my thigh as I ran. I'd never killed anyone before. But I'd kill him if it meant stopping the slaughter.

This enchanted dagger, the weapon that would not stop following me, had the power to murder a demigod. It was designed to split apart inside the body. It would break into deadly shards, each one smaller than the last, and slice an immortal apart from the inside.

It was a ragged, painful death I wouldn't wish on anyone.

Until now.

We dodged a trio of nurses strolling past the OR. The light was off in Kosta's office.

"This way," I said, leading him across the courtyard to the VIP tent.

Marc's expression was tight, focused. "I wonder if Kosta's in there."

Kosta might stop me. He might try to bargain with Nerthus or save Argus if it came to that. Marc might try to stop me as well. I was ready to murder a general, the son of a goddess. The punishment would be brutal.

And eternal.

No sense being polite. We didn't knock. I doubted Marc even considered it. He pushed open one flap, and I did the other as we breezed right in.

"Kosta?" he called.

"General Argus! We need to talk," I said, slipping my hand into my pocket, closing it around the knife.

I swore I'd never influence the prophecies, but when they predicted doom, and when I had been given the means to prevent it...well, it didn't take a brain surgeon to figure out what had to be done.

The inside of the tent was plush, luxurious. Low couches were scattered across the main room. Ornate copper-and-glass lamps cast eerie shadows. A fountain gurgled, which made it impossible to hear any noises the general might make if he drew his own weapon, or if he had already made his escape.

Curtains at the back fluttered, and Eris strolled out wearing a chainmail halter dress. The silver loops did nothing to hide her body. Her pink lips twisted in to a frown. "He's not here."

"What? Your son?"

Marc moved behind her, searching the room and the curtained area beyond.

"Your Colonel Kosta already did that," Eris huffed. "What is with you people?"

We didn't have time for her games. Right now the spy could be delivering our samples, giving our notes to scientists bent on Armageddon.

Golden hair, like spun silk, cascaded over her shoulders and curled at the tips of her breasts. "The little weasel ran off with Nerthus. Can you believe it?"

Actually, I could.

I stood for a moment, stunned.

Eris planted her hands on her hips. "That bitch," she said, watching Marc as he emerged from the back room. "I thought she was after you."

"She was," I ground out. And now it seemed she'd lured Argus.

"Back room's clear," he said to me. "Where are they?" he demanded.

Eris threw out her perfectly sculpted arms. "How should I know where that cradle-robbing bimbo took him? She seduced him right under my nose!"

Well, he was the son of chaos.

"Did he take the notes on the venom?" Marc pressed her.

"Of course he did," she said, her voice rising. "I got him that generalship. I arranged for the downfall of Tantalus in order to get that job. Now Tantalus is down in Hades, standing in a pool of water, reaching for fruit he's never going to get—and how does my son repay me? He betrays our side just to get up some twit's dress!"

"Okay," I said. Focus. "Eris, they're going to kill every human on Earth and in Limbo." I looked her dead in the eyes. "How can we stop them?"

Her brow furrowed. "We don't stop them." She drew a lock of hair behind her ear. "What's done is done."

Marc drew up next to her. "You can fix this, Eris. We know you can."

She wrinkled her nose. "I'm not so good at fixing things. Don't get me wrong. I have a lot of fun with humans." She ran her fingers lightly up Marc's chest, half interested. "You in particular look very tasty." She dropped her hand. "But what's the point? I'm standing here with leftovers."

"Argus is shaming his family," I said, hoping to appeal to her pride, her vanity, anything.

She tsked. "Believe me, nobody thought he was that hot to begin with."

Her eyes fell to the knife still clutched in my hand. "Hello! What is this?"

My fingers tightened around the handle. "It's mine."

"Well, I know it's yours," she said, her eyes roving over the damaged tip.

It was my first, last, and only supernatural tool, and I was going to use it. Somehow.

She held out her hand. "Give it. I demand tribute."

"Why should she?" Marc demanded. His mouth curled in a saccharine smile. "Unless you help us."

Eris let out a high giggle. "I'll get the cradle-robbing bimbo. But I'm not going to start a war over it."

Or save us.

"Now give it," she said, wiggling her fingers. "It's very old and it's very pretty. Just like me."

"I need this," I said, growing desperate. For what, I wasn't sure. But this dagger had come back to me. It had been part of the second prophecy. I couldn't just hand it over to a goddess because she thought it was a cute accessory.

Her eyes narrowed.

"Come on," Marc said, moving between us, backing me up.

She raised her chin. "Gods, you're cocky. I'll bet you would have been delicious."

"We're not going anywhere yet," I said, taking my place next to him. "We need to know. Where's Argus? Where is the weapon?"

The tension in the room built, and the goddess clapped her hands together. "Ahh...I'm going to miss humans." She rolled her eyes when we didn't share the joke. "Fine. Meropis."

What?

Marc towered over her. "Plato made that up."

"You humans are so naive. Meropis is just in the realm of the gods." She licked her lips as she eyed my weapon. "Nerthus has her scientists. She has her weapon. And now, my son." She frowned. "He's probably screwing her brains out."

Marc shook his head. "There's no way we can follow him to Meropis."

It was legendary.

I attempted to slip the knife into my pocket, very casually.

"Stop," Eris commanded.

I drew the blade and held it between us. "What? Are you going to help us?"

She drew up. "Are you threatening me?"

"Yes!"

Her eyes narrowed. "And you wonder why they want to kill the humans."

"Back away," I ordered.

"I want it." Her pearly skin began to glow green. Sparks erupted from her shoulders and arms as she reached for my dagger.

She was going to smite me.

Marc rushed her and she struck him down with a slap. He went down hard against a tent post.

Smoke curled from her ears. "Nerthus's weapon fires at dawn. You'll be dead soon anyway. Now give me my dagger!"

Energy shot from the ends of her fingers. It slammed into the knife, numbing my hands as I gripped it for dear life. It jerked with the energy and shot it right back at her. Eris ducked as the wall behind her exploded in emerald flames.

She popped back up. "You want to burn the tent down? Fine!"

The flames shot out in all directions behind her. The roof caught. Marc rolled away from the wall. He was hurt. I didn't know if he could walk. He certainly couldn't run.

Fire raced across the roof of the tent and she laughed. And, why not? Fire couldn't burn her. She stood in a circle of flame. "Mmm...feels good," she said, running her hands over her chainmail outfit.

"You win," I said, backing up. "We leave. You get the knife." I could only pray that it would follow me this time. "I'll leave it by the front door."

The tent burned as Marc stumbled to his feet. We waited for her to attack as we retreated. I coughed against the smoke, the rising heat.

"It doesn't matter, you know," Eris said, as if we were taking a stroll in the park. "You'll be dead soon anyway. If you kept the knife, you'd just be making me wait. And Hephaestus." She gave a twisted, satisfied smirk.

I glanced at Marc. "God of fire and forge?"

"You should see his biceps," she said, caressing the blade. "He's going to love this dagger. Nerthus will be surprised, too."

I wanted to tell her to can it.

"Why does Nerthus need Hephaestus?" Marc asked.

"He's her son. Hephaestus is working up a big crystal for her. I hear it's amazing."

Titurate.

"This is getting better and better," I ground out.

Or worse and worse.

Eris held the dagger to the burning sky, triumphant, as Marc and I stumbled into the dark night, dreading the dawn.

CHAPTER TWENTY-SIX

It was over. This was it. "I can't believe we failed."

Nerthus had her weapon, her pathway. There was nothing we could do.

On some level, I always thought we'd find a way to beat this. That we'd survive. That we'd come together and somehow make this all right.

I gripped Marc's arm as he led me away. Torches lined the path, crackling in the cold. "Why warn us?" Why give us a shot if there was nothing we could do?

Why make us helpless to stop the slaughter?

His gaze traveled over me, stark and raw. "Maybe we had a chance, and we failed."

"No." I refused to believe that. We'd come together for a reason. And it wasn't to die.

It had never been an option.

"Stop." I stood, throat dry, shaking as I tried to make some sense of it. We were missing something. I wasn't doing enough.

But I'd done everything the oracles had asked. I'd given up my security and my sanity. I'd been willing to talk to a murdered soul, spy on the enemy, sacrifice my mentor. Deny my love. I'd worked days, nights, whatever it took to do the right thing.

And it wasn't enough.

Marc took my hand. He was cold. "There's nothing we can do now."

The camp was settling down for the night. Lanterns blazed. Laughter burst from a tent nearby. My chest felt tight. "Should we warn them?"

"No." He squeezed my hand. "Let them be happy."

A torch bobbed toward us. As it neared, I saw Shirley smiling. "What's up, buttercup?" Her hair hung in twin braids over her shoulders. Her face fell as she drew closer. She narrowed her eyes at Marc. "Is he breaking your heart again?"

"It's not what you think," I said, trying to be chipper. "Where are you headed?"

"Margarita night," she said, still sizing us up. "Holly got ahold of a bottle of tequila. Want to come?" she asked me.

"No," I said, hugging her, saying goodbye to my friend. I squeezed my eyes shut. "Thanks."

"Okay," she said, a little confused as she patted me on the back. "Well, if you change your mind, we're in Holly's tent."

I nodded as I let her go, afraid I'd break down if I said anything else.

They'd have one last girls' night. They'd drink and laugh and find comfort the best way we knew down here—with one another.

"You know, Shirley can get a hangover from half a beer," I said, sniffing. She wouldn't even have to worry about a hangover. The weapon would detonate at dawn.

"Come on," Marc said, handing me a torch. "We need to hit the lab."

"Why?" It was trashed. There was nothing left.

He was purposeful, intense as we made our way toward

the cemetery. "I keep thinking there's something we need to do. We can't just let this happen."

Yes, well, "Unless we can travel to some mythical land, I don't see how we can stop this."

We hadn't even known Meropis was real until five minutes ago. It wasn't like we could book a ship. Or find it on a map.

Meanwhile, they had our breakthrough, a deadly virus, and a fully functioning weapon.

I dodged graves, trying to keep up as Marc quickened his pace. It was hopeless. Impossible. "Even if we could make it there, how do we stop a god?"

"Two gods," he said, as if he were trying to figure it out. "And Argus."

"My thoughts exactly," I said as we hit the minefield.

I stopped for a moment, taking it in. *Merde*. I couldn't believe I was actually going to miss this place. I should plant one last prank, a reminder for after I was gone, but I didn't have it in me.

Our torches cast shadows as we passed the hickey horns van, the burned-out ambulance. "Look, Marc, we don't need to spend our last night beating our heads against the wall over something we can't change."

He spun on me. "What? Do you just want to die? Give up on the whole human race?" His face was a mask of pain and regret. "How can you quit?"

"Why can't you fail?"

He stared at me as if I'd gone off the deep end.

I shook my head. "We can't stop this. We can't change this." I strode up to him. "And you won't admit it. You can't stand the fact that you're not in control. We're not in control."

He looked at me, stunned. "We can be," he said, not convincing either one of us.

"No, Marc," I said, planting my torch as the truth

slammed into me. I was raw with it. "It's all about control with you. It has been ever since you set foot in Limbo." I'd never seen it so clearly. Maybe I'd never let myself. "You couldn't stand being here, so you manipulated it."

"That's not true," he ground out.

But it was. He'd found a way not to care. "You played dead."

He was furious. "We. Settled. That."

I met him, matched him snarl for snarl. "No. We. Didn't." We stood inches apart, like two coiled snakes poised to strike. "You wanted me back, but on your own terms. You wanted to see me and laugh with me. Pretend like nothing had changed. But you don't want to give anything up."

"I was being practical," he thundered, breaking away.

I followed him into the darkness. "You were holding back. You can't let up an inch. You can't let yourself feel what it's like to have your heart ripped out."

We were headed for the lab, like two fools, stumbling through the blackened debris. "Even now, you can't give it up," I called after him. "You want to spend our last night alive running on some hamster wheel, just so you don't have to feel."

He spun around. "What do you want me to do?" he demanded, looming over me. "Do you want me to tell you the first year down here almost killed me? That I couldn't breathe I missed you so much?" The clouds broke overhead, and moonlight shone down. He held back so much pain he was shaking. "I'd sit in my tent at night and grind my fists against my head and imagine you back in New Orleans with some other guy."

"I never—"

"You would have," he ground out, tortured and sure. "It was a matter of time." He shook his head. "I'd never get over you. I had nothing but you. But you'd eventually move on. I watched it happen over and over again to guys in camp." He stood, fierce and alone. "It's what happens when people never come back." He stared at me, hard. "So yes, I let you go. I decided you should be happy." He blinked fast. "I let you off the hook. I gave you up before you could leave me."

I stood, stunned.

He let out a ragged breath. "When I found out you were here, I wanted to see you so bad I was sick with it. But I couldn't. I couldn't let myself. I didn't know what I'd do when I saw you again." He ground his jaw tight. "I wouldn't let myself until I knew I could handle it."

I touched his shoulder, his arm. "You hurt me, Marc."

He looked at me with such love it stole my breath away. "I never wanted to. God, Petra, all I've ever wanted to do is love you."

Tears clung to my lashes. I hadn't even realized I was crying. "Then love me."

His mouth crashed over mine. I tasted his longing, his regret, his love.

He loved me.

He needed me.

It was all I'd ever wanted.

"Petra." He held me tight. "I'm sorry. I'm so sorry. I want to love you. It's all I ever wanted."

I rained kisses on his cheeks, his lips, his chest. "I love you, Marc. I've always loved you." I'd needed him so bad. Even when I thought I'd lost him forever, I never stopped wanting him.

And now he was here. He was mine. I'd show him with every kiss, every caress just how much I'd always loved him. That he was right in coming back to me. That he could love me. That even if we had nothing else, we could have this night together.

It would be our time, and it would be beautiful.

My entire existence drew down to this place, this moment.

His lips traveled to my ear. His fingers found the soft spot behind my neck.

"I'm glad you're happy," he whispered, "because I think it would take an atom bomb to dislodge me."

Or a weapon of the gods.

My heart sank as I caressed his cheeks, his jaw. What I'd give for a lifetime with this man.

"Follow me," he said, taking my hand. He led me through the darkness to our demolished lab.

It looked small and sad in the moonlight. Its door hung open, destruction inside.

"I have an idea," he said. He walked over to the wrecked helicopter and managed to pull out a wound bundle of something. He shook it out, and I saw he'd come up with a climbing rope. "Standard equipment," he explained.

I planted my hands on my hips, half amused, half wondering if he'd knocked something loose back there. "I swear I never know what you're going to do."

"Fess up. You like it that way," he said, tossing one end of the ladder up onto the roof of the lab.

Once he made sure it was secure, and once he'd yanked down about ten feet of excess rope ladder, he offered it to me with a half bow.

"What is this?" I asked, strolling up, giving the climbing rope a test tug.

His lips grazed my shoulder. "I know you're used to taller buildings, but this was the only thing I could swing on such short notice."

"Hmm," I said, planting a boot on the bottom rung, willing to take this gift, this man, for as long as I could.

The roof of the lab was slightly ridged metal. I turned to

see Marc following me up, with a blanket tucked under his arm. "You've thought of everything."

"I wish," he said, shaking an errant piece of glass away.

If we'd only known the dangers of our research. If we'd only treated that with as much suspicion as we'd treated each other.

"Hey," he said, easing me down on the blanket with him. "No regrets."

"No regrets," I promised.

He hovered over me, his face laid bare, his emotions raw. "I love you," he said fiercely, possessively. "I promise I'll never leave you again. If we find a way out of this, I'll always be with you."

It was all I'd ever wanted, him with me. He felt perfect. He filled me on a fundamental level. He was that missing piece that I'd lost so long ago.

We lay down under the stars, kissing tenderly. We loved each other slow. Touching, murmuring, even laughing at times, we stayed awake all night, this last night.

And when streaks of red and purple gave way to dawn, we lay together, bodies and legs entwined, as we watched a gleaming crystal rise over the horizon.

CHAPTER TWENTY-SEVEN

I'D NEVER SEEN anything so large, so beautiful. It rose high in the sky, a glittering beacon of death. The facets sparkled against the dawn. It was the most brilliant sight I'd ever witnessed.

When it had reached the apex of the sky, it exploded in a million flecks of light. Glittery shards rained down. They disappeared in the wind, the deadly crystal powder taking flight, poisoning the very air we breathed.

I swallowed hard.

Soon, humans would inhale the virus. Their bodies would begin to shut down as it attacked the nervous system. Muscles would slow—the heart, the lungs. They'd breathe out the poison, but it wouldn't matter. It would already be in the air, the water, the soil. One hundred percent fatal and designed to kill quickly.

At least it would be over fast.

The virus could move through the portals and beyond. The humans on Earth might have a few minutes, maybe an hour more. No one would understand what was happening as entire cities succumbed. Until there was nothing left.

Marc and I held each other close, afraid to breathe. I closed my eyes as I felt the fine dust brush over my skin. I didn't want to die. I hoped it wouldn't hurt too much. This feeling of my body shutting down, my lungs failing. It would be like drowning. My breath hitched.

I buried my face in the warm crook of Marc's shoulder and waited.

"I love you," he murmured in my ear, as if he had to say it one last time.

It was all so fragile—life, love. Each moment we had together. We could never get them back.

My lungs felt heavy. I could almost feel the virus invading, working its way into me on a cellular level. It was hard to breathe, hard to think. At least the end would be quick. We would die as we'd always wanted to live—together.

I clung to Marc, letting his comfort ease through me. I should be more afraid, outraged even, but I was tired of anger. I was sick of living with injustice.

Death would set me free.

Marc lifted his chin from my head. The air around us lay still, as if the entire world held its breath.

I blinked up at him. My throat and chest felt tight. We shouldn't have survived it this long. "What's happening?" I whispered, afraid to speak.

"I don't know," he said, brushing a smudge of something from my cheek.

It was as if we were alone in the world.

We held each other for a moment longer, waiting. For our deaths, for the deaths of our friends and colleagues, for what I wasn't sure.

"Let's see what's happening," he said, reaching for his shirt.

Right. If we didn't succumb right away, they might need us down there.

We readied ourselves quickly and hurried back toward camp in silence. It was eerie. Not a soul walked the paths. It was so quiet, I could hear our camp flag flapping in the breeze.

"This is so weird," I said, my eyes darting, searching for signs of life.

"I know," Marc said beside me.

We passed silent tents, a deserted mess hall. It was as if everyone was dead except for us.

"Let's check out the clinic," he said as we walked past a discarded boot in the road. Letters from home fluttered in the poison air, scattering down the path like tumbleweeds.

Maybe some of the virus victims had made it there. We could at least do some good before we succumbed.

Hot grief welled up inside me, and I tamped it down. My friends were going to be in there, my colleagues. The least I could do was face the end with dignity.

Marc opened the door to the recovery unit, and I followed him in.

The front desk was stacked with files, as if someone had been working right up until the end. I braced myself and searched behind it, expecting a body. But there was nothing there.

"Where did everyone go?" It wasn't like a virus could consume the bodies.

Marc shook his head and glanced into the first recovery room, then ducked inside.

I joined him.

It was the first time I'd ever seen the recovery room completely quiet. I breathed in the familiar scent, ready for my lungs to give out, for my strength to fail. I fingered the files on the desk, as if they could give me some clue as to what had happened here.

"Hey!" a voice called.

I flung the file sideways as Holly popped out of one of the middle rooms. "Couldn't sleep?"

Marc dashed into the hallway, and Holly gave a little scream, dropping the tray she'd been carrying. Scalpels and medical scissors clattered over the floor. "For crying out loud, those were sterile!"

She bent to pick up the instruments, glaring at Marc and me.

We simply stared at her.

"What's going on?" I demanded.

"Other than him scaring the bejesus out of me?" She shot Marc a look. "I'm just getting ready for the morning shift."

He stood over her. "You haven't been hit with massive casualties?"

"No," she said, gathering up the last of the scalpels.

It didn't make sense. I saw the crystal explode.

"What does it mean?" I asked Marc.

Was there a delayed effect? Did we still have time? I didn't know what to do with it if we did.

He stood, jaw clenched. Finally, he seemed to come to a decision. "Let's go see Eris."

We left a very confused Holly and headed for what was left of the VIP tent.

As we neared, we saw that Eris had replaced the burned red hutch with white limestone. That should be easy to cart around if we needed to relocate the MASH camp.

The goddess was unlocking an ice-blue front door, wearing the same silver chain mail dress she'd had on the night before. Her hair was mussed and...was that a hickey on her neck?

"Hello." She giggled, giving me the once-over. "Glad to see you had fun, too."

I reached to smooth down my own bed head. Come on. I couldn't look that bad.

"Did you save us?" Marc demanded as we stepped onto Eris's new threshold. It was made of a kind of clear glass. Tropical fish swam underneath. The poor things had no idea they were in the desert. I didn't know what to think of this. Of her.

The glass gave way under Marc's foot, and he sloshed his boot in the muddy bottom. The goddess snickered as he shook out his boot and gave her a look. "I had better things to do," she trilled, opening the door. "Let's just say I got mine, too."

"Your what?" I asked, throat tight. I was tired of games.

She pursed her glossy lips. "My sweet revenge. I slept with Nerthus's son."

Marc and I exchanged a look.

"And then you destroyed the virus," he said.

Eris clucked, posing in the doorway as she fondled the frame. "All you humans think about is yourselves. Me, me, me." She rolled her eyes. "I went up to Hephaestus's forge, but he said he was way too busy for me. Luckily I had your knife. I showed it to him, and he completely forgot about the crystal he was working on." She drew her fingers across her collarbone, down her ample cleavage. "I told him it was a gift to his glory, and of course he invited me inside."

Unbelievable. "You gave my knife as a gift?"

"You gave it to me," she huffed. "Anyhow, we did it seventeen different ways, including a reverse Zeus right on top of the crystal he should have been working on. It's my signature move. Hephaestus was so impressed with my flexibility, he decided to etch my name on it. Did you see it? I hope Nerthus saw it. He sank it into that big fiery forge, and of course I told him how hot he was." She notched her chin up. "He wrote *E-r-i-s* right on the front."

I stared at her, trying not to react, as it sank in.

Marc was not so subtle. "Hephaestus sank the loaded

crystal into his forge?" he barked, not even caring when his other foot sank into the goddess's tropical front porch.

Eris frowned. "Well, of course it was loaded. It was the weapon." She brightened. "With my name on it."

I couldn't help but grin. Marc, too. You couldn't heat the virus. Not without killing it.

He will fire the weapon and bring an end to suffering.

Thank God.

They'd fired a deadly weapon—into a very costly tribute to the goddess of chaos.

I kept my face straight as a grin bubbled up inside me. If I didn't watch it, I was going to laugh. Incredible. I glanced at Marc and could tell he was on the verge, too.

"I've got to get out of here," I mumbled.

"Yes. Do," Eris said, dismissing us. "I'm very tired."

We stumbled off her porch, fighting it as we made our way past Eris's limestone pied-à-terre, to the other side of the VIP showers. There, we collapsed in a fit of laughter.

It was too much, too overwhelming that the human race was saved by...her. By a reverse Zeus, whatever the heck that was.

"She killed it." I giggled, tears streaming down my face.

Marc wrapped his arms around me, his fingers tangling in my hair as he pulled me down for a joyful kiss.

I tasted him, savored him. I slid my hands down his chest and under his T-shirt. His skin was warm and alive.

"We did it," he said against my hair, spinning me in a circle until I was breathless. Free. I smiled against his skin.

We did it.

Now we just had to make sure they didn't try again.

CHAPTER TWENTY-EIGHT

"We need to tell Kosta."

His tent was just on the other side of the VIP showers. Hand in hand, we dashed the twenty feet to his hutch and pounded on the wooden door.

No answer. Marc and I exchanged a look as we knocked again, harder.

The door opened a fraction, and Shirley stood on the other side. Her hair was mussed, and her lipstick was gone. I couldn't believe she was going to let Kosta see her like that until... I gasped. "No!"

Colonel Kosta strode up behind her, bare except for a very short towel wrapped around his waist. "What do you want?" he demanded, moving in front of her.

For a second, my mind went blank. *Kosta and Shirley sitting in a tree...* I shook it off. "There's been a new development," I said. "The virus has been destroyed."

The colonel's eyes widened. "That's good news," he said in the understatement of the year. He reached down to touch Shirley's shoulder. I don't even think he realized he was doing it. His eyes flicked over Marc and me. "Meet me in my office at oh nine hundred." With that, the door closed in our faces.

I looked at Marc. "Seems to me he's going to take his time getting there."

But I was wrong. Kosta beat us. We walked into his outer office to find Shirley at her desk, grinning like she'd never stop.

"Way to go," I said, impressed.

"I told you I had a system." She winked as she opened the door to Kosta's office.

The colonel sat behind his desk, mellower than I was used to seeing him. He had his hands clasped over his chest and a cigar dangling from the side of his mouth. "Thanks, Shirley," he said, giving her the once-over.

Shirley needed to write a book. *How to Seduce a Demigod in Just Under Fourteen Years.*

Marc and I stood in front of Kosta's desk.

He plucked the cigar from between his lips. "What do you know?"

I stared at him. Then back to her. Shirley and Kosta. Who would have thought?

"Hephaestus lowered the virus and the crystal into his forge," Marc told him.

Kosta shook his head. "Why would he do a fool thing like that?"

I shook my head, smiling. "He was under the influence of Eris and a reverse Zeus, according to her."

Kosta lowered his cigar and succumbed to a belly laugh. The skin on his face and head grew ruddy. His shoulders shook. I'd never seen anything like it. He'd barely cracked a smile in the seven years I'd known him. Now he was wiping tears from the corners of his eyes.

"Gods," he said, standing, trying to gather himself. "Argus defected. His mother should be leaving for Olympus soon."

He eyed the closed door. "I did some checking when I got here to the office. My sources say the Old God Army is calling the virus a dud. The gods are canceling the program."

Holy Hades. "We did it." I hugged Marc, not caring where we were. Kosta would have to get over it. We were alive.

The door burst open behind us. Shirley clutched the handle, wide-eyed. "I told her you were busy, but—"

With a crackle and burst of feathers, a goddess appeared next to Kosta. She was Egyptian, with long black hair and an ornate headdress with an ostrich feather at the front. She wore a flowing white robe and carried an ankh, which she promptly set on Kosta's desk.

"Who are these two?" she asked, unfurling her wings.

"This is actually the one I told you about," Kosta said, tilting his head at Marc. To me, he said, "This is Ma'at, goddess of justice—"

"And truth and about eight other things," she said, whipping a feather out of thin air.

Nice trick.

"Thanks," she said, holding it out in front of us.

Holy moly. She knew what I was thinking.

"Hello? Goddess of truth," she said, peering through the feather, making a thorough study of us.

"Nerthus isn't too happy," Kosta said. "She's been humiliated because her virus didn't work." He nodded his head toward Marc. "She wants this one back to restart the program."

Ma'at made a face. "Well, she's not going to get him. I'll tell her myself. He belongs with us now."

My heart swelled.

Thank you, God.

"It's Ma'at," she said, "God*dess*. And I'm not doing it for you. Or Eris." She stood in front of Marc. "You are going to be quite valuable to us."

Marc watched her. “I have no idea what you mean.”

The corner of her mouth curled up in a grin. “You will. In the meantime, you two belong together.”

My heart swelled. I knew that.

But how did she know that?

The goddess frowned as a riot of colors burst from the lower right corner of the room. A rainbow blazed arching past Kosta’s desk and over the line of ancient shields. “Iris?”

“Is this a good time?” a timid voice echoed.

Ma’at stuffed her feather back into a fold in her robe. “Spit it out, Iris.”

“Priority message one from the old god leadership. START: Nerthus the condemned has wasted our time and our glory on a futile virus. STOP. Said goddess will be swiftly and irrevocably punished for her vile crime. STOP. Nerthus, venerated Goddess of the Sacred Grove, Creator and Blessed Ruler of Niatharum, Divine Mother of Hephaestus, will be made the slave girl to Argus, High General of the Old God Army, for a period of one thousand years, for him to do with her as he wishes. END MESSAGE.”

Ma’at waved her hand, and the rainbow vanished. “Thank you, Iris.”

She turned to the colonel and reached onto his desk for the ankh. “Good work, Kosta. I just wish I could stick around.”

“Yes,” he said, uncomfortable. His eyes traveled to where Shirley stood at the door.

“Put a sock in it. I know.” The goddess waved her hand and was gone.

Kosta’s gaze traveled to Marc. “We’ll get you set up here in camp. We’ll also put you on the schedule.”

“There’s a free tent close to the tar swamp,” Shirley chimed in from the door.

“I’d like that,” Marc said, wrapping his arm around me.

I couldn't believe it.

At last, Marc was here, with me.

"I'd like to request a change in quarters," I said, unable to contain my excitement.

"Give Shirley your application," the colonel said, as if I had any doubt my friend would rush it through. He looked to Marc. "Make sure she leaves in the mornings wearing more than a robe."

"Something I need to know?" Marc asked.

"I'll tell you all about it," I said as Kosta led us to the door.

"I'd also like to get the lab up and running again," Marc added to him.

The colonel considered it. "It seems harmless enough now that the virus is gone."

Amazing. We could rebuild. Start again. We still had the anesthetic. And now I had Marc as well.

We walked out into the sunshine. It was a new day, a new era. At last, we could see people stirring in camp. Soldiers and clerks, doctors and nurses had made it onto the paths. Voices murmured behind tent flaps. Life went on.

Marc and I made our way to the swamp like excited kids.

We burst into my place, where Rodger now had TIE fighters strung from our laundry line.

He pointed a finger at me. "The decals are drying."

"I don't care," I said with a flourish. "I'm moving out."

Rodger's face lit up for a second before it fell. He recovered quickly. "I'm glad for you," he said.

My roommate set down a large rock he'd been inspecting and went to shake Marc's hand.

"What's that?" I asked.

"Titurate," he said proudly. "The largest piece I've ever seen. And I just found it sitting outside the showers this morning. Can you believe it? My rock-club buddies are going to go nuts!"

"Nice sample," Marc said, walking over to inspect it. It was as clear as a raw diamond and about the size of a basketball. He bent over it, running a finger over a sharp edge. "It's hard to believe this can vanish to powder."

"You just have to hit the right frequency," I said, repeating what Rodger had told me. "It's like eeeee," I added, trying to hit a good pitch.

"No," Rodger said over me. "It's more like eeeee-yeee." He hit an octave higher. We sounded like idiots, singing to the rock. I had a feeling Marc was about to tell us that when—crack—the rock exploded to dust.

I gasped. "It worked!"

Fine powder rained down over us. Marc looked like he'd been hit with a sack of flour.

Rodger's mouth hung open. "My rock!" he said, pointing to the dust on the floor, on Marc, in the air, on a stack of formerly red T-shirts. "That was my titurate!"

"Tough break, buddy," Marc said.

I felt bad for him. I really did. "The least we can do is help you clean up," I said, wishing we had a broom, opting to open a few windows instead. It could just blow out, right?

"Just know you're getting quite a housekeeper," Rodger said, brushing off his stack of shirts.

"We'll hire a maid," Marc said, gathering me into his arms, getting dust all over me. What the hey? I was covered anyway. He nuzzled my cheek and whispered into my ear, "I'm going to keep you way too busy to clean."

My body tingled just thinking about it.

"I think I hear my rock club calling," Rodger said as he banged out of the tent.

We barely heard him.

I ran a hand over Marc's cheek, his jaw. I found the jagged scar at his neck. "I can't believe I have you back."

"Forever, if you want me, Petra."

He lowered his lips to mine, so familiar, so warm. So right.

Forever sounded good to me.

Don't miss the final installment of *The Monster Mash* trilogy *Werewolves of London*

Coming February 2021!

ABOUT THE AUTHOR

New York Times and *USA Today* bestselling author Angie Fox writes sweet, fun, action-packed stories. Her characters are clever and fearless, but in real life, Angie is afraid of basements, bees, and going up stairs when it's dark behind her. Let's face it: Angie wouldn't last five minutes in one of her books.

Angie earned a journalism degree from the University of Missouri. During that time, she also skipped class for an entire week so she could read Anne Rice's vampire series straight through. Angie has always loved books and is shocked, honored and tickled pink that she now gets to write books for a living. Although, she did skip writing for a week this past summer so she could read Molly Harper's Half Moon Hollow series straight through.

Angie makes her home in St. Louis, Missouri with a football-addicted husband, two kids, and Moxie the dog.

If you are interested in receiving an email each time Angie releases a new book, please sign up at www.angiefox.com.

Connect with Angie Fox online:
www.angiefox.com
angie@angiefox.com

FAX Tues 9

757

989

~~3074~~ 3014

989-0734

DOB

CPSIA information can be obtained
at www.ICGtesting.com
Printed in the USA
LVHW031254020221
678115LV00018B/620

9 781939 661760